Somewhere Only We Know

KATE CHAMBERS

To my beloved grandmother Mickie. If you had to leave me, at least you left me with the best of you—your sass and your love of books. Thanks for reading the early manuscript of this book while you were sick and for telling me you loved it. I love you and I wish you were here.

The Puck Stops Here

"Pumpkin frangipane studded with roasted spiced cranberries nestled in a gingersnap cookie crust and topped with cinnamon whipped cream," Jane muttered to herself as her fingers clamored across the keys of her laptop. "The Autumn Immersion Tart," she continued, concluding her email and sending it off with a click. Another click opened an email from her landlord.

"Ms. Mullins, per our discussion last week, the rent on our properties will increase in January per section 7.2b of our lease agreements. The due date for the first increased payment will be January 31. We are certain that with the popularity of Atlantic Station as a holiday shopping locale, all businesses should be able to sustain this increase. Sincerely yours, Alexander Martin, PM4 Properties."

She sighed and closed the email program, rubbing her eyes with her palms. A rise in rent would never be good news, but it couldn't have come at a worse time. The bill for repairs to one of the ovens sat beside her phone and atop a growing stack of bills for supplies, the cost of which increased in the last few months. Not to mention that this was the second rent hike in a year.

"Well Jane," she said to her empty office, "we better sell a lot of these tarts."

Flipping switches, she headed into the kitchen. Rows of minuscule royal icing roses lined one work table, the vibrant purple hue popping against the white parchment paper they rested on. A note from Rachel, one of her part-time staff, listed ingredients they were running low on for Jane to order. Tall refrigerator cases hummed, filled with fruit tarts, cheesecakes, cupcakes, and pies. Large plastic boxes housed macarons and unfilled cream puffs. She loved the kitchen—it was the heart of the bakery, and when the staff was all here, it was full of laughs, too.

The front of the house was her favorite, with all the inspiration taken from her father and his love of hockey. "The Puck Stops Here Bakery," the huge signage over the front counter proclaimed, in bright red letters patterned after a sports jersey. As she turned on the brilliant overhead lights, the room seemed to come to life. Bright white tiled floors painted with red and blue lines, round tables with their legs made of old hockey sticks, and the old air hockey table in the corner made the whole place fun and inviting.

Hockey may not have always been a success in Atlanta—they were, after all, on their third NHL team—but the bakery had been a keeper. Since opening four years ago, they had enjoyed a reputation for beautiful and delicious cakes and for excellent customer service, but with the rise in allergies and intolerances, as well as a shift toward healthier treats, Jane worried that the shop might not survive.

"Morning, boss," Trevor Macías called, his voice booming and grin bright as he came through the swinging door.

"Hey, Trevor! Is your knee feeling better today?"

"Oh, yeah, I'm ready to rock!"

"What are we rocking?" Jane's assistant manager, Nia Pasternak, joined their conversation, her long dark braids swinging.

"Hey, Nia," Jane greeted her.

"Hey, boss. Gigantor." She playfully elbowed the much-taller Trevor. "What's on the agenda for today?"

"Jane! We're out of gingerbread cookies and I can't make the new—" Rayna Maroun called from the stockroom, the others quick to follow her voice. She was tossing empty boxes out of a cabinet.

Ducking as one box headed for her head, Jane replied, "You don't have to hit me over it!"

"Oh, God. Sorry, boss," Rayna gushed, and the group laughed. "I just wanted to get one of the tarts made before opening, but we're out of the cookies for the crust. They were supposed to be in the shipment from Santana's yesterday, but I don't see them."

Jane pulled some papers from a bright blue bin on the wall, skimming the invoice for ingredients ordered from the wholesale market.

"Yeah," she concluded. "Here are the five boxes of ginger-bread cookies I ordered. I'm going to have to have another talk with our rep again." Replacing the papers, Jane turned to her staff. "Well, I'm glad y'all got here early. It's gonna be a big weekend with that music festival across the station. They're expecting about five thousand attendees each day, plus artists and staff. Most, I would guess, will hit this corridor for meals. We should plan on several extra pans a day of the main flavors, definitely of the pumpkin muffins. Those are always a big seller with crowds. Rayna, take some money from the petty cash drawer and run down to the store and grab a couple of boxes of the old-fashioned ginger snaps. We can use those until I get it sorted. Bring back the receipts."

"Yes ma'am." Trevor saluted, pretending to march across

the kitchen. "To work, troops!" The girls joined in, all four of them laughing brightly. Rayna hurried out the door toward the nearby grocery store, while Nia reached over to one of the two large ovens on the wall to warm it up, hesitating when it offered no reaction.

"Jane? Didn't we just have the oven fixed?"

"Um, no," Jane replied. "Not that one." She crossed the room to fiddle with the controls. Nothing seemed to make a difference. She slumped, leaning her hands on the counter. "I'll have to call Roger and see if he can get down here again today to take a look. We will have to do the best we can with one oven until then." Everyone nodded and set to work.

By noon, the front of the shop was bustling with regular customers and festival attendees. Trevor was humming along to a driving song on the radio while he and Jane worked on a four-tier wedding cake for Saturday.

"That's the new single from Ned McMillan and the Rock-eteers called 'On the Floor.' Some people think it's about his breakup with the Swedish supermodel, Taryn, but he's remained tight-lipped about that split. Can't blame the guy, break-ups are tough. You're listening to Nick and Nate on WBZZ, the Buzz. It's a cool sunny day in the city today, which is great for all the shoppers and Turntable Festival friends out at Atlantic Station. We're live out here all afternoon—" Jane froze.

Everyone turned back to their respective projects when Nia moved quickly to change the channel. Rayna poked her head through the swinging door, calling for Trevor, who followed her out front. Nia watched Jane squeeze a fondant acorn in her palm.

"Jane?" she quietly asked, gently placing her hand on her friend's shoulder. "You okay?"

"I'm fine."

"I know—"

"Really, Nia, I'm fine. It's been two years. And it wasn't like he was the love of my life."

Nia gave her a knowing look. "Why don't you take a break for a minute? Give that poor acorn a rest."

Looking down, Jane realized she'd crushed it. She sealed the container of brown fondant and headed for her office. Glancing at the mirror beside the door, she grimaced. Dark circles ringed her eyes, her round face smudged with powdered sugar, her ponytail frizzy after the morning's efforts. Maybe Nick was right. Who'd want the fat cupcake girl?

"Boss?" Trevor poked around the door. Jane jumped. "Nia said you were back here."

"Yeah, I was going to make a cup of tea."

"I know why you came back, Jane, and it's cool. I just..." He hesitated. "I need to tell you something important, and I'm afraid you're going to flip."

Jane eyed her baking assistant suspiciously. "What is it, Trevor?"

"Well, I know you'd decided not to, but Nia, Rayna, and I all discussed it, and we... Well, we submitted you for the Culinary Channel decorating competition open call."

Her eyes widened. "You did what?"

"Please don't hate us. We just..."

"We knew you wouldn't send it yourself. And you're so good at what you do, you'd be amazing at this competition," Rayna added, peering in behind Trevor.

"You'd filled out all the paperwork, anyway," Trevor added.

"Are you mad?" Rayna asked, filling the silence that had settled.

Jane sighed. "No. Honestly, I'm touched that you guys believe we can do it, but it won't matter. That money would be a big help with the rent going up. And now with another stove out of commission. But they never pick people like me, places like us. It's always fancy pastry chefs from hotels or big restaurants." She noticed Trevor and Rayna exchange a glance. "What aren't you telling me?"

"You've got mail," Trevor offered. He pulled a thick envelope from his back pocket and slid it across Jane's desk.

The Culinary Channel logo gleamed in the upper left-hand corner, while her name, barely legible, was handwritten in blue across the white paper.

Jane sucked in her breath. "What does it say?"

"We don't know. Didn't want to open your mail," Trevor chuckled.

Slowly, she lifted the envelope, slid a finger beneath the tab, and drew out a sheaf of papers.

Without a word, they watched her eyes scan the top page, her emotion unreadable.

"Okay, boss, you can't torture us like this. What does it say?"

Jane grinned, "Dear Miss Mullins, we are pleased to inform you that you are selected as a competitor for our upcoming Sweet Tooth cake decorating challenge." Her friends erupted into whoops and cheers, wrapping her in a hug.

Nia, drawn in by the noise, cheered. "I guess it's okay that we submitted you after all?"

"It's only okay if you agree to go as my assistant, ma'am!"

"Let's see, a week in New York with my boss and dear friend, baking in a major competition *plus* a chance to see my hunky boyfriend? Yes, please!"

Jane skimmed the letter again and began to flip through the other papers. "Wow, lots of releases. Oh, a schedule! Makes sense." She nodded as she spoke. "A day of competition, a day of rest. So, if you win out, it's seven days. Nine, I guess, if you count travel days. *Oh*!" The papers dropped to the desk.

"What?" the trio asked anxiously.

"They... They want to come here to film B-roll at the bakery and at Gramma's house, to show my first kitchen apparently, and the host is coming to interview me, since I'm a new competitor."

"That's awesome," Trevor commented. "I guess the other three people are regulars? No worries. You can handle—"

"That's not it," Jane interrupted, breathless, picking the paper back up, and rereading to confirm the contents. "I knew they'd be regulars. They hardly ever have new folks. It's the host of Sweet Tooth. Coming here."

This time Nia's eyes grew wide. "Oh. My. God. Jane. Is it him? Really?"

Jane grinned. "Yes! He's going to be here. In my town. In my bakery. Holy mackerel." Then her face shifted. "They want to film at my grandparents'. I'm going to look like an idiot."

"No, you won't. It'll be great!"

"I'm confused," Rayna said. "Who's the host and why is it a big deal?"

"Yeah," Trevor added. "Is the host some rock star hottie?" He laughed.

"Actually, it's Jane's long-time celebrity crush," Nia chuckled. "She's going to be all swoony."

"Don't say it like," Jane admonished. "Crush makes it sound so shallow and silly. I respect him, admire him. That's all."

"Right," snorted Nia. "Not to mention that you think he's ridiculously attractive and you want to jump him." Jane swatted her friend's arm.

"It's those dark curls," Rayna added. "You just want to tangle your fingers in them."

Jane blushed bright red. "I do not!"

"Who is it?" asked Trevor, perplexed.

Nia swooned, draping herself across the arm of the office couch dramatically. "The real love of Jane's life."

Poor Trevor looked even more confused. "Who?"

"Lincoln Bainbridge," Jane answered, dreamily.

Easy Mac

In the bright lights of the Culinary Channel studio, Lincoln Bainbridge tried not to sweat. He grinned at the camera, waving a large chef's knife across the butcher block countertop.

"Here is where we have an ordinary dish and take it on a little trip. Into the pot with your boiling pasta, add some fresh basil and a pinch of oregano. This will infuse the pasta itself with a subtle, herby taste." Laying the knife to the side, he moved to a second pot that bubbled on the stovetop. "Now, into your cheddar-mozzarella cheese sauce, add a dash of nutmeg before dumping in the cup of grated Parmesan. Continue stirring for about five minutes before turning down the heat to simmer. You don't want this to boil, nor do you want to scald it. Both will produce not only an unusable sauce, but a terrible smell." He laughed. "Okay, we're going to stir this for a bit longer. When we come back, I will show you what we're going to do with the hot dogs."

As the little red light clicked off on the camera, Lincoln let out a long sigh.

"Take five, Lincoln," the director called. "We need to make some changes on our end, and we'll be ready to finish up."

"Thanks, Bryant." Lincoln put his spoon on the counter and stepped off the set to meet his agent. "Antony, really? Mac and cheese?" Lincoln implored, watching the impeccably dressed older man type aggressively on his phone.

"Everyone loves macaroni and cheese, Lincoln," he replied, not looking up.

"Of course they do, but this is the best the writers could come up with? Did you tell them I wanted to branch out more?"

More typing. "I did, but the heads didn't go for it." Lincoln wasn't surprised. The network heads hadn't agreed with any idea he'd had for the last five years.

Finally raising his head, Antony smiled at him. "Oh, come on. You are the great Lincoln Bainbridge. You are a culinary legend."

"And I'm standing here adding a handful of herbs and spices to a completely basic dish. I just feel like everyone else gets the freedom to create, to do new things. I just wish they'd let me be more..."

"More exciting?" Antony offered.

"More creative, more skillful. I could be doing—"

"Lincoln, honey. You're a heartthrob. From Next Top Chef to Guess This Dish and Slice N Dice, you are practically a household name. Women adore you. Hell, some men adore you too! You were engaged to a supermodel for god's sake. What more do you want?"

Lincoln winced at the mention of his ex. "I don't want to sound ungrateful, Antony, but—"

"Sorry, Lincoln. We need to finish this episode before you leave for Atlanta," Bryant interjected.

"Right you are, Bryant." Antony nodded, firmly patting Lincoln on the shoulder. "Lincoln has to be on that plane so we can start filming the Sweet Tooth segment down there the day after tomorrow."

Lincoln's shoulders drooped before he took a deep breath, plastered his brilliant smile on his face, and stepped back into the glaring lights. He gracefully sprinkled more cheese into the creamy sauce bubbling on the stovetop, stirring smoothly as he did.

Under his skillful hands, pasta joined the cheese, hot dog rounds sizzled in a skillet, and a dish came together.

He offered portions of the pasta as they wrapped the shoot, thanking the camera crew as he gathered his coat and his messenger bag to head home.

"Hey, Lincoln," Bryant called. "Antony had to leave, but he wanted you to stop by his office before you go home. Something about the Atlanta trip."

Another sigh. "Thanks, Bryant. See you guys when I get back," Lincoln called over his shoulder. A quick trip up twenty floors, and the elevator doors opened into the lobby of the producers' offices.

Sunset made a swirl of gray and pink over the Hudson as Lincoln waited in the open space. He tapped his fingers impatiently on the dark wood counter. It was almost seven and he was starving, which was ironic considering he'd spent his day cooking, and he had to pack before he left for Atlanta the next morning.

"What on earth is taking Antony so long?" he muttered, staring at the polished wooden door to his right. The voices inside were hushed and indiscernible, piquing his curiosity.

Few meetings at the network occurred so quietly, but as Antony was one of the top producers and agents, sometimes confidentiality was of the utmost importance.

Lincoln jumped as something crashed within the office and someone yelped. A woman's voice responded in a shrill, harsh tone, but he couldn't make out words. The door opened, revealing Stefanie Bauer, a tall, wispy woman with a heavy Dutch accent, even after years of living in the States. Lincoln had met her several times before in his work for the network.

The last time they had met, it was across the stainless-steel battleground on Slice N Dice when his command of the secret ingredient had left her fuming and screeching at him in Dutch from the sidelines. He knew her to be an arrogant woman who could not tolerate losing. More than once, he had seen her eviscerate an opponent through nothing more than mental intimidation. Between her own ferocity and the well-tempered, barbed wit of her assistant Luka Heidlemeir, she was practically unstoppable. Only two people besides him had ever beaten her, and they were both Champion Chefs.

She grinned menacingly at Lincoln as she crossed the room. "Well, Mr. Bainbridge. Having fun on your little show, are you? I just love the oregano macaroni and cheese you made today. Looks delightful." She cackled all the way through the lobby and into the elevator. He shook his head—he should defend his show, but he couldn't. She was right, it was hardly gourmet fare.

"Hey, Lincoln. Come on in," Antony said from his office. Lincoln stepped in, not bothering to shut the door, but taking in the improvements Antony had made since his last visit. Along one wall was a high shelf, populated with the awards Antony's shows had won, more than half from Lincoln's own shows. His desk, a black wood and chrome monstrosity, was neat as a pin, flawless stacks of papers with pale yellow sticky notes attached, his lamp spilling warm gold light across the surface, brightening as the light outside diminished. At home in his perfectionist paradise was the man himself, a longtime producer for the Culinary Channel, responsible for some of the most popular shows on the network for the past decade. He'd been only a rookie producer when Lincoln showed up at the audition for Next Top Chef and immediately saw the younger man's ability and charisma.

"You wanted to see me before I left?" Lincoln asked, settling into one of the large leather chairs across the desk from the power producer. "Though I still don't understand why I have to go to Atlanta at all. We haven't done profile pieces like this on Sweet Tooth in seasons. We usually run B-roll of the—"

"We haven't had a first-time competitor in years, Lincoln." Antony interjected, leaning against his desk. "The last one was Emily Grammercy six years ago. Cute little blonde, very perky. She had owned her own shop for about two years and she was good, don't get me wrong, but she couldn't handle the pressure. She had a meltdown when the blown sugar globe on her back-to-school-themed cake shattered at hour three. Couldn't even finish the cake. It was brilliant—huge rating spike for us." Antony grinned broadly.

Lincoln just shook his head. "I remember. Poor girl, she was a wreck that day. I thought the network decided it was better to use all pros after that."

"More or less, but really, rookies stopped entering, stopped applying."

"So, this girl in Atlanta?"

"Apparently braver than most. Oh, she seems sweet. A little Southern belle who opened her shop a few years back and is pretty successful in the city. She does nice work, but we'll see how she does against Findlay, Ryan Watson, and Stefanie."

"Speaking of Stefanie—" Lincoln started, but the office door opened and Antony's assistant entered, interrupting him. As with everything in his office and his career, Antony had been both specific and expensive about his taste in assistants. Julia Fordham was twenty-two, five-foot-nine, and weighed exactly one hundred and five pounds when soaking wet. She also had a penchant for designer clothing, which highlighted the assets atop her chest that Antony had purchased for her four years ago when she began working for him.

"Yes, Julia?" Antony asked.

"Mr. Perandin, you said you had some files for me to put in the system?" she asked, her voice husky and flirtatious.

"Oh, yes," he said, reaching for the nearest stack of papers, dotted with notes. "The invoices need to be in by the end of the week, and the other files are to be input as soon as you have time after that. Thank you, Julia. And you look lovely today." She smiled as she brushed past Lincoln, bending to take the papers from Antony at a perfect angle so Lincoln got a straight shot down her silky blue top, before she sashayed back to the door.

"Nice to see you, Mr. Bainbridge," she murmured as she closed the door behind her.

"You should take her out sometime," Antony suggested, cocking his head toward the door. "It might help break you out of this post-Railey funk you've been in."

"Antony, you know me better than to even suggest that," Lincoln countered, irritated. "I'm not interested in dating right now. I barely see my apartment as it is."

"Who said date? And who says you have to be at your apartment? Take her to a nice dinner, then go see her place. She might be difficult to explain basic accounting procedures to, but she's easy everywhere else." Antony winked conspiratorially.

Lincoln rolled his eyes. "Not interested."

"Whatever. So, where were we?"

"Atlanta."

"Right. Just get some sappy stories about this new girl. Make the audience love her, make everyone fall in love with her."

"And if she crashes and burns?"

"Then every single viewer in middle America will root for

her and cry buckets when they all watch it happen. We can't lose!" He chuckled. "Either she shows the other three up, which isn't likely, or she fails and our ratings are massive. I'm happy either way."

"Right. Well, I suppose I will see you when I get back." Lincoln reached across the desk and shook Antony's meticulously manicured hand.

"Have a good trip, buddy. Maybe you can find one of those hot southern girls to keep you company," he encouraged as Lincoln stepped back into the lobby. Julia looked up from her desk, where she was scrolling through a designer purse website.

"Good night, Julia," he said with a nod as he gathered his coat and scarf from the rack and bundled himself up. "Have a good night, Natalie, Fred," he called to Antony's other assistants.

"It'd be better if we were together," Julia offered through lowered lashes. "I could skip out a little early and Antony won't mind."

"No thanks, Julia. I have to get home and pack," he answered, as he stepped into the open elevator and pressed the button for the downstairs lobby. The doors closed between them as he saw her stand from her desk to follow him.

Lincoln sighed. Even if he were interested in meeting someone, which he was not, he would not pursue someone that shallow ever again. And a one-night stand with Julia? Definitely not. Flings were fine for some people, but he had enough trouble trusting women in general that the idea of barely knowing one before falling into bed didn't appeal to him at all. He tucked his head under as a sharp breeze whipped around the building when he walked to the black car at the corner. Climbing in, he shivered. At least Atlanta would be warmer.

"Victor, can you swing by Moon Blossom before we head

home? I'm craving soup and some crab Rangoon." The driver nodded and pulled away from the curb into the early evening traffic.

Lincoln thanked Victor as the car slowed to a stop at his building and nodded at Winslow, the doorman, as he opened the shining glass door with a flourish. The lobby was quiet, his footsteps tapping across the tiles, until he stepped into the elevator and turned his key in the lock for the top-floor apartment.

Lincoln's apartment was a thing of beauty-a gleaming homage to the finest furniture, appliances, and fixtures money could buy; it was a shame he rarely used it. The apartment, like most things, had been Antony's idea in their last contract negotiation. According to him, a star deserved a star of a place. Lincoln would have preferred a smaller, cozier apartment.

His impression was that the whole apartment was cold, sterile, and polished. The walls were painted in a shade of grey, with hard marble floors framing grey, white, and black furniture. Stainless steel took the focus in the kitchen, gleaming icily from every corner. Even though he'd lived in the penthouse for nearly a decade, it still looked more like a rental than a home.

With a sigh, he dropped his bag by the umbrella stand at the door and trudged to the sofa, where he dropped onto the black leather. For all its starkness, he had to admit he wished he spent more time in it. Dreading sounding demanding, Lincoln knew others would give their teeth for his life. But he longed for a home; somewhere warm and inviting, full of life and color. Mostly, he wanted more out of his job, more than peddling rudimentary recipes. He'd much prefer days updating the foods his grandmother had taught him or foods he learned as he traveled. Sure, hot dog macaroni and cheese was accessible, but he wanted more.

He couldn't escape the desire for more, not just in his

work, but in his personal life. A smile to come home to at the end of a long day, a warm embrace on a bad one. But that was something he'd never quite seemed to find. Love broke him twice, and he'd spent the last two years pretending that he was fine alone. Life was easier that way. But that didn't stop a memory lingering in every place he went, including his apartment. Railey, his ex-fiancée, spent more time here than he had, residing in the penthouse when she was in town for fashion shows or fittings or photo shoots, and it wasn't unusual for him to return for the weekend to find her shampoos and body washes in the shower, and a fridge full of celery, spring water, and pears. Her fragrance lingered in his mind; a sweet combination of peaches, expensive perfume, and hairspray.

Lincoln stared at the heavy iron table by the door, remembering its role in the day the engagement ended. He'd returned home from a long day in the studio, filming another episode of Slice N Dice, to find a folded piece of ivory paper and the seven-carat diamond and platinum ring waiting for him. What a note she'd left. She'd run off with Dylan, his best friend, and was headed to California for some soap opera. Of course, she cared for him, but she didn't want to get married. Oh, and they hadn't wanted to face Lincoln because they didn't think he'd take it well.

On that, he supposed they were right. After three days of melodramatic moping, Lincoln emerged, pressed and dressed, and headed off to work, stopping at the jeweler where he had bought Railey's ring. Even though she had designed the ring herself, the jeweler was confident that he could resell the magnificent modern piece and bought it back from the stone-faced, jilted lover.

He hadn't dated since. Most of the women he met were fans of an image anyway, and the thought of a relationship with such a woman didn't thrill him at all. It wasn't even the thought of an obsessive girl who had memorized his favorite kind of sandwich that repelled him most, though there was little appeal in such a prospect, but he felt that he could never trust a woman like that. A woman who had spent so much time poring over his life and his activities would surely be waiting for an opportunity to sell a story to the tabloids.

One of his friends, Arthur Dunner, who was a writer in the city, fell victim to a journalist posing as his date to get the "inside story" on the well-known writer. Lincoln shuddered at the thought. He wanted to trust people again, to stop believing that they were going to hurt him, that they would leave, but maybe he was just too broken. He hadn't had any luck getting where he wanted to be in his job, so why would he think he'd be any better at a relationship? He dug a plastic fork into a takeout container of rice and began to look over his notes for the trip. No sense in focusing on something he couldn't solve now, and Atlanta was his next stop.

Don't Meet Your Heroes

Jane surveyed the bakery like a proud parent. It took three full weeks, but her crew had not disappointed; the place sparkled in the bright lights.

Trevor had pulled all the decorations down from the walls and both he and Rayna had scrubbed everything. Even the nets had gotten a wash. Nia hand-washed the jerseys as well as the bakery team's uniforms. Rayna's husband, Sully, had repainted the marks on the walls where chairs and tables had scraped and bumped, and even fixed some places on the floor where the marks were noticeable. The counters were spotless —the glass cases reflecting the illuminated shop.

As fantastic as the storefront now appeared, the kitchen looked even better. Jane had gone over every single stainless-steel surface until it shone in the fluorescents and even straightened and relabeled every item in the pantry. Freshly frosted confections crowded cooling racks along the far wall, ready for their debut out front.

"All right, Culinary Channel. We're ready for you," Jane murmured into the silent space. The clock above the swinging door read 7:45; the team was supposed to arrive early to complete the prep, and the cameras were slated to show up at eight. When she spoke to Antony's assistant, Julia, two days before, the annoyed-sounding woman listed off a litany of information on how to prep for the shoot, times, and other information Jane had frantically scribbled on her notepad.

"It's a big day, Dad," Jane said, face toward the ceiling. "Culinary Channel is coming here to see your little girl in action. I hope I make you proud."

The door chime rang and in tumbled the crew, faces bright, though she noticed they'd all put in some extra time getting ready. Nia's long hair was braided over her left shoulder, and she had flawless eyeliner behind her glasses. Trevor had styled his hair into a swoop, opted for jeans without holes, and sported the cleanest jersey she'd seen him wear.

"Rayna, are those Stanley Cups on your earrings?" Jane asked, leaning in to see. Rayna's head wrap was a dark blue, and she had added clever hockey accessories to her ensemble.

"I thought they'd be appropriate today," Rayna replied, reaching for her apron. "So, what do we need to do? Should we be baking when they arrive or what?"

"The woman I spoke to said to have the place clean and looking like we wanted it to be on camera and then wait until the camera crew gets here. She said they'd tell us what to do after that."

"What time are they supposed to be here?" Trevor called, hanging his jacket in the hallway.

"Any minute now, actually. They wanted to start early so they could get this part done in one day. Remember, they said they want to shoot some at my grandparents' house tomorrow, too."

"Cool. So, are you nervous about meeting your future husband?" he taunted, waggling his eyebrows.

"I'm kind of terrified. I've always heard don't meet your heroes, but no one ever gives you advice on meeting your celebrity crush, though I still hate that phrase. I guess I'm hoping I can just... Not sound like an idiot," she admitted, wringing her hands.

"You'll be fine," Rayna assured her. "We'll make sure you shine like the star you are. And he's gonna love you."

Knock! Knock! Knock!

"Oh my god, they're here," Nia whispered, her eyes bright with excitement.

"It's fine." Jane smiled, taking a deep breath. "I'll go let them in. Y'all wait here." She headed for the door to the store-front. "Oh, Nia!" She stopped short. "Will you please close my laptop for me? I'd be mortified if he saw his face pop up in the screensaver." All four laughed as the swinging door shut behind her. A dark-haired man in jeans and a black polo shirt smiled warmly through the glass door. Jane twisted the lock and pulled the door inwards.

"Good morning." She spotted the embroidered Culinary Channel logo on his shirt. "Come on in. Can we help carry anything?"

The man chuckled, waving a hand toward a van parked at the sidewalk edge. "My crew's got it, but thanks. I'm Jordan Maxwell, the shoot director."

"Nice to meet you." She shook his outstretched hand. "Come on in." They stepped inside, the crew following, carrying various pieces of equipment.

"Right," Jordan began, looking around the room. "Wow. This is one of the coolest places I've gotten to film. Honestly. We see a lot of pink and fluffy bakeries, but this is just really cool."

Jane grinned. "Thank you. We definitely like to be a little out of the ordinary."

"Lincoln will be here in a few minutes, just to talk with you and kind of get a feel for questions to ask you and the staff and for the story behind the bakery. We'll shoot out here in front first, probably some exteriors, when the light gets a little better, and then into the bakery. And we're shooting at your grandparents' place tomorrow. I thought that was what was in my notes."

"Right. My first kitchen," she nodded. "Apparently, Mr. Perandin thought it was good color commentary for the story."

"I'm sure it will be." The kitchen door swung open, her staff bustling into the room, all smiling like the Cheshire Cat. "This must be your team."

"Most of them," Jane replied. "These are my full-time staffers. I have two part-time workers as well, mostly in the afternoon and evenings because they're students. This is Trevor Macías, Nia Pasternak, and Rayna Maroun." Each person waved as she introduced them.

"Nice to meet you." Jordan nodded. "It'll take us about twenty minutes to get set and we'll get started. I told Jane that Lincoln will—"

"Lincoln will what, Jordan?" a rich voice asked, stepping through the door, held open by a crew member. "I hope you haven't been spilling all my secrets."

Jordan chuckled. "You have secrets? I thought the world knew everything about the culinary Casanova." He followed a skinny man in a blue t-shirt outside.

Jane, the crew, and Lincoln stood in silence for a beat.

"Well, I guess you already know who I am," Lincoln muttered.

Jane could only stare, agape. The man in front of her was much more than the pictures and the videos she had seen. Lincoln Bainbridge was six foot three and built more like an athlete than a professional chef. His hair was a rich chocolate brown, and it curled loosely across his forehead, framing his dark brown eyes. A crisp blue and white button-down and dark-washed jeans hung on him as if they were tailor-made.

"Of course we do. Our boss is in love with you," Trevor blurted, immediately covering his mouth.

"Ah." He half-frowned, turning to Jane. "So, I have a fan?"

"No! I mean, yes. I mean," she stammered.

His smile was cold. "I understand. It's nice to meet you, Miss Mullins. Always nice to meet an admirer."

"Welcome to my bakery." She smiled, regaining her confidence. "It's an honor to have you and the crew here."

By the time she'd finished the sentence, Lincoln had turned to a passing camerawoman to ask her a question. Jane's face fell, and she turned to her friends to hide her disappointment.

"Well, that was... Something," Nia whispered.

"I sounded like an idiot!" Jane spat. "Every nightmare I have ever, ever had about meeting him pretty much came true."

"I don't know, Jane," Trevor said, eyeing the chef. "He seems like... Well, he seems like a jerk." Jane looked at Nia and Rayna, who nodded in agreement.

"Jane, he didn't even let you finish your thought before he stopped paying attention."

"He's not a jerk. I just sounded like a moron." Jane took a deep breath. "I'm good. I've got it together now. We'll fix this." Straightening her shoulders, she strode across the tiles to where Lincoln stood, now conferring with Jordan.

"Sorry about that, Mr. Bainbridge. This is a big day for us and I got a little flustered. Where would you like to start?"

"It's nothing, Miss Mullins. I get the doe-eyed, tongue-tied, fawning all the time. Fangirls are part of the day-to-day for me."

She frowned. "I'm not a... I'm not sure that's what

happened, but anyway..." She shook off her rising annoyance. "Jordan mentioned you'd want to talk to us to get a feel for who we are at The Puck Stops Here, so would you like some coffee and one of our peach Danishes while we talk?"

"No, thank you," Lincoln replied, eyeing the pastries in the case. "I know the questions they'll want to be answered on camera, so we'll wait until the crew is ready and go from there." The shrill chime of the telephone echoed through the shop.

"Pardon me." Jane stepped away, disappointed even more in her second encounter than her first.

Trevor answered the phone by the time she reached it, taking an order on the notepad. Jane noticed Rayna and Nia had disappeared into the office while the camera crew continued to set up.

"Hey, y'all, what are you doing back here?"

"We're taking a minute to get ready before they want to film," Rayna answered.

"Are you sure you weren't talking about what an ass you think Lincoln is?" Jane grumbled.

"Well, that and how cute Jordan is," Nia grinned and Rayna laughed, too.

"He reminds me of Sully when he was young, all cute, with that clean-cut black hair."

"The muscles! Good lord, he must live in a gym. His arms are incredible."

"He does look like he could sweep a girl off her feet," Jane agreed as Nia fanned her face with an order form.

"Ladies, they want to get started," Trevor called into the office. "So, stop talking about who has the cutest butt." All three women rolled their eyes as they walked back to the front of the store. "Cause we all know it's me," Trevor added, eliciting a fresh round of laughter.

Huge lights now illuminated the storefront, and three different cameras were positioned around the space.

"Wow," Nia breathed.

"Hey, Jane." Jordan smiled, "We're going to start with you behind the counter, introducing us to the shop, and then Lincoln will come in and ask you some questions. Just real easy stuff, okay?"

"Sure," she nodded, "That sounds great."

For hours, the bakery crew followed directions, pretending to serve customers or bake different items, stopping for the cameras to move or to reshoot a certain motion. Jane answered Lincoln's questions, which he turned on the charm to ask, before immediately reverting to the taciturn man who'd shown up that morning. While she was proud of her team and what they'd showcased all day, Lincoln himself was proving to be a bit of a disappointment.

The sun was setting behind the Atlanta skyline when Jordan called, "That's a wrap, folks!" on filming. While the equipment was packed away, Jane's staff left for home or deliveries. Jane sighed contentedly as she packed up treats for the crew to take with them. Everyone had worked hard and deserved a goody.

"You did well," Lincoln commented, looking over the space again.

"Thank you," she replied, determined to not say anything stupid.

"You've made some," Lincoln paused, reading her menu boards, "interesting choices here in your offerings and your decor."

"I've never been much for convention," Jane said with a shrug. "I like to think it's one of the things that really sets us apart here."

"Or holds you back."

"What?"

"Most successful bakeries limit their offerings to the most popular items, or at least to a specific range of items like cupcakes. But you're all over the place here. Pastries, cakes, muffins, pies, tarts. And you've got bizarre flavors, too. You'd do better for yourself to stick to a more mainstream offering."

"You mean like adding marshmallows to basic brownies and calling them elevated? If that's your idea of mainstream, then I'm sorry, Mr. Bainbridge, but I'm not interested."

He narrowed his eyes and stepped back. "I was only offering my experience, Miss Mullins. You don't have to take it. Doesn't make my commentary any less true."

"You think you're always right just because you're a big shot? That anything that deviates from your normal is unacceptable," she seethed. "You make glorified kids' food, Lincoln Bainbridge. Where's your imagination? Where's your creativity? You've spent less than a day in my shop and less time actually learning anything about me. Does that give you any right to pass judgment on me or my work?"

Jordan stuck his head back into the shop, and the interruption shook Jane from her simmering rage. "Hey, Jane, we're all set. I've got the address for your grandparents' place, but I'll call if we have any trouble. We'll see you about ten?"

"Sounds great, Jordan. Thanks." She waved as the door closed behind him. Lincoln hadn't moved, still staring into the glass case.

Jane hesitated. She'd managed to insult her crush and denigrate his work in about two sentences. "Mr. Bainbridge, I'm sorry I—"

"I think you have said enough, Miss. Mullins. I'll see you tomorrow morning with the others."

She swallowed. "Can I send you back to the hotel with something?"

"If you must," he replied, his eyes meeting hers. She'd

always thought his deep brown eyes were warm, but today they were empty. Not cold or angry, almost sad.

She sliced and wrapped a piece of the Autumn Immersion tart and handed it across the counter to him. "I hope you like it."

Wordlessly, he turned and left the store, the ring of the door chime echoing in the empty room.

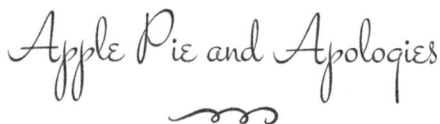

Apple Pie and Apologies

The city hummed far below Lincoln's window as he stared over the illuminated skyline. High above Atlanta in his suite at the posh Twelve Atlantic Station, he should have been enjoying a quiet night off; it had been months since he'd had one. The room was open and bright, with an incredible view, and the sofa, at least, was even more comfortable than his apartment back home. Still, the afternoon's events played out on repeat, Jane's words pricking his ears.

He wasn't one of those celebrities that never had people tell him off or, at least, he thought he wasn't. Most people told him he was charming and witty, slightly sarcastic. Lord knows the fangirls had no problem telling him how "incredible" he was.

He shook his head, fighting away the vision of the fiery Jane, arms akimbo, green eyes blazing.

"She's right, though," he groaned, sinking back against the turquoise and grey cushions. "When is the last time I actually created something instead of just parroting someone else's recipe for creamed kale?" The last word caught in his throat. For the first time in a long time, he felt tears in his eyes. He used to be proud of the work he did, but it had been a long time since it felt like a passion and not just a job. It had been years since he'd felt as zealous about his work as this woman was about hers.

He shook off the tears and shame and thought about dinner, looking around for a room service menu. His suite included a kitchen, an obvious amenity for a professional chef, but there wasn't anything in it to cook. And if he was truthful, he didn't have the desire at the moment. The white bakery container on the kitchen counter caught his eye. He opened it, revealing the sumptuous slice of tart from Jane, cranberries dotting the surface beneath the pale orange cream. Lincoln searched the drawers for a fork, but came up empty.

"Oh well, guess I'm eating with my fingers."

He took a bite, noticing that even after sitting for several hours, the tart shell was perfectly crisp. The mix of flavors hit him instantly: tangy cranberry, sweet and creamy frangipane, sharp gingerbread crust, and the light and airy whipped cream.

"Whoa." He downed the rest of the slice in two bites, licking his fingers. "That is incredible!"

Shame crept over him as he eyed the empty container. He'd been cruel about her food without ever giving it a chance.

"I am an ass," he said out loud. "Maybe I can make amends tomorrow." Lincoln was uncertain any apology would be acceptable, but he needed to try. And he still needed dinner. He spotted a menu for the hotel restaurant attached to the mini-fridge. The offerings looked good enough, but as he read the list of sandwiches and bistro fare, he realized he needed a walk in the cool night air as much as he needed food.

A quick zip down the glossy elevator and Lincoln stepped out onto the busy sidewalk. He knew from previous trips that Atlantic Station boasted some great cuisine, but also tended to be crowded this time of night and he was definitely hoping for something a bit more subdued. The crosswalk changed, and he headed down State Street, past the park and rows of townhouses, watching young families in their yards, young professionals arriving home from work, looking exhausted, when a warm, spicy smell reached him. As State Street opened onto 14th, he turned left, his nose following the aroma, like a cartoon character, stopping in front of a rustic storefront that read, "Mike's Barbecue."

It was almost nine, but the tables looked fairly full. He hesitated for a moment, but the smell was too good to walk away from.

"Hi there, sir. Can I get you a table this evening?" a lanky, bearded man asked.

"Yeah, I caught a whiff of whatever you've got cooking about two blocks over and followed it. I need to try this," Lincoln laughed.

"We get that a lot, actually," the man chuckled. "Can I get you a table or would you rather sit at the bar?" Lincoln glanced around. The bar faced the kitchen, and the tables near the door were fairly full and boisterous, but the place was emptier near the back.

"Can I get a table near the back? Hoping for a nice, quiet evening."

"Sure thing." The host grabbed a menu. "Follow me."

They wove through the tables to an empty one in the corner, where Lincoln sat with his back to the wall. "Thanks, man." He nodded to the host.

"You're welcome. A server will be by to get your drink order and fill you in on the specials. Enjoy." And he was gone, back to his post at the front doors.

The menu was full of classic barbecue joint foods: ribs, baked beans, and pulled pork. He realized how hungry he was as he read the descriptions of all the choices, but a nearby familiar voice distracted him.

"Thanks, Andy," she said. Lincoln turned and saw her dark red hair twisted in a bun, bouncing as she spoke. "I needed it today," she explained, leaning over to smell the food that had just arrived at her table in the opposite corner.

She didn't look like the woman who had verbally eviscerated him that afternoon. Her eyes weren't bright as they had been, but were a softer shade of deep green that caught the lights as she spoke. She'd traded her work shirt for a black tank top and a gold sweater, both of which fit her snugly. Sitting alone in the corner of the restaurant, she seemed more like the sweet girl who'd greeted him that morning.

Quietly, Lincoln got up from his chair and, as the server returned to the kitchen, approached Jane's table.

"Come here often?" he asked amiably, sliding into the chair across from her.

Her eyes widened. "What on earth? I thought you were going back to your hotel."

"Funny thing about hotels, even fancy ones: they don't automatically feed you. I needed to eat, and I decided I wanted to take a little walk. Found this place on the smell alone."

She just stared at him, her head cocked to one side and an eyebrow raised.

"Seriously though, is the food good? It looks fantastic. What is this?" He gestured to her plate.

She lifted her left eyebrow. "Brisket, broccoli slaw, and Brunswick stew. And yes. It is pretty good."

Andy, the server, returned, having noticed Lincoln's change of scenery. "Can I get you something to drink, sir? Or do you know what you'd like?"

"Yeah, can I get a sweet tea and the brisket with broccoli slaw and Brunswick stew? Looks delicious."

"Sure thing." As he headed for the kitchen, Andy glanced back at the pair, shrugging his shoulders.

When they were alone again, Jane stared at Lincoln. "Why

31

did you sit here? You didn't seem to want much to do with the little fangirl this afternoon," she commented sharply. He knew he deserved her scorn.

"I'm beyond sorry for how I acted. You were right. I was horrible to you when you were nothing but kind and welcoming. You should have thrown a cupcake at me."

Jane snorted, then hastily tried to recompose the scowl she'd been sporting. "I should have," she replied, looking him up and down. "But that wouldn't have been very ladylike or hospitable of me. It wouldn't have reflected well on the bakery."

"Maybe not, but those cupcakes looked rather remarkable. I might have just licked it off my face and it turned into an advertisement for how good your stuff is. That slice of tart you sent back with me was one of the best things I've eaten in ages."

She waved a hand at his expression. "The frosting would have ruined your hair, I'm afraid, since we use the good stuff. Butter doesn't make for good styling gel."

Now he laughed. "Is that an assumption or personal experience?"

"I may or may not have gotten into a frosting battle in college," she reported. They both laughed, as Andy returned with Lincoln's dinner. Jane couldn't miss how much freer this Lincoln seemed as opposed to the one who had brooded around the shop that afternoon. His brown eyes were bright and his smile was... Well, it was the smile she'd fallen for in the first place.

"You haven't touched your food!" he exclaimed. "I've been monopolizing your mouth." He stopped; eyes wide at his own words.

She stared at him, the innuendo hanging in the air. "You should occupy yours before you say anything else."

Lincoln blushed. "Sorry!" He speared a piece of meat with his fork and dug into the meal. Jane watched him, eyes wide.

"What?

"Um, you've got a little sauce," she gestured at her chin.

He swiped a finger, smearing the brown sauce across his chin, causing Jane to giggle. She reached across the table with a napkin, clearing the offending substance from his face.

Lincoln groaned. "Please don't tell anyone you saw that."

"I'll keep your secret. Just don't do it again." They both dug into their meals and, for a few minutes, the only sound was muffled chewing and an occasional "mmm" from the pair.

"This is remarkably good," he said, his plate about half cleared. "Do you come here a lot? Since it's near the bakery?"

"It's actually closer to my house, but no. Most of the time I go home and cook. If I go out, it's with friends and it's usually to one of the pubs in the area. I really only come down here when I have a bad day."

His face fell. "Bad days? Today was a bad day then?"

Jane grimaced. "Well, it certainly was not the day I expected." She stared at her plate, determinedly not looking at Lincoln.

"No, you're right. You were obviously excited for the crew and I to be there, to show off your hard work, and I stole your spotlight." Embarrassment flooded his expression.

"I put too much pressure on it," she reasoned. "I had a vision in my head that would have never happened, but it wasn't a bad day. I mean, I got interviewed because I'm going to be in a Culinary Channel competition. How bad can that be?" She smiled, the brightness in her eyes he noticed earlier returning.

"So, what made you want to apply?" he inquired, taking another bite of his slaw.

"I didn't actually," she admitted sheepishly. "Nia and Trevor found the application I'd filled out and submitted it without me even knowing. I'd talked about it for..." she thought, "years probably, but I was always too afraid to do it."

"Afraid? With a successful bakery under your belt?"

"Cakes are a whole different ball game in eight hours with only two people. We do some spectacular projects at the bakery, but they take days of effort and a ton of teamwork. I'm still not sure I'm capable of the challenge. I'm sure I'll be the first to go." Jane paused, looking past him, past the window, and out into her imagination. "But even when I do, at least I got the shot in the first place."

"You don't sound very confident," Lincoln said, surprised that the girl who had so eloquently put him in his place that afternoon was so self-deprecating on her own work.

She blinked. "It's difficult to explain. The bakery does great work. We've been praised as one of the best bakeries in the city. And I realize that even getting picked as a first-timer for the challenge is a big deal. I guess I'm just afraid of screwing something up and embarrassing myself, or embarrassing my team." Wiping her mouth, she laid her fork onto her now empty plate and tucked a wayward strand of hair behind her ear.

"I don't think you do yourself credit," Lincoln murmured, patting her hand. "You're going to knock 'em dead in New York."

She shook her head, smiling. "You're sweet, but I know that realistically, unless it's a competition of rookies, I don't stand a chance. They never win. And I know my limits."

Andy appeared at the table. "Can I get those out of the way for you?" he asked, seeing their empty dishes. The duo nodded.

"The food was excellent; give my compliments to the chefs," Lincoln said, sipping from his water glass.

"Sure thing," Andy replied, eyeing Lincoln. "Can I get you two a dessert?"

"How about a slice of the apple pie I saw earlier?" Lincoln requested.

"The pie? Always a great choice. And you, Jane?"

"Nothing for me. Thanks, Andy," Jane answered. "I best not."

Lincoln watched her face. "Let me get two," he said, stopping Andy as he started away from the table. "They just look really good."

As Andy retreated, Jane admonished Lincoln, "You shouldn't have done that. I...I don't like to spend that much when I'm out and, honestly, I don't need the calories. Have you seen me?" She gestured up and down her frame. "The curve is not in."

Lincoln followed the trail of her hand, from mahogany curls escaping her bun, to her soft, round face framing deep green eyes, to the curves of her body. She was not a small girl, and he wondered how many times someone else had made comments on her size to her. Just the thought angered him.

"You're a fan of self-deprecating humor, huh?"

"It's saved my psyche for most of my life, so I guess so."

"Ever thought you're too hard on yourself?"

"Occasionally," she replied matter-of-factly. "I know what I am. No point in trying to hide from it." The softness in her voice had faded, the bitterness in her words as sharp as his chef's knives.

"Here we go," Andy called, returning and breaking the string of tension between them. "Two apple pies."

"Wow," Jane breathed, inhaling the sweet scent of the dessert. "I love that smell." Lincoln smiled again, amused that apples and cinnamon could melt her harshness away.

"This does look incredible," Lincoln commented. "My grandmother used to make us pie on the Saturday after report cards came in. She'd get up early, before even my father was up, and make the dough from scratch. Every one she made was flawless, perfectly flaky, and sweet." Jane watched his eyes drift away, remembering something long past.

"And we'd wake up to the smell of these pies coming out of the oven, like cartoon characters being pulled in by a cloud of aroma. If we were up in time, she'd let us help with tossing the apples in cinnamon and sugar or, if she was feeling extra generous, making caramel. My dad hated it. He said it made the whole house smell like a cheap candle, but he always ate them."

"That sounds amazing." Jane took a bite of her own treat, moaning softly. Lincoln felt a twinge in his gut at the sound.

"So, your family was really close? I—"

"What?"

She grimaced. "I remember reading that you had a really big family."

For the first time, he shrugged off her fan status. "It's okay. I'm used to people sometimes knowing more about me than I know about myself. For example, did you know that I only sleep on thousand-count sheets?"

Jane rolled her eyes. "Sorry, I know it's got to be weird to have a conversation with someone whose frame of reference is interviews and articles. I would never assume that I know anything real about you based on that."

"To be fair, you probably know more than most if you've been following me since the beginning. I didn't get really private about my life until down the road."

"That's true. You are just as charming as you've always been, but you give more perfunctory answers and less personal ones."

"Honestly, there's not much personal to tell. It's just me in a big empty apartment eating takeout and streaming movies. I'm sure people think I'm out every night partying and going to new restaurants and schmoozing, and I do have appearances sometimes, but I don't know... I don't really enjoy it."

"You'd rather be at home?"

"Not my apartment, but yes. I am ready to come home at the end of the day to a warm and cozy house filled with family."

"Sounds like that's what you had growing up," Jane said softly. "Big family? Lots of cozy holidays? Must be hard this time of year to be away from them. Can you not go home?"

"Actually, I do have a big family. My dad is one of five, I'm one of four, and all my aunts and uncles had three or more kids. The Bainbridge clan together is an imposing sight. But no, I don't go home for the holidays. I tried to get them to move my show closer to home a few times, but Antony, my manager, said they wouldn't go for it." He finished his pie, swirling a piece of the crust through the last bit of filling.

"I'm sorry," she murmured, sensing a much longer story in his silence. "My family isn't quite that big, but we're close and loud and we get together as much as we can. My dad had three sisters and they all have kids and a few of my cousins are married and have kids of their own. We'll all be together for Thanksgiving this week. It'll be loud and wild and there will be enough food for several armies, but it's home."

"I'm envious. I'll stay in the apartment because the city is crazy with the parade and all. I might actually cook something, though. Maybe basil mac and cheese," he laughed drily.

"You'd be welcome with us," Jane blurted. "I mean, if you didn't want to hurry back or you didn't have something to do with the network or... Something."

It was a moment before he responded. "Maybe. I don't have any meetings until Monday since nothing really happens except the live chat on Thursday, and I'm not on that crew."

Jane's phone buzzed on the table, making them both jump. "Oh, wow!" she exclaimed. "It's almost eleven. And if y'all are heading to my grandparents' house to film tomorrow at ten, I need to get home." She waved a hand at Andy, gesturing for a check.

"I've got this," Lincoln declared, pulling out a credit card.

"No, I can't let you do that," Jane retorted.

Andy stopped at the table, two slips in his hand. "They'll get you up front. Thanks, guys." Lincoln snatched both papers, grinning and moving quickly through the empty restaurant toward the register near the door.

"Mr. Bainbridge, I really can't let you do that," Jane called, following behind.

Lincoln reached the counter and dropped the receipts and the small plastic card on top. The cashier, a slender girl with long brown-blonde hair, smiled broadly as she noticed the name on the card.

"Oh, my god! I thought you were familiar. You're Lincoln Bainbridge from the Culinary Channel!" she squealed. "I'm like, your biggest fan ever! My last boyfriend had a fit any time I made that cheeseburger casserole!" Jane rolled her eyes.

"Nice to meet you..." Lincoln paused.

"Kellen," the girl gushed, "Kellen McCoy. I just adore your show so much!"

"Always nice to meet a fan, Kellen," Lincoln acknowledged, reaching a hand out to her. She grabbed it and pulled him in, embracing him tightly against her chest. "Oof," he grunted and pulled away. "Thanks for that. I hate to run, but it's late and we've got an early morning appointment," he explained, gesturing to Jane at his side.

Kellen noticed the other woman for the first time, with an appraising up-and-down glance, ending with a small sneer. "Of course. You'd like me to combine your tabs?" she asked with a surprised tone.

"Yes, please. I'd be a bad date if I made her pay, wouldn't I?"

Kellen's eyes widened. "Uh," she looked at Jane again,

"sure. Let me just get that for you." She took the papers and punched some numbers on the register screen in front of her, muttering about how much food "she" ate. Jane didn't respond. A new receipt appeared, Lincoln signed it, and passed it back.

"Thanks so much, Kellen. Have a great night." He took Jane by the elbow and led her out the door. As they stepped back out onto 14th street, Lincoln heard a ripple of laughter and "He's going out with her?" He stiffened, glancing at Jane, trying to read her expression.

"Don't even worry about it," she said, her eyes straight ahead. "It's not the worst I've gotten. And I expected it when she knew who you were." Turning to face him, she smiled. "Thanks for tonight, though. You really didn't have to pay."

"Technically, I didn't," he chuckled. "That's my work card and I barely ever use it. Thought it might be good to knock the dust off of it."

"Well, okay." She turned left, facing Atlantic Drive.

"Is your car this way?" Lincoln asked, looking down the dimly lit road.

"I walked actually. Needed to clear my head. No worries though," she added emphatically, "It's only two blocks from here. Easy walk."

"I'll walk you home," he decided.

"No, really, you don't—"

"I want to. I'll feel better knowing you got home in one piece," he insisted. "Which way?"

"Mr. Bainbridge, I—"

"Lincoln. Please, Jane, I think we can go by first names at this point, and you're not talking me out of this. If it's a haul back to the hotel, I'll call for a ride. Now, which way is your apartment?"

"This way." She pointed. "Two streets over, then left and up to 16th."

"Oh, that's easy," he explained as they began walking, "I'm over on 17th, so I can just stroll back after I make sure you get home."

"You're far too chivalrous for your own good," Jane told him, tucking her hands into her sweater pockets.

"You can take the boy out of the South, but you can't take the South out of the boy," he joked, shoulders softening. "Honestly, it's just nice to have someone to talk to who isn't my agent or a show producer."

"Or an overzealous fangirl?" Jane mocked. "Oh, my god! It's Lincoln Bainbridge!" she mimicked Kellen, her voice breathy and high-pitched.

"Ugh," he groaned. "She's not even the worst, but she was pretty awful, especially to you."

"Tell me about the worst groupie experience you've ever had," she changed the subject eagerly, moving closer to him as a family passed on the inside edge of the sidewalk.

"The worst? Oh, wow... That's difficult to narrow down. There was a woman in London who stole a staff uniform and got upstairs and pretend she was delivering room service. Or the guy in Milan who literally ripped my shirt trying to get me to take it off and put on the one he had brought me, allegedly from Prada. But I'd guess that the one that really stands out was in California. A woman, probably close to my mother's age, somehow got into my dressing room for a wine special we were shooting in Napa and I found her there stretched across the sofa, naked, except for a cloud of whipped cream and a few precisely placed cherries."

Jane was aghast. "Are you serious? What did you do?"

"Backed away slowly and called security." Lincoln shuddered. "Even the security guards were scratching their heads at her. She was completely convinced that we were in love and going to run away together, presumably after our sticky tryst backstage. As they led her out, wrapped in a big blanket, she kept yelling that she loved me and was going to have my baby."

"Holy crap. People are wilder than I thought."

"I guess a lot of it is in the way Antony's pushed the shows. He's always pushed me as more of a sex symbol than a chef. I certainly wasn't the only person on Slice N Dice, but you'd never know that from the promotional materials."

"That is true," Jane remarked. "I've seen interviews with you where they don't even talk about food."

"Yeah," Lincoln trailed off.

The street was mostly empty as they moved along, the house fronts illuminated from within, their owners tucked in for the night. Conversation flowed easily between the pair, ranging from work to favorite books to music. Lincoln stole a glance at Jane, hastily turning away when he realized she was looking at him, too.

"Sorry," he muttered, embarrassed at his own obviousness. "I was just... I don't know what I was doing."

She blushed as red as her hair. "It's fine," she replied. "So, do you come to Atlanta often?"

"Not really," he admitted. "I don't travel as much as I used to, but even then, it was mostly international, for Slice N Dice."

"You grew up in Nashville, right?"

"Yeah, in Brentwood." He grew quiet again; the only sound was their shoes crunching along the pavement.

"I'm sorry." Jane reached for his hand.

Lincoln stopped walking and turned to face her. "Don't be. I don't talk about them for a host of reasons, but I did have a very nice upbringing in Brentwood. My family is still there, all except my YaYa. Like I said, I don't go home much." He started walking again. "I really don't go home at all."

Taking a few long strides to catch up to him as they approached 16th Street. "No more questions," she declared.

"At least not about family." They turned right at the corner and made their way to the last house on the set of four. "This is me."

Lincoln looked over the house. It was a pretty little grey, craftsman-style house with a tiny covered porch and a bright yellow front door. It was obviously an older house, but had been lovingly kept.

"It suits you," he declared. "Bright but homey."

"You're sweet," she laughed, but blushed at his words. "It cost a fortune to rent anywhere in the city, but I got lucky with this place. Can I offer you a cup of coffee or something?"

"Thanks, but we both need sleep."

"Are you sure you're okay to walk back to the hotel alone?"

"I think I'll be okay," he chuckled, "since I can see it from here." Jane glanced over his head and realized for the first time just how close the building really was.

"You're right." She grinned. "I guess you can walk a block. Maybe just text me when you get back to the hotel." She froze.

He didn't hesitate. "Sure. Nice to know someone is looking out for me. Here," he said, pulling his phone from his pocket and handing it to her. "Go ahead and put your number in. It'll be helpful if I need to get a hold of you tomorrow, too."

It was an excuse, and he knew it, but he wanted her number, wanted to keep talking to the first person to make him feel like himself in a long time. "Now you're in good company, just above Dan Greenberg." He noticed her eyes widen.

"Yeah, cause that's a totally normal thing for me."

"Does it make it better or worse if I tell you that August Black is further up the list?"

"Uh, I don't know, but here." She handed his phone back

and turned to unlock the door. "I can't be trusted with that kind of information."

Lincoln laughed, his voice booming into the night air. "I see. Thanks for the honesty."

"Well, thanks for walking me home."

"The pleasure is mine, Jane Mullins. Sleep tight. I'll see you in the morning."

"Goodnight, Lincoln." She smiled as she stepped inside, slowly closing the door as Lincoln retreated down the lamp-lit street to his hotel.

* * *

He flopped across the hotel room bed before pulling out his phone.

Lincoln: Made it back to my hotel in one piece, though I did nearly get pummeled by a man on a bike. Thanks for having dinner with me tonight. It was a really nice change. See you tomorrow.

He grinned. It wasn't an exaggeration to say it was one of the best nights he'd had in ages, though he was surprised at the source. Before he could stop himself, he sent a second text.

Lincoln: P.S. Be sure to save my number. I like having a friend to talk to.

Thoughts of her coworkers' earlier words sent a cold drip down his spine. She was a fan, a long-time one. She had followed him since the early years and knew all about him. God, she'd known about his family. This was exactly what he didn't need. How had he let himself forget that over pie and a late-night walk? He trusted too damn easily. His phone trilled, and he glanced at the message.

Jane: Thank you again for walking me home. I will save your number, but I promise not to abuse the privilege.

43

Well, that didn't sound like a girl ready to sell her story to the tabloids.

"What the hell are you doing, Bainbridge?" He groaned to himself. "Just do your damn job and stop flirting with the talent."

Garden of Memories

~~~

There was a knock at the front door; Jane knew it had to be Lincoln and the crew because friends came through the back. She checked her reflection in the hall mirror as she stepped into the foyer and opened the door. Jordan stood on the flagstone porch, grinning, with the crew behind him.

"Morning!" he called brightly, as she stepped to one side to let them all in.

"Hi, Jordan, guys. Come on in," she laughed as they entered. "Where would you like to set up? There's a whole house for you."

"Wow, you grew up here? This is a great house," Jordan said as Jane peered over his shoulder, looking for Lincoln.

"Yeah." She smiled, looking around at the familiar walls. Her Gramma's teapot collection lined narrow shelves above the sofa, a tall rack of her quilts tucked by the door to the back porch. There was nothing fancy to be seen, but pictures of children and grandchildren rested on every surface. It was definitely a family place.

"They haven't changed it much since, to be honest. It was

45

a wonderful place to grow up," Jane explained, the crew bustling about her.

"I know we need some B-roll of the kitchen, and some exteriors definitely," Jordan decided, peering down the hallway.

"Whatever you need," she agreed, nodding. "Do you need me now, or should I just stay out of the way?"

"We'll need you later, but I want to get the exteriors before the light shifts too much."

"Sounds good," she agreed, nodding. "I'll be outside."

She slipped out the back door, onto the screened-in porch. How many hours had she spent on this porch? Summer dinners and autumn breakfasts, long nights, wrapped up in a blanket, reading cookbooks and novels. Here were the enamel-coated flower pots that had housed her herb garden, the rocking chair Grampy had rocked in her in as a little girl, when she couldn't sleep. Even the backyard had remained unchanged, with its tall border of pine trees ringing the open lawn and dense, wooded area.

Grabbing a nearby watering can, she stepped onto the open wood porch and down the steps to the patio beneath. Using the hose hanging on the wall, she filled the can, and began to water the wide pots of pansies her Gramma planted every fall. As she worked, she began to sing.

She jumped a foot when a hand touched her shoulder.

"Oh jeez," Jane muttered as she steadied herself. Lincoln laughed.

"Sorry! Sorry! I had no idea I'd scare you!"

"I wasn't expecting anyone out here." She brushed a smudge from her jeans.

"I was on the phone when the guys came in, and Jordan said they want to do some shots without me, so..."

"Yeah." They were quiet, the distant noise of cars hummed.

"This is a really nice backyard," Lincoln commented after a moment.

"Grampy has always taken a lot of pride in his yard. But this isn't the best part."

"Really?" Lincoln asked, looking at her as she stared across the lawn.

"No, and I'll show you." Without thinking, she grabbed his hand and started toward the tree line. She stopped when he hesitated, and she dropped his hand. "Sorry. I guess I should have asked."

He chuckled. "No, no. I was just surprised. Sometimes I forget how to act like a normal human. Lead the way," he offered, reaching for her hand. She grinned and moved again.

The pine trees soared above them, dappled in the morning sunlight, as they wove through the rough-barked trunks. Jane stopped abruptly at a wooden gate set into a dense green hedge wall.

"Whoa," Lincoln said softly.

"The hedge runs about half of the property in the woods," Jane explained, hushed.

"Wait, why are we whispering?"

"Because it's a secret," she grinned again, reaching along the gate edge and drawing out a key, which she deftly used to open the door. "Welcome," she invited, reaching her hand for his as she stepped inside.

Lincoln checked before the threshold, watching Jane, her copper hair shimmering in the sunlight, swishing as she turned her face to the brilliant sunshine. He stepped through the shadowy doorway and emerged into a magnificent corner of creation.

There was no pavement, stone, or otherwise between his feet and the thick, green grass that spanned the whole of the enclosure. In the center of the garden soared a massive oak tree with an aged tire swing dangling from one of its lower branches.

To his left, in the closest corner, was a softly cascading waterfall, splashing into a clear pool edged with stacked stone. On his right was a collection of thin but tall birch trees and a vine-wrapped trellis that reached to the top of the hedged wall, a few feet beyond his height. Several trees dotted the rest of the space, surrounded solely by the dense, vibrant grass. In the far corner, all he saw was a wall of thin grey-green vines, shifting slightly in the autumn breeze.

"Over here," Jane's voice called from behind him, and he promptly followed. Brushing aside the curtain, which he quickly realized was composed of the lowest branches of a large weeping willow tree, he saw Jane perched on a stone bench, ankles crossed and swinging, smiling. A string of paper lanterns crisscrossed the nature-made canopy, and a hammock on a wooden stand swung on its own accord near the wall.

"This was my playhouse as a kid. Even in the rain, it stays almost completely dry under here." Tapping her knuckles on the tree's trunk, she grinned as she reached a spot with an echo. With a flick, she pulled away a piece of trunk, revealing a small cabinet that had been carved into it.

"Grampy made this for me so I could have a place to store my outdoor things. As I grew older, it was mostly full of books. This was my sanctuary. I could completely shut out the world here. I never wore shoes; I'd leave them outside the door, if I left the house in them at all. We kept small fish in the pond for a while, but my grandparents can't really care for the place now, and it was too much upkeep. I used to have dreams about the best moments in my life happening here. Some of them actually did. I opened my acceptance letter from culinary school here. The phone call telling me the owners had accepted my application for the bakery location came while I was here." Her feet had stopped swinging.

"Your father built the garden?" Lincoln asked, sitting beside her.

"He did, for my Gramma. He was the oldest, and the only son, and he built this for her before he went off to college. We've added things here and there, Gramma, Grampy, and me, but the walls, the trees, that was all him. I think he missed it when he and my mother married, because sometimes he would disappear on the weekends, and come here. We lived in a tiny little apartment in the city when I was born, closer to Dad's job. We didn't have a lot of money, partly because my mother stayed home with me, but Dad worked hard to make things good for us." Lincoln watched Jane's expression shift, from softly remembering to pained.

"Once, after he'd vanished for a few hours and come home, I remember them fighting. She was angry that she had left school and come here, that she'd gotten pregnant and that she was still living in a tiny apartment with little to show for her life. I was not a part of my mother's plans, apparently. She blamed him for everything and swore she was done. She slammed the door so hard when she left that the picture of them the day they brought me home from the hospital fell off the wall and shattered. The last thing she yelled was that nothing would ever change; we would be stuck like this, living paycheck to paycheck, struggling to get by, for our whole lives."

Lincoln reached forward, gently taking Jane's hand.

"Daddy came into my room and sat on the edge of my bed, realizing that I had heard everything that she'd said. He hugged me tightly, both of us crying. He looked at me after a few minutes and said, "Janie, don't you ever think you're not the best thing that ever happened to us.'

"I was only five," Jane continued, a half-smile on her face as she looked at Lincoln, "But I remember those words, clear as day."

"Did your mother come home after that fight?" Lincoln asked quietly, his thumb absently stroking her knuckles.

"She did. They never talked about it again, but I came across a brochure for a community college that offered an art degree tucked in her purse one day a few weeks later. I saw her buy a set of paintbrushes and some paints, too, and I could hear her talking to someone on the phone about going to the park to paint again. I'd like to think that it all would have come out alright in the end." Jane fell silent, her eyes fixed on a spot far from the present.

"But?" he prompted, after a moment.

"But about three months after that fight, I was curled up in the window seat of the apartment, reading, when our phone rang. I heard my mother answer it, and then scream. Mrs. O'Callahan, our next-door neighbor who had our spare key, came rushing in, thinking we were being attacked. She must have called Gramma and Grampy because they came to get me while my mother left. All I really remember from then is asking where Dad was and Gramma telling me that he was gone to heaven and I would have to wait to see him again."

"What happened?"

"He was driving home that day and a car coming the other direction had kicked up a piece of tire tread into the wind-shield of a moving van, which swerved across the yellow line and hit him head-on. They said it would have killed him instantly."

The breeze rustled the willow branches.

"I can't imagine how hard that was, especially at five." Lincoln paused, feeling Jane's hand tighten around his. "So where is your mom now?"

The expression of sadness on Jane's face was replaced with bitterness. "After the funeral, I was staying here while she went back home to England to find a place for us to live, or at least, that's what she said. We got a call a few weeks into her trip that she'd met a man who'd asked her to marry him, and they were going to travel. She said she thought I'd find it lonely to be away from my friends, so I would stay here, with Gramma and Grampy."

"She left you?" Lincoln asked, horrified.

Jane was quiet, her hands dropping in her lap, feet planted on the grass. "I didn't want to go, anyway. And I never regretted not fighting to go with her. Not that it would have mattered."

"Did she ever change her mind?"

"I think she did once. I was about thirteen and she wrote me a letter, the first one in a long time, and told me they were all settled, with my first half-sister and a second baby on the way, and she suggested I go live in England with them. I told Gramma I wrote back, but I really tore the letter to bits without answering. A month or so later, she showed up at my school, right around lunchtime, in the courtyard between the buildings. She had a teddy bear and a balloon in her hands, like she was expecting her five-year-old to still be five. I saw her and didn't recognize her at first. She looked so different. Older, obviously, but her hair was blonde and much shorter than the long brown wave it had been in my childhood. Her outfit was tailored and neat, but the unmistakable early bump of an expecting mother was obvious. She was smiling, but it wasn't a warm smile. It was expectant, as if she believed I would run to her like a long-lost child when she called my name. My friends were all whispering among themselves. They didn't know who she was, and I never talked about her to them."

"She was so hopeful," Jane admitted, "So confident that I would be happy to see her. But I was fueled by abandonment and teenage hormones so I basically shouted at her to leave me alone and that I didn't want to leave when I was five and thought my mother loved me, and I certainly don't want to leave now, when I'm old enough to know that she didn't."

Lincoln grimaced. "Ouch."

Nodding, Jane agreed, "Not my finest moment."

Jane stopped. Her eyes were dry, but he could hear the strain in her voice. "Sorry to dump all that on you," she looked at him.

Lincoln smiled, playfully bonking his head against her shoulder. "Hey, I asked! And we all have family trauma, right?"

"I guess," Jane said with a shrug, "I've come to realize, as an adult, she's not a bad person, really. She made the choices she thought were the best for her, and I believe she did want to make me a part of it. But I wouldn't have ever been happy that far from here, from my family."

"You didn't think you would adjust?"

"Maybe if I'd gone when I was little, but by thirteen, I was rooted here. I've never regretted it," she repeated.

"You amaze me, Jane. You fought for where you are, every step of the way."

She smiled for the first time since they entered the garden. "Grampy likes to tell me a wise woman makes her own opportunities. I guess I'm proof that he was right. I had to work for everything, but I have mostly made it to where I want to be."

"And this opportunity? The chance to win twenty-five thousand dollars and international fame?"

"I don't know about the fame part, but the money would be a big help to us right now."

Lincoln looked puzzled. "Why now, in particular? I thought things were going really well for you?"

"Things are going... Okay." she wrung her hands together, not meeting Lincoln's eyes. "Our business is down from this time last year, the landlord is raising the rent, and both of our stoves have gone down in the last few months and required several thousand dollars in repairs."

"Wow. That's a lot to handle."

"Yeah, especially when I didn't..." she stopped.

"You didn't what?"

"If I tell you this, you have to swear to keep it a secret. Not even my crew knows this."

He gestured across his chest in a big X. "Cross my heart."

"I didn't want to go the whole bakery route. I had dreams of opening a family-style restaurant using my family recipes and just making this whole cozy atmosphere where people feel loved. But they kept telling me in culinary school that I was too soft for restaurant life and plenty of people told me that trying to open a place like that in Atlanta was a pipe dream. So, I took part of my inheritance from Dad and opened the bakery. And it's worked. I mean, it's been successful so far. I just..."

"It's not what your dream was," he finished, patting her knee. "I know that feeling. I really do. I wanted to be a chef in my own restaurant, too. My grandmother was the one who thought I had the face of a TV host. I'm sure everything will work out, though, Jane."

"I hope so. I can't fail at this." She looked at him; he was staring intently at her, his body turned straight at her, and his face inching closer to hers.

"Miss Mullins? Lincoln?" someone yelled, startling them both so that they jumped back.

"We'll be right there, Jordan," Lincoln called in reply. Jane was straightening her sweater's collar. "We should head back up." He adopted a game-show host voice. "Time for your big debut!" She laughed.

"Then what was yesterday?" she asked as they walked. She locked the gate, tucking the key back behind the greenery, and he offered his arm gallantly.

"Yesterday was the day you met someone you'd dreamed of meeting for," he paused. "How long?"

"Only about a decade." Jane admitted.

"And how did that go for you?"

"A little rough, if I'm honest."

He stopped walking, but held her arm in his. "I'm sorry for that. I really am." She started to interrupt but he continued. "You weren't what I expected. And it kinda threw me off."

"What were you expecting?" Jane asked, turning to face him.

"I don't know," he admitted. They started walking again, emerging into the sunlit backyard. "But I'm glad I was wrong." He watched the sun dance through the strands of her hair as they crossed the yard, resisting the urge to brush a wayward curl from her face.

Jordan and the crew were standing in the living room, cameras focused on the narrow kitchen when the pair walked in. Jane immediately dropped her arm from Lincoln's.

"Hey, Jane, we want to get some shots of you working in the kitchen, then we'll do some static roll of you talking about growing up here and the inspiration for the bakery."

"Alright. Let's go," Jane agreed, her smile brightening.

For the next two hours, Lincoln watched her cheerily recount learning to cook with her grandmother, spending holidays with her aunts and uncles, cousins and friends. She pretended to mix up a cake, cheerfully moving about the kitchen. It was captivating; the way she spun through the galley-style kitchen with a confidence and poise he'd never seen, the way she held not just his attention, but everyone's.

"That's a wrap!" Jordan finally announced. Turning to Jane and Lincoln, he continued, "We've got everything we need. It will be great background and color for your introductory segment for the show. Thank you for letting us visit your home," he smiled earnestly.

"Thank y'all for coming!" Jane replied heartily. "Y'all have been so wonderful. I can't wait to see what you put together."

Jordan set off with the crew to pack, leaving Lincoln and Jane alone again.

"I need to call Gramma. Can you help the guys get sorted?"

"Sure thing."

The crew was packing up as Lincoln watched Jane talking happily on the phone with her grandmother. After everything she'd told him today, he couldn't help but smile as she chatted about filming and the competition itself, asking questions about the trip her grandparents were on. Even with her occasional sharpness, Jane Mullins was perhaps the warmest and most kind person he had ever met, and despite his usual reserve with people, he wanted to spend more time with her. It should scare him, but somehow, he felt safe with her.

"Lincoln?" Jordan asked. "We're all set. We have to take the rental van back and then head to the airport. They've got us in LA tomorrow for the remote part of the Thanksgiving show, so we can't take you back to the hotel. Are you alright to get back?"

"Yeah, I'll call a car. It's fine. Y'all be safe, and thanks for all the work you've put in these two days."

"Hey, no worries. These are fun. The nice ones are easy to work with," Jordan admitted, gesturing with a head nod to Jane. "Take care and we'll see you back in New York, brother." The men shook hands, and the crew was off.

Jane ended the call as she heard the door close. Disappointment settled as she saw the empty house. They'd all gone while she was talking to Gramma. She supposed it was time to head home. She rounded the corner to the kitchen and jumped when she saw someone leaning against the cabinet.

"Ah!" she cried, heart racing, before she recognized Lincoln. He doubled over laughing as she tried to catch her breath. "I thought everyone left!"

"The guys did, but they are going straight to the airport. I was waiting to tell you goodbye before I call the car to take me back."

She shook her head, chuckling, "Well, that was nice of you. Until you scared me half to death. Again."

Lincoln bowed dramatically. "I am terribly sorry, my lady. Let me make it up to you?"

Jane hesitated, her heart racing. "I suppose I can do that. How will you make it up to me?"

He paused, then grinned. "If you can give me a ride back to the city, we can grab dinner?"

"Again?"

Frowning, Lincoln nodded. "Unless you're tired of me already."

"No, no!" she hurried to reassure him, patting his arm. "I just...we had dinner together last night and I didn't think you'd want to spend more time with me."

"I absolutely do," Lincoln said firmly.

She hadn't thought her heart could go this fast, but she might rival a hummingbird at the moment. "Sounds great. You had home tomorrow then?"

"Actually, I got a call from Antony's office and they booked my return flight for Friday since Thursday was so full. I've got tomorrow and Thursday free in the city. I guess I'll find somewhere that's open to eat some turkey."

"My offer still stands. You're welcome to join us here, if you're brave enough to face the Mullins clan."

"You're sure your grandparents won't mind?"

"Lincoln, there's so many of us, they might not notice." He laughed. "I'm just kidding, but yes, they'll be fine with it."

"That really sounds lovely," he admitted, smiling widely. "It's been a very long time since I've had a family Thanksgiving."

Jane glanced at the time on her phone. "We should head back. Traffic will pick up if we wait much later." She grabbed her messenger back from the counter and the pair moved out the door, which Jane locked promptly behind them. Lincoln climbed into the passenger seat, but his knees were practically at his chest in the compact car.

Taking in the sight as she climbed in, she said, "There's a seat adjuster on the side, so you don't have to ride like that. Usually, I'm hauling orders in here so I don't need lots of room."

He shifted the seat back, stretching his long legs as space appeared.

"Better?" she asked.

"Much. Thank you."

She set off back to the interstate that would take them back to the city. "What do you think you'll do tomorrow with your free time?"

"I'm not sure. I know there's all the touristy things, but I don't really want to do them alone," he said, eyeing her as they drove. "I'm sure you are working, right?"

"Umm, actually, the crew will be running things tomorrow, but we're mostly open for pickups. People who ordered pies and things for Thursday. I will be grocery shopping and cooking at my apartment." She glanced at him, "I like to put on Christmas music and this apron my grandmother bought me a few years ago, and open the windows and just cook all day."

"Do you do most of the cooking?" Lincoln asked.

"It's pretty evenly split, actually. We all do several things and then bring it all together. Gramma and Grandpa always make the turkey and the cornbread dressing, which is a closely guarded family recipe."

"You'd tell me, but then you'd have to kill me?" he chortled.

"Something like that. My aunts make casseroles and vegetables and desserts. My uncle Cole makes a seven-layer salad with peas and bacon and cheese that everyone loves. And I make hash brown casserole, celery stuffed with cream cheese and olives or pecans, and some kind of dessert."

"Pumpkin pie?"

"I usually do something different each year. Last year it was an apple spice Bundt cake with salted caramel glaze. Year before that it was a pistachio-chocolate pie. Gramma always makes a sweet potato pie and a pecan pie, and my cousins usually bring cookies they've made."

"That is a lot of food!"

"It is, but we do always have leftovers. Gramma has an entire cabinet full of plastic containers that we use to pack them up and take them home and then eat turkey sandwiches and dressing for a week." She was smiling broadly as she spoke.

"Sounds like it will be fun." Lincoln thought for a moment. "Maybe I can join you for shopping and cooking tomorrow?"

Stealing a glance at him, Jane saw a hopeful smile on his face. "Are you sure? You could do anything around the city. Why would you want to spend it with some silly baker you hardly know?"

"Two dinners and the girl still thinks I don't like her!" Lincoln cried exasperated. "This may come as a surprise to you, Jane, but I have truly enjoyed my time with you. And rather than spend a day in a city that I don't know very well all alone the day before Thanksgiving, I would like to spend it with a lovely woman, doing something enjoyable."

Chastised, Jane was silent. They drove like that for a while, before she hazarded a glance at Lincoln, who was watching her.

"Tell me a story?" Jane asked abruptly, trying to ignore the way his glances made her feel as they made their way up the interstate, the city coming into view in the distance.

"What kind of story?"

"Any kind. Just a story."

"Uh, well, let's see... When I was turning twenty-one, my friends at Vanderbilt decided that the only way to celebrate was to take me out and get me very, very drunk."

"As one does," she playfully agreed.

"So, we bar hop for a while, and I'm drinking like a new twenty-one-year-old, but I'm not really drunk, just kinda buzzed, mostly just really loud and stumbly. It's closing time and we're stumbling out of a bar on the riverside and we pass a dumpster that was full of clothes, and I decided to look through it. I found this hideous, fuchsia dress and, because we're all drunk, we added some sequined silver heels. I started yelling about how great I looked, then wobbled down the side-walk. The guys follow me down the street, where I fell into a fountain outside of a restaurant and started singing at the top of my lungs. Lesson learned, I should not have tequila. Ever."

Jane wove through the streets of Atlanta, laughing so hard she could barely breathe. "Wow! Are there pictures of your birthday?"

"Not from that portion of the evening," he said, relieved. "Thankfully, that was back before everyone had camera phones. Your turn. Tell me something no one else knows about you."

She wrinkled her nose. "Really? I'm pretty much an open book. I'm the poster child for wearing your heart on your sleeve."

"Oh, come on, there must be something you do that no one else knows about."

Thinking for a moment, she responded, "I love the cold weather, even the darkest days of winter here. I adore it. It wakes me up from the inside out, like my soul just comes to life in the fall and winter. I even enjoy cold showers."

"Really? Cold showers?"

"Not all the time, just cold water at the end. Although, I

have to admit that sometimes, after one of the sticky humid days we get in the summer, I will take a totally cold shower just to cool down." Lincoln shook his head, trying to not imagine Jane in the shower.

She pulled into an alley that ran parallel to 16th street, moving slowly down the grey paved path. "We're home," she informed, pulling into the driveway of her little house. Lincoln noticed a dark green bicycle, a basket attached to the front handlebars, leaning against the far wall.

"You ride?"

"Sometimes to work, when the weather is nice." She smiled. "Or I'll ride over to the farmer's market to get fresh bread and spices. Thus, the basket."

"Very cozy," Lincoln acknowledged, shutting the car door as they climbed out.

They made their way across the porch, and Jane unlocked the yellow door. "This is home."

Lincoln turned slowly on the spot, taking in the open room. The walls were a pale grey color, and the floors a dark hardwood, golden-hued in the setting sun that filtered through the wide windows at the front of the house. A squashy dark blue sofa, lined with brightly colored pillows, stretched along the wall in one room, facing a wall-mounted television and flanked by an old upholstered armchair. Jane reached down and turned on the closest lamp, one of a mismatched pair.

"It's definitely not fancy, but it's homey enough. Everything is second-hand thrift store bought or gifted by friends and family. I actually rescued the dining room table from the dump and painted it. Maybe one day I'll have my own house and yard."

"You wouldn't want to stay in the city?"

"Not really. I mean, I moved up here because I was tired of fighting traffic every single day, especially in the beginning, when I was pretty much running the bakery on my own. I still hate traffic, but I'd like to have a house with a yard and big trees that cast shade in the summer and drop leaves in the fall." Jane moved across the room as she spoke dreamily. "I have dreams of a farmhouse with big windows, a huge kitchen where I can host my whole family, and a garden bathtub." She chuckled at the last item.

"I'm sure you'll get there someday," Lincoln replied, resting a hand on her shoulder.

"I don't know. That would be a lot for one person to take care of, especially when the bakery takes so much time. Another reason I moved here was to rent instead of buying a place. No real upkeep for me. I was always afraid that if I bought a place, I couldn't take care of it."

"You won't be on your own forever, though. You never know," Lincoln suggested.

Jane turned to face him. "With my history, I might be."

"What's that loaded comment supposed to mean?" he asked, brows furrowed.

Jane took a deep breath. "The short version of the story is that I dated one of the radio DJs in town for about a year before he broke up with me, on air, but not before calling me a gold-digging slut." Lincoln's expression twisted angrily as she spoke. "Then he had the nerve to come drunkenly into the bakery and try to get me to give him permission to use the whole ordeal, since the station was concerned I'd sue them over it, and then when I refused, told me the only reason he'd dated a 'pig like me' was because his agent thought it would be good for his image after his last breakup, where his ex accused him of abuse."

Lincoln slumped onto a nearby chair, flabbergasted. "Are you serious? He broke up with you on air?"

"I wish I was kidding. It was pretty horrible. We lost some customers, and some others were, let's say, less than kind.

Fortunately, most of our repeat customers, the ones we've been working with since the beginning, didn't believe any of it and stuck with us."

"Jane, I'm so sorry. This guy sounds like an ass."

"Oh, he was, even when we were dating. But I... I hadn't dated much before him and he was nice enough when we were in public until the end. But we never spent time alone if he could help it, and I was always the initiator. It didn't surprise me to learn that he'd done it for his image. Before me, he'd dated models and dancers and last I heard, he still was."

Lincoln stood and crossed to her, embracing her gently. "He didn't deserve you."

For a moment, they stood together, his arms wrapped around her. She breathed deeply, inhaling his scent. "You know my story, everything about Railey, I suppose."

Jane pulled away. "Not the details, but yes, the basic story. She ran off with a photographer and now she does soap operas out in Los Angeles."

"Not any photographer," he corrected, leaning against the kitchen counter. "My childhood best friend. One of my closest friends at the time. He'd been squiring her around town when I traveled and I thought it was just innocent at first until I came home from an on-location in Maine and found the ring and a letter. And she still wanted to be friends. Like we'd ever been friends before."

Jane grimaced; his story was as bad as hers. "Do you talk to either of them?"

"Not since that day. Dylan has tried to reach out a few times, and Railey did once or twice in the beginning, I suspect because the paparazzi were making her out to be pretty frigid. They're not together anymore, I do know that."

Silence swept around them, Jane sitting in a kitchen chair, Lincoln leaning against the counter, ghosts of the past lingering heavily in the air.

She shook her head adamantly. "Nope, not tonight. We've been hurt, and it sucks, but tonight, we are going to eat dinner and enjoy ourselves and forget them." She stood, crossing the room and opening the refrigerator.

"Well," she began, "we might have a slight problem."

He moved around the counter and peered into the fridge. "Oh. Running on empty?"

"Since I'm going to the market tomorrow, I guess I let myself run out of actual food," she laughed. "Must have missed that detail when I was grabbing the cream for my tea this morning. Well, crap. I invite a chef for dinner and I can serve him," she rooted through the remnants of items, "a crisp salad of olives and Monterey jack cheese or a peanut butter and jelly sandwich."

Chuckling, Lincoln admonished her. "You do not have to feed me. We could go out or get takeout. I'm an easy date."

She flushed at Lincoln referring to himself as her date. "Well, I have been craving Chinese. We could get delivery from there and if we're still hungry, walk down to Edelberg's for ice cream later."

"I love Chinese. Sounds perfect! I have to admit, I'm kind of starving."

"Me, too. Skipping lunch wasn't the best idea we've had." She opened a drawer and pulled out a thin binder, which opened into a sheaf of papers that he quickly identified as takeout menus.

"You order out often?"

"Not really, but I had menus from all the nearby areas from when I moved in. They came in a welcome packet for the apartment, so I organized them."

Lincoln examined the menus and saw sticky notes marking certain dishes and larger notes with totals for specific orders. Jane noticed the look on his face. "Saves time." He raised his eyebrows at the meticulous notes on each menu.

"I'm an organizing freak. Okay? I like labels and color coding. And you can pry my fancy pens from my cold, dead hands" She smacked his arm with a menu.

He ducked, laughing. "No judgment. I'd be a mess if I didn't have an agent who keeps track of things for me."

Jane held up a menu. "This is the best place in miles and they always give you twice as much as you need." She handed Lincoln the paper. "I get the sesame chicken with wonton soup, and I think I'll get an order of crab Rangoon..."

"Oh, those are my favorite. I get them all the time from Moon Blossom, the Chinese place between my apartment and the studio. They're so crisp and creamy, and just a little sweet... Mmm."

"Definitely an order of those. And fried rice. Lots of fried rice." Jane made notes on a small pad she'd grabbed from the drawer. "What about a main dish for you?"

"Anything spicy? I like good spice."

"They've got General Tso's chicken or beef and Szechuan chicken, beef, and pork. I got the Szechuan once by accident and it nearly took off the roof of my mouth."

"Okay, maybe not that spicy," Lincoln laughed. "It all sounds good. Can we share?"

"Sure! Like I said, they always give me a ton of stuff." She grabbed her phone, scrolling through the saved numbers until she found the right one. "Hello, Mrs. Yanchen. It's Jane." Lincoln watched Jane while she ordered, amused the restaurant knew her by name. "Fifteen minutes? Thanks!"

"They know you by name?" he chuckled.

"Yeah. I don't go out a lot, but Panda Wok is pretty cheap and it's great when I have a busy day and can't be bothered to cook something. Or for nights when I have company and don't have real food that's not pop tarts in the house."

"Well, Miss Mullins, why don't you give me a tour of your lovely home while we wait for our food?"

"Umm, sure," she responded hesitantly.

"Unless you don't want to or it's a mess or something," he added. "I can totally sit on the couch and watch TV."

"No, it's fine. I just don't really have people here much. And honestly," she gestured to him, "I'm still a little in shock that you, of all people, are standing in my kitchen right now, talking about Chinese food, so the thought of you touring my house, seeing my bedroom, is a little tough to comprehend. But, let's go!" She waved a hand around. "This is the kitchen. It's way smaller than I'd have liked, but larger than most places I looked, so it was a winner. The breakfast slash dining room." She gestured to the round wooden table with a dark wood top and cream-hued legs ringed with matching chairs. She moved back toward the front door, Lincoln at her heels. "My living room and office and sometimes bedroom."

"And down the hall?"

"The bathroom, a tiny storage closet, and my bedroom." She walked through the open door and he followed, unable to keep from smiling at the cozy space.

Jane had fashioned a canopy above the double bed, which was covered with a vibrant green comforter and piles of pillows. There was another slightly worn armchair tucked in one corner, facing the small television situated atop a dark wooden dresser. Two wide windows overlooked the street, the city lights beginning to illuminate in the autumn twilight.

"It suits you," he declared. "It's quirky and colorful and warm."

"It's something," she agreed, nodding. "Nice home for my books and a pretty cozy place to sleep." He noticed the book-shelves that ran along the wall opposite the windows, all of them stuffed to bursting with books of every size, shape, and color. Small paperbacks wedged in between worn hardcover cookbooks. A bulletin board layered with handwritten recipes, photos of houses, kitchens, even a glittering cocktail dress and printed images of decorated cakes hung nearby too.

"Wow, the entire collection of August Black," he noted, impressed, picking a brightly colored book from the top of a shelf.

"Isabella Goldman, too," Jane replied. "They're my favorites, but I have others. Ani Gregory, I think there might even be a beat-up copy of Jenny Youngman in there somewhere."

"*Synonymous Flavors.*" He flipped through a smaller tome, its cover adorned with a color pie chart of flavors. "You're a student of food and flavor."

"I guess." Jane shrugged, kicking her shoes off and into the closet. "I love to look at what combinations make sense, and experiment with ones that aren't obvious. Umm," she paused awkwardly, eyeing her dresser, "Would you mind stepping out while I change clothes?"

Suddenly, he felt awkward too, standing in the room of a girl he barely knew. "Oh sure. I'll just go back to the living room and watch TV until dinner gets here," he blurted as he hurried out the door. Dropping onto the sofa, Lincoln realized how tired he'd gotten. He found the remote and wasn't surprised that the Culinary Channel turned on.

"We're going to add in the blackberry preserves here. If you're not a fan of seeds, you can always substitute blackberry jam. Just use about a tablespoon less since jam tends to offer more moisture than preserves." The bubbly presence of Eloise Hardaway, the "Cheap Chic Chef" beamed from the screen.

"Do you know her?" Jane inquired, stepping off the last stair, now wearing slim black leggings and a dark blue tunic. He noticed she'd let her hair down from the plastic clip she'd used to hold it away from her face and wanted to run his fingers through the mess of curls that tumbled to her shoulders.

"Eloise? Not much. She's fairly new and she films mostly at her home studio in Chicago, so we don't cross paths. I've met her a few times. She seems sweet, though."

"I can see that. She's almost a little too sweet sometimes."

"Yeah, but that's just her show persona; she's more normally sweet in person," he chuckled. "So, you watch the Channel a lot, then?"

"Only certain shows," she insisted. "I'm not a total junkie. I watch a lot of documentaries and other shows, too. Wow, I never realized how nerdy and sad that sounded until just now."

"I get it, though. You work hard and you work a lot; when you get home, you just want to relax and unwind, so you find things that take your mind away."

"Exactly! I watch hockey, too, so there's that. But that's not a relaxing thing so much as a wild, unbridled passion that usually leads to me yelling at the television, occasionally so loud the neighbors complain."

Lincoln guffawed. "Really? That is amazing."

"Really. Not every game, but big games, playoff games especially. I get a little, um, into it."

"I think I'd like to see that."

"I don't know; it's not very ladylike of me."

"Being ladylike is overrated. Trust me, I know." He waggled his eyebrows, and she chuckled.

"I like people to see me as put together and polished. Playoff hockey doesn't bring that out in me."

"Why do you care what people think?"

She half-shrugged. "I was always the weird kid, the kid with no parents, when I was younger and I hated the way people looked at me, treated me. Even in culinary school, they all acted like I was a cushion, too soft to make it. Then when everything happened with Nick, and people believed I was this

67

gold-digger... I just worry that people don't see me as I am, or as I want to be."

"But you realize what they say about you is more about them and less about you."

"That's all well and good, but I don't like people to think things about me that aren't true."

"I had to let that go," Lincoln said, looking right at her. "After the first episode of Next Top Chef. Some of the things people said about me, or wrote about me on the internet, some of it was really terrible stuff. People are always going to assume things, you just can't let them get to you."

Jane started to reply when the doorbell rang. "I'll get it," she announced, rushing to the front door. Carrying two loaded bags, which she deposited on the kitchen bar, she pulled plates and utensils from their respective cabinets.

"What can I get you to drink? I've got tea, water, milk, and ginger ale."

"Tea sounds great."

They settled onto the couch and ate in silence, except for the television. As one show ended and another began, Lincoln commented, "This is exceptionally good Chinese food. Even better than the place I get mine in New York. Thank you."

"My pleasure," Jane replied, staring at the television. How had she managed to forget how to speak in the last half hour?

"So tomorrow," Lincoln began.

"You certainly don't have to help me shop and cook," she rushed. "I'm sure there are things you'd much rather do. I won't hold you to it."

He shook his head. "I was just going to ask what time you want to get started."

"Ten? The market shouldn't be too busy and it'll be a nice day to walk there."

"Sounds good. Maybe I can make dessert this year while you make the other things."

"Only if you want to."

"Jane," Lincoln tucked his fork into the container and turned to face her. "What can I do to make you believe I like you? That I want to be with you?"

She gulped. Was this even real? "I just have a hard time believing someone like you would want to...would want..." she trailed off, ducking her head.

Lincoln slipped a finger beneath her chin and lifted her face, waiting until her eyes met his. He saw the hesitation in the emerald green, but didn't pull away. "I want. I want to spend time with you. I want to get to know you better. Please let me."

Jane took a deep breath. "Okay."

"Good. Now, let's eat!"

They dug back into their Chinese food and made a list of ingredients to buy the next day.

Turkey Day

"Are you sure you're ready for this?" Jane asked Thursday morning as they stood, hands full of casserole dishes and containers, in front of the bright red door.

"Do I really need a warning for your family?" He chuckled.

"You know those Thanksgivings on television where everyone dresses up and you all eat around a beautifully covered table with candles and the whole turkey in the middle and all?"

"Of course. That Norman Rockwell, idyllic holiday?"

"Well, we're not anything like that. We use paper plates and everything is served buffet style and we sit all over the house, most of the men in the den watching football, the women in the dining room sharing recipes for every dish, and the kids at the folding table in the living room playing table hockey with a roll."

He laughed aloud, imagining the scene she described. "Sounds like more fun than my family's holidays. Of course, we have to go inside the house for me to fully appreciate this scenario you're painting."

She took a deep breath. "You should also know that I have only brought one other guy home and they like to *remind* me, for lack of a better term, that I'm still single. They interrogated Tim, the guy I dated in college, about 'his intentions' almost the whole day; I'm not convinced it didn't play a role when he dumped me a week later."

He snorted derisively. "What an idiot. So, what's our story?"

"What story?"

"Are we dating? Are we friends? Should I know your whole life story?" a pull in his gut made him need the answer in a way he didn't expect.

She hesitated, thoughts racing. Did Lincoln Bainbridge just ask if they were dating? Or were they fake dating? She knew how that trope tended to play out in her favorite books. Another beat passed. "I don't know. I guess our being friends is a safe enough plan. Not that they, my Gramma in particular, will stop questioning you anyway."

"After eleven years of interviews and paparazzi following you around, you get used to deflecting questions." He cocked his head. "Unless, of course, you're simply embarrassed by me, Jane."

She punched him lightly on the shoulder and opened the old screen door.

"Jane!" Several voices rang out in unison as she and Lincoln stepped into the brightly lit kitchen. Two small objects flew at her knees, knocking her back into Lincoln, who caught her gracefully.

The pint-size perpetrators grinned up innocently, one a flushed face, redheaded little girl, the other a dark-haired, bespectacled, blue-eyed boy. Jane ruffled both heads, prying the children from her shins before dropping to kid level.

"Hi, Cam! Hi, Mikey!" she cried, wrapping both in a wide

embrace after she placed the containers of food on the counters. "Have you been good?"

Both kids nodded, then looked up at the unfamiliar figure towering above them; Jane noticed and raised back to her feet.

"Cam, Mikey, this is my friend Lincoln Bainbridge. Lincoln, these are my two youngest cousins, Cambria Hillman and Michael Rochester."

"Hi, guys," Lincoln said, reaching into his leather messenger bag and pulling out two plastic-wrapped cookies, a Santa head, and a snowman. The kids' faces brightened, and they scurried away into the throng of people. He and Jane moved deeper into the room, more people greeting them.

"Janie!" one woman exclaimed as she embraced the blushing girl. "It's about time. I thought you'd gotten lost!" The boisterous woman, with tight, dark curls framing a cheerful face, hugged Jane and kissed her cheek.

"Hey, Aunt Kay. Sorry we're late. I couldn't find the lid for my casserole dish."

"Not to worry, sweetheart! And who is this handsome young gentleman?" Kay asked.

Holding out his hand, Lincoln replied, "Lincoln Bainbridge, ma'am. Pleasure to meet you."

Lincoln stifled a laugh at the look on the woman's face. Obviously, Jane's family would know of her long-standing crush on him.

Finally, Kay spoke, shaking his hand. "Kay Wilfred. It's a pleasure to meet you. We've heard so much about you."

Three other women appeared in the long, narrow kitchen, and Lincoln thought the older one with wispy salt and pepper hair had to be Gramma.

"Well, hello ladies," he grinned, as Jane struggled for words in the crowd. "I'm Lincoln Bainbridge."

"Malinda Hillman," replied the brunette.

"Anna Rochester," said the blonde.

"And you must be Mrs. Mullins," Lincoln addressed the matriarch. "I've seen your lovely home before, but am glad to finally have the pleasure of meeting you, ma'am."

"You too, sweetheart!" she exclaimed, wrapping Lincoln in a hug. Jane blushed as she heard him "oof" in her grandmother's eager embrace. "Please call me Annie. Janie's been talking about you forever!"

Quickly, her blush spread across her cheeks, and Jane interrupted, "Gramma, I think we're all starving. Maybe we should eat?"

Releasing Lincoln, Gramma nodded. "You're right. Alright. Anna, would you round up the kids, please?"

The women retreated into the larger room, and Jane moved close to Lincoln, taking his hand. "Well, she loves you already. And the cookies? Such a sweet idea."

"You said you had seven cousins. I thought I would bring them all a little treat."

She smiled, squeezing his hand. "So far, you've impressed them and me. I think you've earned some turkey and dressing."

Anna returned, seven babbling children at her sides, followed by four men, the other halves of the women he had already met. This time, Jane took the introduction initiative.

"As I told your beautiful wives, it is a pleasure to meet you all. And I am so thankful that I got stranded here over the holiday so that I can share it with this fantastic family." He turned to Gramma. "Jane has been telling me about this world-famous dressing you make, and I have been dying to try it. Shall we eat?"

Jane elbowed him, as her grandfather replied, "Have to bless the food first, son. Adam, will you do the honors this time?"

Lincoln watched Jane's family and the affection they

shared, his eyes welling as he wished his own could be so loving.

The amen was said and in a rush, the kids were squeezing past him into the kitchen, grabbing thick paper plates from the counter and quickly filling every inch of white space with vibrant foods. Cam was stacking slices of ham on her plate architecturally, while Mikey was spooning copious amounts of macaroni and cheese into his dish.

Lincoln felt a tap on his arm and turned to see Jane, grinning broadly, holding out a paper platter for him. "Gotta move fast around here or we might run out."

He eyed the plethora of food, the myriad dishes and thought this unlikely, but asked, "Has that ever happened?"

She laughed brightly, as did her grandfather, who was standing behind them. "Never," her grandfather replied. "We might run out of Annie's dressing or the rolls, but never the whole lot of food. Of course, we do run out of cranberry sauce every year, don't we, Janie?" He winked conspiratorially. Jane blushed, turning to the food table to grab a turkey leg and a few small pieces of dark meat.

"Does your grandmother make really good cranberry sauce, too," Lincoln inquired quietly, gathering turkey as Jane moved to the table laden with casseroles.

"No. My grandmother doesn't make cranberry sauce. I prefer the can-shaped, jellied variety. And I love it. It's my second favorite Thanksgiving food."

"The kind you buy that makes that slurping sound when it slides out of the can?"

"That's the stuff. Just don't tell anyone at the Culinary Channel. I'm sure that's heresy up there."

It was Lincoln's turn to laugh. "You know, I don't think I've ever had it. My grandmother has been making this weird cranberry Jell-O stuff since Moses was a boy, and I don't like that at all. This seems to be my year for new things. Where is this fine delicacy?"

"Over there." Jane gestured toward a cut glass dish at the table's end. She moved into the kitchen, to the stove where the massive pan of dressing waited.

Lincoln looked over the dish with a smile. The can shape was still recognizable, though someone had very neatly sliced the log right along the ridgelines, arraying it prettily on the glistening dish. Resting next to it was a silver spoon with a large round head, which he used to scoop a slice onto his plate.

"Lincoln, would you like tea or a Coke?" Jane called from the other end of the kitchen.

"Is it sweet tea?"

Everyone in earshot laughed. "Where are you from, boy?" Adam asked, clapping Lincoln on the shoulder.

"Forgot where I was for a moment." Lincoln humored them. "I'm from Nashville, born and raised, but I've been living in New York for the past ten years and up there, if you don't ask, you never know what you might get. I will take some sweet southern tea, Jane."

His plate full, small amounts of nearly everything cramming into the rounded corners, Lincoln set his plate on a beautiful old hardwood table, tucked into a bright room off of the food area. Jane followed close behind him.

"You sure you don't want to watch football with the guys in the living room?"

"You know me, Jane," he said, his eyes glinting with the joke. "Am I here for football or you?"

Her heart skipped a beat as his eyes bored into hers. "Fair enough. Just be warned that this is the girls' area and they are going to ask you all the questions."

He intertwined his fingers, popping them outward like a batter at the plate. "I am ready," he said.

She swatted at his shoulder, but he caught her hand in

mid-air, bringing it to his lips for a swift kiss before an "ahem" behind him startled them both.

"Sorry y'all, didn't mean to interrupt anything." Kay grinned like a kid who's gotten away with something. "Should I leave you two alone?"

"No, Aunt Kay, Lincoln was just enjoying my new lotion. It smells like strawberries," she fibbed sweetly, but confidently, though the increasingly familiar blush on her cheek allayed the insistence.

The three of them sat down, digging in to their respective plates, joined quickly by Malinda, Anna, and Gramma. After a few minutes of eager chewing and "mmming" all around, the interrogation began.

"So, Lincoln, you're from Nashville?" Gramma asked, innocently slicing a large piece of squash.

"Yes, ma'am. I was born and raised there, in the Belle Meade area. My parents still live in the same house my father built when they were first married, and all of my siblings live nearby. They all went to Tennessee schools and stayed relatively close."

"You didn't go to college there?"

"I did my undergrad at Vanderbilt. But after I graduated, I left for culinary school in New York."

"And your degree is in?" Gramma pressed.

"Business. My grandfather owns a major supplier of automotive parts. All his sons work there in some capacity, and he intended for me to join the family affair as soon as I got out of school."

"So, they weren't pleased when you chose another path?" Jane glared at her grandmother's nosiness, but the older woman either didn't see care or didn't notice.

"Weren't pleased is a gross understatement, actually. My grandfather cut me off, and my own dear dad threatened to kick me out of the house. Thankfully, I had saved enough money to get to the city and start culinary school, sharing a three-bedroom apartment with five other guys." He glanced at Jane. "But I wasn't there for very long."

Jane looked at Lincoln; she'd not heard this part of the story. He hadn't hesitated to answer the question but she could tell it was a sore subject. Before her aunts could ask another question, she interjected, "Lincoln was a culinary school prodigy and after the first day, his teacher submitted him for the Next Top Chef competition."

"And you're in Atlanta to interview Janie for the competition she's going to be in, right?"

"Yes, ma'am. The crew and director caught a flight out last night. They're filming a featurette on a restaurant in Los Angeles, but I was supposed to head back to New York. I've spent enough holidays alone in the city to know that I'd rather spend it with friendly folks, so when Jane invited me here, I had them change my flight," he explained, smiling warmly at Jane across the table.

"He even went shopping with me and helped cook yesterday."

"I did. I hope I didn't mess up the hash brown casserole. It's been ages since I've made one."

"It's delicious!" Malinda assured him. "Jane's food always is, though." The women nodded in agreement. Everyone tucked into their burgeoning plates as Anna began telling a story about Mikey at school, and quickly the room was filled with anecdotes of all the children at school, even some about Kay, Anna, Malinda, and Jane's father in their school days. Lincoln found himself laughing so hard that his eyes were watering.

"Alright. We'll clean up and then settle in for the tree lighting. Jane, you are exempt this year, since you have company. Why don't y'all walk down to the garden? I'll ring the bell when it's time."

Jane grimaced at the blatant insinuation, but smiled. "Okay."

Lincoln followed her down the deck steps, his bag slung over one shoulder, and onto the flagstone path he had seen a few days before. Under the deck, Jane rifled through a bin of miscellany, withdrawing a dark red flashlight.

"This is a set up you know," she grumbled, noticing his eyes on her.

He nodded, "I thought it was kind of sweet though. They love you."

She smiled at that. "They do. After today, they're big fans of yours too. Come on, we've probably got an hour before the show."

"What tree lighting?" He took her hand as they walked.

"We watch the lighting of the big tree in Atlanta every year on Thanksgiving night. It's just one of those things we've always done." They had reached the gate; she handed him the lantern to hold while she unlocked it.

They stepped inside and he was amazed by how different the place looked, bathed in moonlight. The last few leaves on the oak tree twisted and turned in the evening breeze, their deep red and bronze shimmering in the night. Jane hung the lantern on a peg in the oak tree's trunk, casting a wide pool of warm, golden light on the dense grass. Lincoln sat on the edge of the waterfall's pool, as Jane slid into the tire swing, her dangling feet brushing the tips of the grass.

He reached into his bag, drawing out a small round object. Resting on chased golden feet, the squat circle of gold and emerald green fit neatly in his palm. He wound the small key it bore several times, then released the catch. Softly, a string of musical notes wove around the enclosure, a faint tune echoing against the stone.

Jane turned, her eyes wide as she recognized the tune. He smiled, humming softly along with the melody. Jane sat on the cold ground, picking up the small music box, beginning to sing the familiar song.

"Where on earth did you find this?" she questioned, staring at him.

"A little shop near my hotel. They had a whole shelf of music boxes, but something told me you would like this one."

"It's for me?" she was shocked, both that he'd brought a gift for her at all, and that he'd managed to read her so well. "You didn't have to."

"I know, but I wanted to. A thank you for inviting me today, and for being so nice to me, even though I know I've been difficult to deal with."

She sat next to him on the stone wall with the music box playing quietly in her lap, and he took her hand.

"Jane, I am sorry. I get so used to being around either egotistical imbeciles, overzealous fangirls, or sycophantic simpletons that I forget there are still normal people out there. I'm so tired of all of that, but it's so much a part of who I am that I can't imagine not doing it. Honestly, I can't remember caring before I met you. I was just kinda in limbo," he said, his southern accent creeping in for the first time since their meeting four days ago.

"I had been so driven in the beginning, so consumed with pursuing this new career path that I didn't need anything else, and then I met..." He stopped, staring down at his shoe. "And when I was with her, she was all I wanted and then after, I really just wanted to forget, so I lost myself in my work again. And then they sent me here, and honestly, I was pissed. I didn't want to travel this close to Thanksgiving, and I really didn't want to go anywhere. But then I got here, and even though I was a cranky child at the bakery, you were kind and patient. And I didn't deserve it."

"I haven't been the easiest to deal with either," she admitted. "You've seen I have trouble trusting people's intentions, and allowing myself to trust them. I'm really glad you came today."

The wind whispered past them, freeing a few more oak leaves, rustling the long tendrils of the willow tree as they gazed at each other. She shivered in the chilly air and he pulled her closer, wrapping his arms around her and running his hands up and down her arms, causing her to shiver again, this time unrelated to the cold.

"Lincoln," she whispered, turning to him, his face inches from hers.

An old bell rang in the distance, resounding over and over. She jumped at the sound, his arm dropping from her shoulder.

"That's Gramma's signal. It's time for the tree lighting, and we should head back." She glanced at the music box in her hands. "Tuck this in your bag. They'll never stop with the jokes if they see it." She thrust it back at him as she hustled out of the garden, the lantern swinging in her hand.

Lincoln slipped the gift back into the leather bag and followed her silently, fully aware of how close he had come to kissing her, and how she didn't appear to be as pleased with that fact as he did.

On Your Marks, Get Set, Bake!

Jane stepped into the glare of the blinding studio lights, her glittering green Converse sneakers silent on the reflective black tile floor. How many times had she watched challenges in this very kitchen from the safety of her sofa? Why had she thought herself and her skills worthy of attempting this herself? A hand on her shoulder made her jump.

"Hey, boss. Are we ready?" Nia asked quietly, noting Jane's tension. When Jane didn't answer, Nia patted her on the shoulder. "We can do this. We have eight hours today to prove ourselves."

"Nia," Jane whispered, picking heavily at her cuticles. "This is not a busy weekend in Atlanta. This is the Culinary Channel. Rahul Ingram. Belinda Wilson. This is Dan, Nia. We watched his show. How on earth can I impress them?"

Looking her employer and friend straight in the eyes, Nia asserted, "I've seen your work. Remember that cake for the Ben-Yehudah wedding? With those tiny little Hebrew letters? Did you sweat then? Maybe, because it was the middle of an Atlanta summer, but they loved every detail on that cake." Jane offered a short laugh at the joke. "The Harper Charity dinner? The Moroccan tiles that were hand-painted? The logo mosaic of tiny frosting dots? Jane, you can do this. If anyone, ever, could step into this challenge and be successful, it is you."

Jane took a deep breath, her hands dropping to her sides. "Alright. We can do this." Nia smiled.

"Is the kitchen to your precise standards, Miss Mullins?" someone asked with a gentle laugh that melted Jane's tension.

Jane turned to see Lincoln, dressed flawlessly, as always, but with his black-framed glasses perched on his nose. As he approached, Nia nonchalantly backed into the kitchen and out of immediate hearing.

"Lincoln," Jane breathed. "I didn't think you would be here until we started filming."

"I had a meeting upstairs and decided to hang around. You ready for your first big challenge? Nervous?"

"Terrified," she admitted. "I can't believe I actually chose to do this."

"You will be great," he promised, taking her hands. "I saw photos of that gilded masterpiece you did for the mayor's inaugural ball last year. You belong here, and you can do this." In the shadows, Nia smiled. "Did Nia check out the kitchen? All the tools are there?" Lincoln asked, releasing Jane's hands.

"Everything looks great. We are getting our game faces on," she chuckled.

"Should we find you eye black?"

"Maybe. Would it scare the judges into liking me?"

"Doubtful. Show them your knife skills though, like how you did those onions for Thanksgiving. You'll have Dan shaking in his sneakers."

There was a pause, and they both dissolved into a fit of laughter. At that moment, Antony walked into the studio, followed by the judges and two of the other competitors. Jane and Lincoln both grew quiet, and he stepped the smallest bit away from her.

"Ah, Miss Mullins. They said you had arrived. Everything in order here?" Antony asked.

Nodding, Jane replied, "Yes, sir. We're ready."

"Good." The judges moved to their table, notepads covered with scribbled notes tucked under their arms. Jane shivered as they passed her, and she quickly ducked into her kitchen alongside Nia.

Antony, who had moved behind the bank of cameras, which were quickly filling with crew members, beckoned Lincoln to him. The latter scurried out of the lights toward the executive.

"Antony?"

"Lincoln, what the hell are you doing?"

Startled, Lincoln looked around. "What?"

"With the girl. She's a competitor. More than that, she's just a kid from Atlanta. You're Lincoln Bainbridge. You cannot afford to just be dawdling with some chubby cake maker from the deep south."

"What are you talking about? I was just giving her a little boost. The poor thing is freaked out. She's in New York for the first time and it's certainly the first time she's ever been in a competition this big."

"That's why we picked her."

"I know," Lincoln replied, irritated. "You expect her to struggle".

"No. I expect her to fail," Antony grunted, matter-of-factly. "Chances are strong she'll have a complete freak out a few hours in and collapse. That always makes for good television. Now, I have to go to a meeting with Clarke and Dolores, but behave, won't you?"

Shaking his head as Antony walked away, his expensive Italian leather shoes tapping on the tiles, Lincoln fought the urge to fight Antony for shamelessly desiring a competitor's failure, and he wasn't sure it would be solely a verbal battle.

Lincoln made his way to the judges' table, ready for taping to begin. Three of the four competitors looked around nervously, with the exception of Stefanie Bauer, a five-time challenger and two-time winner. She was tossing her platinum blond ponytail and chattering away to her assistant Luka, while Ryan Watson, a third-time challenger, rearranged the rows of cake and frosting colorings, and Findlay Robertson, a second-time entrant, was muttering in Gaelic while staring at his sketchpad.

The crew signaled they were ready, and Dan, the director, nodded at Lincoln, who moved to his mark. With a countdown, the whole studio grew silent.

"Welcome again to Sweet Tooth., the competition between bakers and pastry chefs worth twenty-five thousand dollars. I'm your host, Lincoln Bainbridge. Let's meet our competitors this time around. From Los Angeles, California, a third-time challenger, Ryan Watson." Here there was a pause; the editors would add in the B-roll from Ryan's home in post-production. "From Philadelphia, five-time competitor and two-time champion, Stefanie Bauer." Another pause. "From Edinburgh, Scotland, second-time entrant Findlay Robertson." He smiled as he read the last name from the teleprompter, "And from Atlanta, Georgia, a first-time competitor, Jane Mullins." He grinned at her as the cameras panned the kitchens. His smile bolstered her own, allowing her to look confident and strong.

"As usual, we have our illustrious judges: the legendary Rahul Ingram, known for his exquisite cakes and sugar details. Belinda Wilson, the queen of fantastic and beautiful desserts. And Dan Greenberg, infamous for his extreme details and awesome three-dimensional cakes." The judges all nodded as their names were read, except Dan who waved.

"The rules of the challenge are simple. We give the contestants a theme on which to base their cake and they have eight hours to complete their piece. Each successful cake will be six feet tall, include at least one extreme element, and be the best example of the theme. Each week, there will also be a fourth judge, someone who represents the theme of the challenge. Judge Dan, would you like to explain this week's challenge to our competitors?"

"Sure, Lincoln. Competitors, your first challenge is a flash-back to a world of neon, big hair, and keytars. The 1980s are your inspiration today and we want to see how you represent an iconic era. We want to see big and bright, and extreme chefs, extreme."

Lincoln looked at the bakers. "Challengers, your fourth judge this week is an eighties legend. She is best known for her number one hit "My Heart's A Neon Sign". Ladies and Gentlemen, Ms. Lara Checkers!"

From behind a row of tall black velvet curtains, a petite woman with a shockingly pink pixie hairstyle emerged, and everyone applauded.

"I hope you're all ready to rock," the bright woman exclaimed, grinning. "The 80s were full of it!" The group nodded, and the judges took their seats.

Lincoln moved toward the front of the platform. "Challengers, are you ready?" When they all nodded, he continued. "You have eight hours. Ready? Go."

There was a flurry as the chefs and their assistants gathered tightly around their sketchpads and began to draw hurriedly. After about five minutes, Stefanie's assistant Luka began rolling fondant on one counter, while Stefanie made some marks on a large sheet of plywood laid across the other counter.

A minute later, Findlay and his daughter and assistant Sarah both started pulling their cakes from their cooling rack. Jane and Nia moved next; Jane to tinting frosting, which she parceled out into several small bowls and Nia, to covering the baseboard with black fondant. Ryan was the last to move, turning to rifle through his fridge.

Time ticked by and the cakes took shape. Down in Stefanie's kitchen, a towering black and white spire rose above the counter, accented by bright details along the board. Periodically, angry shouts erupted from that end of the room.

Findlay's cake base was sparse, but appeared to be a stage from a rock concert. Sarah was busy molding figures from gum paste while he wired something through the cake itself. In Ryan's kitchen, little was visible, except for a length of neon green fondant draped over a foot-high platform of stacked cakes.

Jane's cake had started slowly, but was moving along. Nia had covered the board flawlessly, and then an offset tiered stack of cakes went up, each one covered in a different neon hue. Working on the lowest layer, cutting wild geometric shapes from the remnants of the other colors and placing them on top of the vibrant pink base, Nia brought the large base layer to life. Working meticulously, Jane was crafting familiar characters for a middle tier, trying to ignore the cameras constantly weaving in and out of their workspace.

They could hear the judges filming their commentaries, even a smattering of the comments they were offering about the competitors, but all eight continued working busily. Hour after hour passed, and the creations came to life. Even as the last few minutes ticked off the clock, all four stations hummed with movement, but at the buzzer, everyone stepped back, pleased with their work.

Now was the tricky part; each team had to move their cake from the workstation to the judging tables. More than once, Jane had seen this end in tragedy, but she had planned for the move in her cake's construction; she, Nia, and one of the crew members transferred the confectionery giant without much drama. Stefanie and Findlay followed suit, but Ryan's cake didn't look steady, even on the stable surface of the countertop.

As he and his assistant Micah lifted the board and began to move forward, the towering cake began to wobble in earnest before the top two tiers slid off the top, hitting the black-tiled floor with a sickening squish, amplified by an audible groan from the audience and an anguished cry from Ryan.

Jane and Nia looked at each other, horrified, as Ryan and his team tried to piece together what they could salvage. Stefanie, a haughty look in her eyes, wheeled her cake, on its judging table, toward the panel. They couldn't hear the judges, but even at a distance, they could see the magnificent work Stefanie and Luka had done. The cake was covered solely in black and white, but accented with bright pops of color in bold shapes. It was an abstract cake, and judging by the irritated look on her face, the judges weren't exactly huge fans of it.

Findlay was next, and his cake was a musical explosion. The colors were similar to Jane's-vivid neon and black, but he focused on the varied kinds of music. Each tier rested on its own pedestal, all of which rotated like records, decorated in the theme of a popular 80s song. As the girls watched him present, they noticed he was holding a remote and as he explained the cake, he subtly pushed a button and suddenly the studio was filled with 80s music.

Nia looked at Jane, who glanced at Lincoln and all three of them laughed. Findlay made a brilliant move that even the judges seemed to enjoy. Stefanie's face was so puckered that it looked as if she swallowed a lemon. It was obvious that the veteran decorator thought Findlay's 'extreme' element was foolish; hers had been a far subtler set of lights that flickered while wrapped around her black and white tower.

Ryan and Micah moved their belatedly repaired creation to the judging area; neither of them looking overly positive.

What was saddest was that the cake was really well done. The men had taken great care to shape the video game joystick that served as a topper, and the multi-colored cube underneath had been so flawless, but both were now hastily patched up.

Jane picked at her cuticles again, nervously waiting for their opportunity to present when she heard Lincoln announcing, "And our final contestant, Jane Mullins."

Nia took a long look at her trembling boss, and together they pushed their creation forward. Rahul eyed the cake, undoubtedly scrutinizing the smallest of details, and Belinda seemed to be doing the same. Dan however, eyes bright and smile wide, appraised the cake with a nod and a wow.

Jane had to admit it was one of her best works, and Nia's as well. The lowest layer was a shocking shade of pink with neon geometric shapes scattered over it. Above that was a black-cloaked tier arrayed like an arcade game, with small white dots, vibrant fruits and bright creatures chasing around it-this layer rotated slowly. Next up was a bright blue piece decorated with a spaceship, more dots aimed at small aliens-this one also rotated, but in the opposite direction. Next was a simple white backdrop covered in airbrushed graffiti, spelling out slang and phrases from the 80s; this was Nia's handiwork, and it was perfect. Jane was sure the top tier was her absolute favorite; the cake itself had been decorated like the face of an 80s hair band rock star, down to a black-tinted chocolate tongue protruding from its mouth, with a wild mane of black licorice cotton candy forming the tangle of hair. 80s music streamed from the top of the cake.

"First, I have to say that this may be one of the finest showings we have had by such a novice," Belinda began. "You certainly gave us the 1980s as well as the extreme elements." Jane was smiling as the judge continued. "However, some of your execution is sloppy, and you could have illustrated another aspect of the era instead of representing two video games. But overall, a nice piece."

Disappointed, Jane nodded and sighed. "Thank you."

Rahul's judgment was next. "I agree with Belinda, overall, your piece is well done, but there are definite errors in your work. The airbrushing is bleeding into the fondant in places, and some of your edges are not neat." Crestfallen, Jane eyed her own work, struggling not to cry. This was a major competition, and criticism was to be expected.

"I think this is my favorite cake," Dan gushed, and Jane perked up. "The cotton candy hair is a brilliant idea, and the moving video game levels are just fun. I look forward to seeing more of your work, Miss Mullins." With a grin and a nod, they were dismissed to the green room to wait while the judges deliberated. As they passed him, Lincoln flashed a thumbs up, earning a weak smile from Jane as the two girls slunk out of the studio.

Muted emptiness hovered in the green room. Stefanie was primping in the mirror, undoubtedly planning for the close-up she'd get as the winner of this round, while Luka fiddled with his cell phone. Findlay and Sarah were both on one sofa, leaning back, eyes closed. In one corner, Ryan and Micah were mourning the destruction of their piece in hushed, pained tones; Ryan's face was a mask of sorrow, contorted with both rage and sadness.

Jane and Nia settled into two armchairs in the opposite corner, and Nia immediately reached for her cell phone.

"Important call?" Jane joked.

"Actually, the crew wanted me to text as soon as we were through with judging. I promised Trevor," Nia explained, her fingers flying across the touchscreen of her phone. Jane rifled through her messenger bag before she found the battered copy of her favorite book; she didn't see Stefanie staring menacingly at her as she opened the book to her bookmark and began to read.

A few pages in, and she was calm. Her mind was off in the English countryside, far from the sleek, sterile green room of the Culinary Channel studios. Nia was still typing away next to her, but Jane barely noticed, plowing along through the text.

When one of the crew opened the door to call them back, she jumped, momentarily forgetting where she actually was. All four teams got to their feet, Stefanie at their head, of course, smiling smugly as she sashayed back into the studio. The group formed a semi-circle in front of the judges' table, with the chefs in front and assistants behind.

Lincoln was in the corner, explaining the scores before he moved over to where the competitors stood.

"And now ladies and gentlemen, we find out who has the sweetest tooth in this round of competition, and who will be going home," Lincoln declared. Findlay, Ryan, and Jane eyed each other nervously, while Stefanie smiled proudly.

"After round one, we've had triumphs and tragedy, and in the end, that is what will send our first competitor home." Lincoln turned. "Ryan, I'm sorry, but you don't have a sweet enough tooth." Ryan nodded, half-smiling.

"Thank you," he replied softly, bowing his head to the judges and then turning to leave the studio.

"And then there were three," Lincoln continued. "In third place after round one, Jane Mullins." Jane smiled, pleased enough that she at least had another round to go. "In second place, Stefanie Bauer." Stefanie looked as if she'd swallowed worms, her face contorting into a bitter, bizarre smile. Findlay, however, was grinning, as Lincoln turned to him. "Congratulations, Findlay! This puts you ahead of the game for next week. We'll see you then on Sweet Tooth!"

The red lights atop the cameras went dark, and everyone

exhaled deeply. Stefanie stomped off immediately, raging to Luka in rapid German, the judges close on her heels. Findlay had picked up Sarah and was spinning her around, tears in his eyes. Jane and Nia couldn't help but feel happy for the pair.

"Congratulations, Findlay!" Jane called to him.

Setting Sarah on her feet, he turned to the other girls. "Thanks, lass. Your cake was pretty great, too." He grinned as he spoke. "Course, that's probably what pissed off Miss Perfect. She wasn't expecting you to be so good. Or to make it through the first round."

"To be honest, Findlay, I wasn't sure I would make it through either." Jane agreed. "This is certainly the most intense thing I've ever done. In fact, I think I'm due for a nap about now." Findlay nodded.

"Aye. We're going to meet my wife for an early dinner and then who knows?"

"See y'all day after tomorrow!" Jane called as she and Nia headed for the doors. "So, what are your plans, Nia?"

"I'm taking the bus down to Eddie's. We're having dinner, then he's taking me to see whatever show he got tickets for." Nia was smiling brightly. It had been difficult for her and her boyfriend when he was accepted to a doctoral program at NYU, but they had worked very hard to ensure that their three-year relationship survived. "What are you doing, boss?"

Jane sighed. "I think I will just stay in, order some room service, and watch a movie."

Nia rolled her eyes. "I'll call you tomorrow, okay?"

Chuckling, Jane patted her assistant on the shoulder. "Have fun!"

Nia bustled out the door, while Jane turned to the narrow hall where she could hear Lincoln's voice. She figured she would thank him for the encouragement today before heading out. As she drew closer, she realized he wasn't alone.

"YOU SPENT THANKSGIVING WITH HER?

Damnit, Lincoln. I can't believe you'd put any trust in a gold-digging, fame-hungry amateur." She recognized Antony's nasal tone immediately, and it stopped her in her tracks. "She's lucky Watson's cake fell, because she would have been gone otherwise. Of course, that would have been better for you."

"How would that have been better for me, Antony? Why is it so awful that I have made a friend with her?" She gulped. It shouldn't bother her that he called her a friend; that's what they were, right?

"Because, Lincoln, there are two roads here. One, you date her, you sleep with her, whatever, and you end up linked with a chubby baker from Nowheresville, USA, which will do *nothing* for your image." Antony was almost screaming at this point. Jane, who had dropped onto a nearby plastic chair, was struggling to breathe while not weeping at the same time. "Two, she will rip your heart out, use you for her career and end up with some other guy and you, my boy, will end up locked in that big apartment of yours, wondering why yet another one slipped through your fingers."

"Antony, you are my producer, not, as you constantly remind me, my friend, so if and or when I want your opinion, I will ask for it. Jane Mullins is a kind-hearted woman who recognized that I was alone on a holiday and invited me in. Nothing more." He paused." Also, as I am not a judge in this competition, it is absolutely not a problem for me to spend time with her. Goodnight Antony."

Jane heard footsteps, but Antony wasn't done. "Lincoln, she isn't worth it. She's nothing. She won't even make it past the second round, then she'll be back in Atlanta."

She sat in silence as one set of feet echoed away from her, and one moved closer. Tears dampened her face, which she had tucked into her chest, her hands tightly clutching her messenger bag.

"Jane?" She jerked her head up at Lincoln's voice.

Plastering on a smile, she stood. "All set?"

"How much did you hear?"

"Not much." She sniffed. "Hardly anything."

Lincoln could see the tracks of tears on her cheeks. He gently wiped the remnants of a tear away. "Jane, you're a terrible liar."

"I'm fine. I promise."

"It's not. He shouldn't have said any of it, especially where you could hear it."

"He's a bit demanding, isn't he?"

"Most producers are," Lincoln muttered. "But yes, he can be incredibly demanding at times." He didn't miss her changing the subject. "Hey," he gently took her by the shoulders. "I don't want you to think I agree with him at all. Because I absolutely do not." She stepped into his embrace and he wrapped his arms around her. "Do you have plans tonight?"

"Just hotel room service and reruns."

"We can do better than that for your first time in New York. Wanna get out of here?"

"I thought you'd never ask."

High Hopes and Hockey

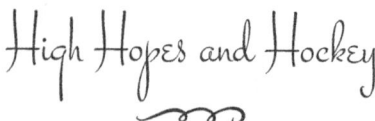

"Well," Lincoln began awkwardly as they stepped out into the dwindling afternoon light. What was it about this woman that made him stammer like a schoolboy? "We both have a free night and my team is playing yours. Are you up for a game?"

She brightened, glancing at him, the slightest hint of red in her eyes fading. Whatever she said, she'd taken more of Antony's words to heart than she'd let on. He took her hand, "Are you sure you're okay?"

Jane nodded, straightening her shoulders. "He won't intimidate me. I've been called worse anyway."

"That doesn't excuse it!" Lincoln cried, still furious over Antony's behavior.

Jane reached up with her free hand and touched his cheek. His ire on her behalf warmed her, even in the November chill. "He's wrong, right?"

"Of course. He's an ass for even—"

She pressed a finger to his lips. "Then he's wrong and we're not going to talk about Antony Perandin anymore, okay? In answer to your question, I would love to go to a hockey game with you, but can I go back to the hotel and shower some of this frosting off first?"

He stared at her, her newfound confidence made him want to sweep her up and kiss her in the middle of the street. Probably a bad idea... "Of course." He agreed. "Actually," he hesitated, realizing that no other woman had ever been to his place, "my place is way closer. Just a block or two. Is that okay with you?" he blurted, running the sentences together.

Jane paused, staring intently at Lincoln. "Are you sure that's a good idea? What if someone sees you bringing a girl back to the apartment?"

"Hasn't happened since—in a long time. I can more or less come and go as I please here. But if you're uncomfortable, I can hail you a cab."

"No, it's fine. It makes way more sense this way."

"Okay." He turned and led the way down the street, slowing his pace when he noticed she was merely ambling, taking in the sights, sounds, and smells of the city. "I forgot this is your first time here," he said warmly.

"Does it show that much?" she asked with an embarrassed giggle.

"Don't worry," he replied with a chuckle, "I actually walked into a street sign my first week here. I was walking from the studio down to Times Square and I was so preoccupied with the lights and signs that I walked straight into a no parking sign."

She stopped, doubling over with laughter.

"It's not that funny," he said, laughing himself. "Alright, maybe it is."

"Actually," Jane added, "I think I can top that. I tripped over a speed bump one time and was almost hit by a car."

Lincoln's eyes widened and he stopped walking. "Are you serious?"

"Completely. Some friends and I had stopped in the store

on our way to see a movie, and as we were coming out, I was trying to stuff my change in my wallet and BAM! My flip-flop caught on the cement and down I went. They *still* remind me of that story to this day."

"Glad to know I'm not the only clumsy one around here," Lincoln added. "For all I must've impressed my teacher in culinary school, I was a mess with a knife for the first five years I was in the kitchen. They used to have to keep a big box of bandages on set for me."

"My crew bought me a box of sparkly band-aids to keep at the bakery. I rarely cut myself, but I burn fingers and hands often."

They both chuckled as they rounded the corner. "Ah, here's my building," he said, stepping a bit away from her and gesturing to the magnificent structure, with a glorious marble edifice framing the doors, which were flanked by crimson coated doormen. "The Monte Carlo Building. Once home to a number of famous people. Now just home to a bunch of normal ones."

"This is really beautiful, Lincoln. You're incredibly lucky to live here."

He nodded, waving to one of the doormen. "Hey, Simon. This is my friend Jane."

"Pleasure to meet you, miss. Mr. Lincoln hasn't had a lady visitor since Miss R—"

"Thanks, Simon," snapped Lincoln, cutting him off. "Let's go Jane."

Simon nodded at her as he held the door open to the exquisite, dark wood-paneled lobby. Antique chandeliers illuminated the lobby, casting a warm glow on the marble floor.

Jane stopped, taking in the decor, her mouth agape. He just smiled.

"Come on, Miss Tourist." Lincoln mashed the up button

for the elevator, which promptly dinged, and the doors opened with a swoosh.

They both stepped in, and Lincoln drew his keys from his pocket, pulling one from the jangle, and inserting it into a lock beside the button marked P. With a twist, then a push of the adjacent button, the elevator began its ascent.

"Wow. The penthouse."

"Impressed?"

"Nah. Owning the building, maybe. The penthouse is just the penthouse."

He rolled his eyes. "Yeah, yeah."

"So, you have to have a key for the elevator to go to your floor?"

"Yes, and then another key to actually get in my apartment. We're big on security here."

The elevator slowed to a stop, and the doors opened, revealing a polished, modern entryway. The double doors were heavy, black wood with shimmering chrome handles. Lincoln paused only a moment before his shoes tip-tapped across the gleaming marble floor and he unlocked the door.

Jane checked on the threshold, completely aware that she was entering her long-time celebrity crush's apartment. Somehow, this was more nerve-wracking than having him in her house. Unlike her cluttered home, this could be a hotel suite. Everything was chic and clean. The open living room barely looked lived in.

As if reading her mind, Lincoln said, "Told you it wasn't like yours. I don't spend as much time here as I'd like. I guess I've never collected any knickknacks or things that really made the place mine."

"It's lovely, though. Very hip."

Lincoln shrugged. "I guess. Maybe I'm not the hip one."

"Oh, you're hip," Jane argued, "The hippest of hip. Is it weird that I want to see the kitchen?"

He grinned "I somehow expected that. It's right through here."

Jane stepped into the brightly lit room, momentarily blinded by the setting sun on the horizon that left her in awe.

"Wow. This may be the most beautiful kitchen I have ever laid eyes on. Even after some of the studio kitchens at the network. Everything is so pristine. It all matches."

"It does. I certainly don't use it to its full, majestic, potential."

"You don't?"

"I only ever cook for myself, maybe one of my few guy friends, but definitely not enough to need a lot of stove space. And I used to go out all the time with—"

"I'm sorry. I made you think of her again. I don't mean to."

"It's alright. It's been over two years; I should be able to talk about her." Lincoln sank into one of the dining room chairs.

"I think you're better off," she said quietly. "She sounds like a flighty, inconsiderate person. And you deserve more than that."

Lincoln just stared out the window, and Jane quietly backed out of the room, off to find the shower. He sat in silence, gaze fixed until he heard the shower in the guest room turn on. Resignedly, he shook his head.

"You invite the girl to a night out and all you can do is ramble about your ex. Well done, Bainbridge. You should probably go change clothes, idiot," he mumbled to himself.

By the time he stepped back into the living room, dressed in jeans and his Rangers jersey, Jane was sitting on the edge of the sofa, the curls of her hair falling alongside her face, brushing the top of the book she was reading. She looked up and made a face.

"I should have expected the jersey, I guess."

He laughed. "They are my adopted team. I moved up here before we had a team back home so I had to cheer for somebody! We should get going. The car should be here by now."

They rode in comfortable silence, interrupted only by the driver informing them they had arrived at the arena. Again, she was struck by New York-even living in a big city like Atlanta was no preparation for being here, in the bustling streets. And she wished she had her Phoenix jersey because her sweater wasn't exactly festive for the occasion.

"Are you coming, Jane, or do you intend to just stare at the city all night?" Lincoln teased from the sidewalk.

She moved quickly to join him as cars behind them honked. "I think you're mocking me, and it's not quite fair. Surely you were dumbstruck when you first arrived."

"I was completely in awe of the place," he said, remembering. "But," he took her arm, "we are not here to discuss my arrival, nor the grand city itself. We are here for some hockey."

She laughed as he led her to will call, where the woman handed him two tickets which, even though Jane couldn't see them in their entirety, certainly led them to seats much closer to the action than she was used to. They moved through the entry doors and were immediately surrounded by a red, white, and blue crushing mass of people. This was not Phoenix territory alright.

Lincoln was pulling her toward one of the shops in the arena, forcing his way through the throng. When they finally broke free of the pressing crowd, she noticed they were in a large merchandise venue where, lined up along the wall, they had jerseys from every team in the league.

He moved quickly toward the wall, losing her hand as he did so. Thumbing through the jerseys, he looked for a particular one before drawing it from the rack.

"What do you think? This one?"

Jane gasped at the dark blue jersey in his hands. "Dominic

Fremont, our goalie. I can't ever find his jersey back home. They are always sold out. How on earth?"

"I called ahead and talked to one of the merchandisers. He found one. I paid for it, and made sure it was waiting when we arrived. I didn't think you would want to wear a hometown jersey." He was grinning broadly now, obviously proud of his efforts.

Jane was stunned. No one had ever gone to that amount of trouble for her before. She ran, throwing her arms around his neck.

"Thank you so much! You are amazing!"

He blushed. "If you say so. There's a changing room back there, so go get into fan mode. We still need hot dogs before we go down to our seats."

"Down to our seats? Oh, my god." She practically bounced into the dressing room.

Her absolute joy was infectious. The more he was able to make her smile, the more he wanted to keep the smile on her face. When he'd seen her tears after overhearing Antony, he'd felt as if he could punch through a wall. Something churned in his stomach, but for the first time in a long time, it was a good feeling.

Jane emerged from the dressing room draped in the jersey which, in true hockey fashion, was baggy on her frame, but she was grinning like a child on Christmas morning.

"You look marvelous," he said with a slight gulp. Marvelous didn't begin to cover how she looked, the bright smile, her curls spilling over the dark fabric but not hiding her curves.

"Okay, so hot dogs? Is that a local tradition? Because at our games, we go for chili cheese fries," she reasoned as they left the store.

He shook his head. "Anything you want, Jane, absolutely anything."

"Be careful of that challenge," she taunted. "You've never seen me at a sporting event. You think I'm nice, but...I am not nice when it comes to my team."

Lincoln flung an arm around her shoulders. "I can already tell this is going to be the most interesting and exciting hockey game I have ever been to. And that's saying something. I was here the night Sjöström and Jerković got into that massive fight, where both teams ended up on the ice, the referees were jumping out of the way, and three guys ended up unconscious by the end of it."

"I remember that game! We were watching that one the weekend before the bakery opened!"

The pair stopped at a concession stand and waited in the line crowded with a mass of fans. When they finally stepped up to the counter, Lincoln ordered.

"Two New York dogs and a soda. And for the lady," he gestured to Jane, "Chili cheese fries and a cola. Anything else, Jane?" He chuckled as she punched him playfully on the arm.

"Not at the moment. But thanks." They gathered their food and began the trek to their seats. Lincoln stopped in front of one tunnel, balancing his meal as he pulled the tickets from his pocket to check them.

"This is us," he confirmed as he moved through the tunnel doors and then the curtain that separated it from the concourse.

As they emerged into the arena, Jane gasped. They were only a few rows back from the ice, and Lincoln kept moving closer and closer. She stopped dead when she realized that he had slipped into the row directly behind the glass. At center ice.

"Are you serious?" she called to him, still a few feet away.

He grinned again, and she realized how much more that smile made her swoon in person than it ever did on television.

"Do you think I would have done all this just to joke with you now?"

Jane scurried to catch up with him, settling into the seat at his side, still amazed by the turn of events. Watching as Lincoln dug into his hot dogs, she remembered how stoic he had been this afternoon, and how distant he had been since their first meeting in Atlanta, barring, of course, the few fleeting moments of insight scattered into the mix. She almost wished she could read his mind. There was no doubt how her heart was tumbling quickly, despite her best efforts to curb its runaway pace, but this was not a boy in her math class in high school. This was not the boy from down the hall in college.

This was Lincoln Bainbridge, the internationally famous chef who she just happened to have been in love with since her freshman year. He dated supermodels and actresses. She worried that this night, and everything wonderful about it, was just an anomaly, but she was determined to make the best of it. If this was the only night she ever got to spend with him, then she was going to enjoy it.

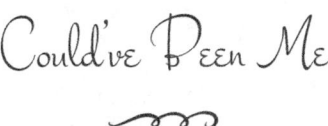

Could've Been Me

The second day of competition dawned early and Jane, as usual, was the first to arrive at the studio. Nia wasn't far behind, her arms full to bursting with auxiliary supplies, all of which tumbled to the stainless-steel countertop. A veritable cornucopia of edible pearl dust and glitter in every color imaginable clattered down, Jane's smile brightening to see them.

"Where on earth did you find all this, Nia? And do you really think we'll need it?"

"Well, after the last round, I thought we might need some pizzazz. No matter what the theme is," she winked.

The studio doors swung open, revealing a swaggering Stefanie and Luka, snobbishly ignoring their fellow competitors. When they reached their kitchen, both women overheard Stefanie whisper loudly, "I guess it's easier to proceed through the competition when you're sleeping with the host."

"No one is sleeping with the host," Nia countered, moving defensively in front of Jane.

Stefanie glared, "Why else would she be in his apartment then?"

Nia whirled on Jane "What? I thought you were just going

to stay at the hotel. Why were you at his apartment?" Stefanie smirked, disappearing to her own workstation.

"Nothing like that," Jane assured adamantly. "He took me to a hockey game."

"You went on a date with Lincoln Bainbridge?" Nia whispered sharply.

"Not a date," Jane countered uncertainly, unsure of that fact herself. "Just hanging out with him. You were out with Eddie and Lincoln felt bad after Antony said some things about me. We hung out, nothing more."

"Jane, if they think you've been trying to get an edge..."

"Nia!" she yelled, startling Stefanie and Luka. She lowered her voice. "He's the host, not a judge. And there's nothing going on between us." She paused, saddened by the truth of her own words. "Nothing like that anyway. We're just friends."

The doors opened again and a mass of people entered. Findlay and Sarah, the crew members, and Antony, who, Jane noted, glared at her with the venom of one of Cleopatra's asps. Her fellow competitors stopped and talked for a few minutes before the doors opened again, this time bringing in the judges, with Lincoln in the rear, who winked stealthily at her as he passed.

The challengers settled into their kitchens, Jane and Nia carefully arranging their new products along the side of the counter so they wouldn't be in the way. Off in the corner, the judges were speaking to Lincoln, who was nodding furiously. With one hand raised, the director called for quiet, and they began to film the introduction segment for the second round, pausing this time after each contestant's name where they would insert footage of the previous round.

Focus shifted when Rahul stood and addressed the bakers. "Competitors," he announced. "You will, as always, have eight hours to complete your showpiece. Again, it must be at least six feet tall, and contain one extreme element. Today, you will also have a guest judge. Lillian Markowitz, editor-in-chief of *Bridal Style* magazine, is here to evaluate your adherence to the theme." He sat down and the woman on his left stood.

Lillian Markowitz was just a little older than Jane, and she wore a suit that would have cost Jane a year's rent. Her black hair fell flawlessly, spun into loose curls at her shoulders, and she was as slender as any supermodel Jane had ever seen. Chef Dan was subtly ogling her, as was Luka, though the latter was far more obvious, but Lincoln, Jane's heart skipped to note, was barely looking at Lilian.

"Ladies and gentlemen, your theme today is our main focus on at *Bridal Style*: Weddings. But you're not just making a wedding cake. Each of you will choose an envelope." She gestured to three pale blue envelopes lying on the judges' table. "Inside is a theme. Your job is to produce a cake that fits the initial requirements *and* realizes the theme you selected. You will choose in order of your current place in the rankings. Miss Bauer?" Stefanie stepped forward, grinning like a crocodile; she obviously felt that choosing first would give her an advantage. After a moment, she picked up the center envelope and returned to her station.

Findlay took less time, opting to quickly pick the envelope to the right, under the watchful gaze of Judge Ingram. He and Sarah also retreated quickly to their kitchen, leaving Jane to select the final envelope, earning her a grin from Judge Dan as she did so.

"Competitors, you will have ten minutes to open the envelope, strategize with your assistant, and sketch your showpiece," Lincoln announced. "Ten minutes on the clock. Go!"

The kitchens were a frenzy of movement as all three competitors tore into their envelopes. A whoop of delight from the kitchen suggested Findlay had gotten something he liked, and Stefanie didn't seem disappointed in her selection either.

Jane drew out the card with her theme on it and exclaimed brightly, "Happily Ever After! Oh, Nia!" Nia was grinning too-the pair couldn't have been given a better theme. They set to work sketching, as had the other teams. Ten minutes passed quickly and the buzzer sounded.

"Teams, your preparation time is over. Before you begin, please tell us what theme you will be executing. Stefanie?"

"Modern love."

"Findlay?"

"Love is in Bloom."

"And Jane?"

She grinned excitedly at Lincoln, confident she and Nia could nail this theme. "Happily Ever After," she replied.

"Very well, competitors. Eight hours on the clock this time. And, go!" Lincoln announced.

Another flurry of movement, and the teams were off, all-in differing directions. Nia set to work on the board and building up the base structure they would need. Jane began to tint the large sheets of fondant she needed to complete her design.

The hours ticked past and each station's masterwork began to rise from each metallic surface. Findlay's piece resembled a towering hillock, dotted with beautifully formed flowers and a soft, flowing drape, while Sarah appeared to be crafting an arch out of gum paste. Down at Stefanie's station, a massive stacked cake had appeared, but it was very plain, each tier edged in a dark blue shade.

Jane smiled as she worked, humming as she worked. The basic form of a princess's castle had emerged and Nia was painstakingly painting the bricks onto the gray fondant while Jane formed the tiny crenellations for each tower and turret. Even from across the studio, she had heard the judges murmuring that they felt her piece was too ambitious, that she wouldn't finish. This round, she knew they were underestimating her, but she was alright with that; they would see her masterpiece in judging.

"Nia, did you check the dance floor?" she asked quietly, referring to the extreme element at the center of their piece. "Does it work okay?"

"It's flawless, Jane." Nia smiled. "After this, I'm going to get the figures finished, then I'll glitter the roofs. Did you get the clock piece put in?"

"Yeah. It works. I'm just nervous that it will decide to malfunction at judging." She looked down at the rows of minuscule decorations. "Hand me that tube of royal frosting, will you? I need to start getting these on."

More time ticked by and tensions mounted. Findlay snapped at Sarah when the isomalt she was working with splattered onto the counter. Luka and Stefanie had been bickering in sharp German almost non-stop for the last three hours; their piece still looked remarkably stark.

Meanwhile, even Lincoln had to admit he was impressed by Jane's handiwork. The magnificent castle was unmistakable, and every detail was flawless, down to the small, hand-dotted mural in the castle's archway.

The judges, talking among themselves, remarked upon the fantastic attention to detail, particularly when Nia situated the hand-molded bride and groom figurine on the cake, in front of the tower.

Time was ticking away faster, with only minutes left, and each pair was affixing their final elements. Findlay's piece had a flowing fountain at its center, surrounded by an Eden of vines, flowers, and trees, and a canopy above a beautiful, hand-crafted couple. Sarah was frantically dotting the finishing touches on the fountain's edge.

Stefanie was attaching a small, yellow butterfly to a wire

which was rotating above the topmost tier of her cake, while Luka attached a few last gray ones to the middle tiers.

The buzzer sounded, and the teams dropped their tools to the table, two of the three embracing their partners. Then came the tedious, strenuous moment where each pair had to move their cakes; all of them recalling what had happened to Ryan in the last round.

There was a smattering of applause while Stefanie and Luka moved their cake to the table for judging. Next up were Findlay and Sarah; their piece must have been astoundingly heavy because they needed three crew assistants to move it, but it met the table with a soft thud and everyone breathed a sigh of relief.

Nia looked at Jane, who motioned for two of the crew to help them and together they hoisted the showpiece onto the judges' table. The spires glittered in the studio lights, and both girls exhaled deeply as the piece rested on the table. Judging would be in reverse order this time, so Nia and Jane quickly moved the table, which was on wheels, over to the judges' area.

This time, Rahul was the first to address them. "Well, well, Miss Mullins. I see you took what we said last week to heart and took more risks in this piece and it shows beautifully. The details are well attended. Can we see your extreme elements?"

Jane nodded and pressed a small button on the board. On cue, the bride and groom figures began to waltz around the courtyard of the cake. "The clock also functions," she pointed out, and the judges eyed the small clock on the castle's front.

Judge Dan was next, and he was grinning as he spoke. "Jane, this is one of the most beautiful cakes I have ever seen. The detail is meticulous, and it exudes romance. I agree with Rahul. Well done!"

"I'm not sure what else there is to say," Belinda spoke. "My colleagues have echoed my thoughts exactly on your work.

Beautiful, detailed, somewhat risky in the narrow towers and tiny crenellations. Overall, a remarkable piece."

Jane thought her heart might pop as their guest judge perused her cake. "I have seen hundreds of wedding cakes, some by decorators at this very table, and I have to say this is one of my favorites. You captured the theme perfectly."

Jane and Nia bowed in thanks to the judges, then moved quickly to the green room to wait. They burst through the doors and exclaimed for joy.

"They loved it! Nia, did you hear them?"

Nia laughed, embracing her friend. "It's a wonderful cake! They were bound to love it. Now we wait."

They both settled onto one of the long, low couches, Nia pulling out her cell phone and immediately texting Eddie. Jane envied her, wishing very much that she could be sharing this moment with Lincoln, though she knew he had heard everything the judges said. Friends would share a moment like this, right? It surely didn't mean anything that she was so eager to have him as part of such a major moment.

After a few minutes, Findlay and Sarah came back to the room, both smiling, apparently pleased with their judging. They sat across from Jane and Nia, commenting on Jane's work, when the doors crashed open.

Stefanie, face red as a length of silk, thundered over to Jane. "You little tramp! What did you do with your man to get them to like your cake better?" Luka stood behind her, his expression like granite. Jane was so stunned and startled she could say nothing as Stefanie raged on. "Do not think that you will beat me just because your boyfriend got them to like your work. I've been doing this for longer than you've been alive. I will win. And you will crumble."

At that moment, Lincoln came to the door, along with one of the crew, to call them back to the set. Jane hesitated, waiting for everyone else to leave before slowly shuffling to the exit. Lincoln was waiting in the shadow on the other side.

"I heard yelling. What happened?"

"Nothing. She was just upset," Jane lied.

"Jane," he admonished, staring deeply into her eyes. "We could almost hear her in the studio. I know she said that it's because of me that the judges liked your piece. Jane, I swear—"

"I know. She's wrong about all of it. I just... I've never been good at handling people yelling at me. I'm okay now."

"Are you sure?" He said, taking her hand.

"I am. I swear. She's just mad because our cake was better. I'm fine." She looked at their joined hands, then to Lincoln's face, which was still laced with concern.

"All I wanted to do during judging was tell you how proud of you I am. Is that weird?"

Jane squeezed his hand, feeling like her heart might jump from her chest. "Nah. All I wanted to do was tell you how giddy I was about their feedback, so I think it's fair." They reached the closed studio doors where Nia was waiting and he dropped her hand. "Let's do this," she said quietly.

She took Nia's arm and marched through the door, stopping next to the other teams at the judging table. Lincoln moved past them to his post at the end of the table.

"Here we are again, and for two contestants, this will be a happy ending to today, while one will not enjoy the fairy tale. Who has the sweetest tooth and who is going home? We saw three very different interpretations of romantic, bridal themes, but one just wasn't happy enough." He turned to them. "I'm sorry Stefanie. You do not have the sweetest tooth today."

Jane was grateful the cameras were there to capture the look of pure incredulity that slowly spread across Stefanie's face. Luka's was a mask of utter shock. The angry woman spun on her heel, spat at Jane's feet, and stomped out of the studio. The judges looked confused, but no one said anything as Lincoln continued.

"Jane, Findlay. You both offered up magnificent creations for us today, but one rose far above. Second place today goes to," he paused dramatically, as he was supposed to, "Findlay."

Jane staggered, her mind reeling, into Nia's waiting arms. Findlay smiled, shaking Jane's hand, and trooped out of the room with Sarah at his side.

"Which means, Miss Mullins, that you are today's winner." Lincoln said, the smile evident in his voice. She cried with delight, embracing Nia, spinning around like children on the playground.

"Thanks for joining us, and be sure to catch next week's finale where we will see who truly has the sweetest Sweet Tooth. Goodnight!"

The cameras shut off, and Jane stopped herself from running to Lincoln in excitement. She noticed the judges were still standing around, and Dan quickly motioned her over.

"Miss Mullins, we just wanted to let you know how impressed we were with your work today. We have rarely seen such enthusiasm and improvement in a first-time competitor."

Blushing, she replied, "Thank you so much!"

"Keep up the good work, and you just might find yourself with a winner's medal and twenty-five grand."

He and the judges left the room while Nia moved to a corner to text their team members. When Jane was certain no one was watching, she dashed into the shadows where Lincoln stood, grinning.

"You did it!" he cried, sweeping her up. "I told you that you could!"

"Oh my gosh, I thought my heart was going to explode," she gushed. "Findlay's cake was so beautiful."

"Stefanie's face was priceless," he whispered. "Did you see it?"

Jane giggled. "I don't know whose was better, hers or Luka's."

"You should go quickly, before Antony shows up again or Stefanie gets feisty. Go home and get some rest. You've more than earned it. I'll text you tomorrow, okay?"

Jane nodded as Nia grabbed her arm and pulled her away.

"Stop looking at him like that," Nia hissed as they hurried out of the studio.

"Like what?"

"Like you want him to sweep you off your feet and kiss you like Prince Charming." As they stepped into the bright lights, Jane was startled by shouting.

"You slept with him and got the win!" She ducked as Stefanie sent a roll of paper towels flying at her head. "You are just some upstart who slept with the host to get ahead."

"What on earth is going on here?" a man's voice echoed in the hall. Jane grimaced as she saw Antony turn the corner, his face red.

"You." He brandished a finger in Jane's face. "I knew you were trouble. Here you were just supposed to be an easy out and you're sleeping with judges and cheating rightful contestants out of their spots. I should have them disqualify you now."

"But doing so would make you a liar and a fool, Antony Perandin." Lincoln's voice boomed into the hallway; even Jane jumped at the sound.

"First, no one has slept with anyone else, at least not in regards to me or the judges. Ergo, there is no fault or cheating. Second, the very fact that you cast a bright entrepreneur as the 'easy-out' makes you more of a fool, and I am sure if such information were to leak out, it would not bode well for the network or your tenure with them. You have done nothing but belittle and berate this young woman and I, for one, think it abominable. Continue on this path, and I will go straight to

Edwards," he spoke forcefully, referring to Geoff Edwards, CEO of the Culinary Channel.

Stefanie shouted more insults at Jane, grappling at her. Jane shrank behind Lincoln.

"You, Ms. Bauer," he roared, "are an ambitious, vengeful, sore loser. You have won twice in this competition. You of all people should know what it takes to win. And you should also know that the host has no jurisdiction over the outcome of the show therefore, even if I were sleeping with this young woman, which I am not, I cannot stress that enough, it would be to no fault, no issue, no breach of ethics. I suggest that we all go home and stop all this childish behavior."

Jane grabbed Nia's arm, their bags, and bustled out the door into the snowy afternoon. She struggled to catch her breath, adrenaline rushing through her system. They should be celebrating, should be dancing through the streets of New York together, not hiding from an angry competitor and worried that Lincoln's producer was going to find a way to get them out of the program.

"My god, Jane. What have you done?"

"Not you, too, Nia." She stared at her assistant. "You know I haven't done anything wrong!"

"I know you've apparently been spending all your spare time with him, even after he spent Thanksgiving with your family."

"That's hardly scandalous. I'm not sleeping with him, Nia. You should know me better than that."

"But the world doesn't, Jane, and people have seen you two together now. They're bound to talk."

"So, they'll talk."

"That idea alone used to break you down. I mean, every-thing with Nick—"

"This is not remotely the same situation. And I cannot live my life, a life here, in this competition that will be on television nationwide, by what people might think or say about what I do. All I can do is the right thing and trust that those who know me the best will know the truth."

Nia was quiet, the sounds of the busy city swirling around them. "Just be careful, Jane. Don't forget who he is, or who you are. I'm going to Eddie's. I'll call you tomorrow." She turned and trooped to the stairs down into the subway.

"Someone has taught you a lesson, Miss Mullins," Lincoln said behind her. "A lesson about perception. And in the nick of time."

She turned into his arms, the tears that had long formed tracing hot lines down her icy face.

"Shh," he calmed her, stroking her hair. "They were all out of line back there. I'm sorry."

"I'm the one who should be sorry. All of this casts you in the same unfavorable light, just because of me. And I'm not worth it."

He spun her around to face him. "Jane Mullins, there is no truth in that statement. I made the choice to repay the kindness you showed me when we first met. There is nothing wrong with our relationship. We know the truth, those we love know the truth." She looked down the street where Nia had disappeared. "Or at least, they will. Do the right thing, know the truth, and everything else will sort itself out." He embraced her again, shielding his face from the sharp breeze cutting into them. "We should go somewhere warm. Have some hot cocoa or something."

Jane nodded. "Chai?"

He tucked her arm into his. "Sure. I think there's a tea shop near here. Let's go."

When Words Fail

～⌒～

The sunlight filtering through the curtains spilled a subtle wake-up call across the pale lids of Jane's eyes as she yawned and stretched under the smooth cotton sheets. Smiling, she drew herself into a sitting position and reached for her cell phone and the television remote, which were side by side on the night table.

Flipping the TV on, she searched for someone who would tell her the weather, settling for a local news program that advertised the weather every ten minutes. One problem solved, she opened her phone and scrolled through the messages. Having ignored all the ones from the night before, she checked that none were overly important. Mostly they were "just checking in" type notes from Nia, Trevor, and her grandmother, all of which earned a very basic response of "I'm fine. Talk to you soon."

At the bottom of the list was a newer message, sent just a half hour before from a name that made her smile instinctively.

Lincoln: Had such a great time the other night. Let's hang out today.

For a brief moment, she regretted not staying at Lincoln's the night before. They'd sat at the tea shop until long after dark, Lincoln doing his best to distract her from the disastrous end of the day. Since they both had the day off, he had offered for her to stay with him instead of having to take a cab back to her hotel, but she turned him down, insisting that she should head back. But he had that massive guest room, nearly bigger than her whole house. And he'd offered to make her breakfast... She stopped her rambling, romantic reflections, shaking her head. Going to the game with him was one thing, and she had seen the ramifications that had produced. Spending the night at his house would just fuel that fire. But there wasn't any harm in spending the day with him, was there? It was her first time in New York and she'd rather be able to see the city with someone who knew the ins and outs of it. And she could deny it all she wanted, but she was enjoying the time they spent together more and more.

On the TV, the meteorologist shared the forecast for the rest of the week, but all Jane heard was one word: snow. And it was supposed to start that evening. She clapped her hands, leaping from the bed and sweeping back the curtains to look out on the city, shrouded in light gray clouds. Christmas lights dotted the scene, and she swore she could hear the chiming of bells in the distance.

In the tangle of sheets she'd left behind, a chirp sounded, signaling a new text message. Rifling through the blankets, she found the blinking phone and opened it to see the sender. A girlish giggle escaped her lips when she saw Lincoln's name on the screen as she opened the text.

Lincoln: A friend of mine is stage managing for Winslow Gorman's concert tonight. Would you want to go with me?

Jane promptly dropped her phone, then scrambled to find it again when it began to ring.

Lincoln barely greeted her when she exclaimed, "Are you serious? Do you have the slightest idea how long I've been dying to see Winslow Gorman? Yes. Yes, a million times, yes I want to go!"

He was laughing on the other end of the line before she finished speaking. "I somehow figured you would. Did you get my earlier message?"

"I did. Can we still hang out if it snows?"

He laughed again and her excitement. "Yes, we can. New York doesn't shut down for snow the way Atlanta, or even Nashville, does. I thought we could do some shopping and then come back here and make lunch and then who knows? The show isn't until eight, so we have plenty of time."

"Give me a little bit to shower and get cute," she chuckled, "and I'll get a cab."

"I'll send the car," he insisted. "You have an hour. See you soon, Jane."

Feeling like she should pinch herself, Jane sat on the edge of the bed. She eyed the handful of clothes hanging in the closet across the room, wishing he had thought to pack more nice things; she had no idea what she would wear to the concert later that night.

Forty-five minutes later, she was showered, made-up, and dressed in her dark wash jeans and a sapphire blue sweater, encased in the thick herringbone wool coat she had splurged on before this trip, her hands wrapped in silver grey gloves that matched the scarf around her neck. She waited in the hotel's magnificent lobby until she saw a sleek black car slow to a stop at the front steps. Rolling down the passenger side window, the driver, Victor, spoke to the doorman, a kindly older gentleman who smiled at Jane as she exited the building.

"Miss Mullins?" He gestured to the car.

"Thank you, Floyd," she replied, slipping him a five-dollar bill.

He tipped his hat as Victor opened the door and she slid inside, feeling very much like a celebrity.

"Mr. Lincoln asked if you would be okay with meeting him at Le Marché Abondant to shop," Victor asked from the driver's seat.

"Of course." She smiled. "I'm afraid I'm a bit at his mercy. I have no idea where anything is here."

"Well, you're in good hands with Mr. Lincoln. He's a great man."

Jane nodded eagerly. "I agree. You've known him a long time?"

"Almost eight years. You take care of him now. After Miss Railey, it was a long time before he trusted anyone, much less a woman. But he likes you, he trusts you."

"He does?" Jane asked. Victor nodded, and her pulse fluttered. "I like him too," she admitted before she realized what she was saying. "And I won't hurt him."

Victor smiled at her in the rear-view mirror as they wove in and out of the holiday traffic. They slipped down a narrow side street and out into a big open area and across from the space was a park with children running about. Finding a spot close to the curb, Victor slowed to a stop and suddenly Jane's door opened, revealing Lincoln standing on the sidewalk, hands tucked into the pockets of his black wool coat.

He offered his hand to Jane, calling over the seats to Victor. "Can you meet us in two hours at Foster's?"

"Yes, sir, Mr. Lincoln." Victor tipped his hat and was gone, disappearing into the congested streets as Jane looked around, taking in a new corner of the Big Apple.

"I think you're right about the snow," Lincoln said, his gloved hand taking hers. "This is how it always looks before a good one." He smiled down at her, and she, reflexively, snuggled against him, cutting the chill of the late autumn wind. "Shall we then? I was just going to make you a nice lunch, but then I realized I had capers and baking soda, so I figured we could have a nice field trip to the market."

They stepped inside the spacious building, which had once been three smaller stores but now housed a cornucopia of products. Jane marveled over the different produce items, exotic fruits and vegetables she could rarely find at home.

"Bilberries!" she exclaimed. "And durian." She gestured to the hideous shapes stacked alone in one corner. "Wow. They really are as potent as they say."

"I used them once on Next Top Chef, but not since then," he remarked, catching a whiff of the signature, "dirty socks" smell. "I think we should leave those for another day," he said, steering her to the fresh herbs.

She smiled. "Then what shall we have for lunch, Mr. Big-Time-Chef?"

"I was thinking I could make some baked chicken and herbed couscous, maybe a salad."

She stopped, and turned to face him, hands on her hips. "Baked chicken? That's what world-famous culinary champion Lincoln Bainbridge is going to make me for lunch?"

He laughed, a deep belly laugh. "Okay, okay!" His hands raised in defense. "I get it."

"I just meant..."

"I know what you meant, and you're right. I've become so accustomed to doing such simple meals that I forget that in my own kitchen, I can do whatever I want." He stepped to her, placing an arm around her shoulders. "What if we really mix it up and you make the entrée, and I'll make dessert?"

Her eyes lit up. "Okay."

"Let's split up," he suggested. "You grab what you need, and I will get what I need. We'll meet at the registers." He gestured to the far corner of the store. She nodded and they parted, baskets in hand.

Fifteen minutes later, she found Lincoln scanning a rack of dried spices waiting for her.

"So, what did you come up with?" she asked, eyeing his basket when they found each other.

"I think I'd rather surprise you, to be honest. What about you?"

"Liver and onions with mashed Brussels sprouts and Limburger smothered yams." He tried, unsuccessfully, to keep a straight face, but couldn't help but grimace. Jane laughed.

"I'm completely kidding. But if yours is going to be a surprise, then mine will, too."

They paid and stepped back out onto the sidewalk, the gray sky still lingering high above them. "So, we're supposed to meet Victor at Foster's? What's that?"

"Ah, you'll love it. Come on." He took her empty hand and began to lead her up the street, turning down one street, then crossing and turning down another until they stopped in front of an old storefront.

The wooden panels were a deep burgundy color, and the lettering above the door shimmered slightly in a gold hue, while the windows were illuminated with Christmas lights and a large tree on one side.

She turned to look at Lincoln. "Well?" he asked.

"What is it?"

"It's a bookstore. One of the oldest in the city and my favorite. Come on." He led her inside. "Mr. Foster?"

An older man, his hair still dark but leaning heavily on a cane, came into view around one towering stack of books.

"Lincoln! It has been too long, dear boy!" The man's accent was undeniably British, and Jane smiled as he embraced Lincoln like family. "And who is this lovely young lady?"

"This is Jane Mullins. She loves books even more than I do, so I thought she should see how a real bookstore operates." The older man smiled proudly.

"It is a pleasure to meet you, Miss Mullins. Always a pleasure to meet friends of Lincoln's, but especially such a beautiful woman."

Jane blushed as she shook his hand. "It's a pleasure to meet you as well."

"Mr. Foster, can we sit our bags in your fridge while we look around? I don't want our food to get too warm."

"Of course. Here, I'll take it." He took the shopping bags from the two of them. "You two head on up and look around. There are some new arrivals in the blue room. And the lady might like to see the tower." He winked slyly at Lincoln, who grabbed Jane's hand and took her up a narrow flight of steps, past stacks upon stacks of books, some bright and new, others so old and worn you could hardly make out the names on the spines.

"Where are we going?" she asked as he hurried her through a big room with tall windows facing out over a backyard garden.

"Just follow me," he said, smiling sneakily.

They walked through another room into a small space, dimly lit and narrow, with a spiraling metal staircase at its center. Up the stairs they moved, winding around and around until they stopped in the center of a bright room with windows on every wall and books stacked high from the floor, surrounding a squashy, hideously floral sofa.

"Wow," she breathed. From every window was a view of the city outside, but she was as entranced by the view inside. Stacks of books were her aim as she beelined to the one nearest the sofa. "Some of these aren't even in English." She rifled through a few until she found a familiar tome.

For several moments, she stood there and stared at the worn blue cover. Lincoln was absently pillaging a stack facing the windows, but he turned when there was only silence behind him.

"What is it?"

"It's a copy of Hans Christian Andersen's fairy tales."

He moved closer, placing a hand on her shoulder. "And?"

"It's just like the one my father used to read for me. It was in the car with him the night he died, and I never saw it again after that." She was still staring at the cover, and he could see the faintest of tears in her eyes.

"Here," he murmured, sitting down with her on the sofa. Lincoln slipped the book from her hands with little resistance and began flipping through the pages.

"There," she exclaimed, pressing her finger to the title on the page. "*Under the Willow Tree.* We would lay in the hammock in the garden and he would read this little part of this story to me. Here," she pointed again, and Lincoln began to read. His voice was warm, soothing as she laid her head on his shoulder. The familiar story of the star-crossed gingerbread man and his honey cake lady who fell in love but never told the other flowed through her mind, Lincoln's storytelling bringing them to life. When the poor maiden broke in two, he hesitated.

"Wow. That's sad," he whispered.

"'It is enough for me that I have been able to live on the same counter with him'," Jane murmured.

Lincoln closed the book and looked at Jane. Her eyes were closed as she whispered, "My father would tell me this story so often that, by the time I was five, I could recite it by memory, and then he would hold me very close and say 'If you love someone, tell them. If you don't say anything, you may wait around until you crack, waiting for them to say it first.'"

"Your father was pretty smart," Lincoln said softly, stroking her hair as it fell over his arm. "Thank you for sharing such an important memory with me." She nodded, threading her fingers through his. After a few moments, he murmured, "I don't know about you, but I am desperately hungry. We should probably get going." On cue, her stomach made a spectacular burbling sound.

He moved to drop the book into the nearest stack, but she grabbed it from his hand. "I want to buy it," she said quietly. "It doesn't feel right to leave it." She hurried down the long flights of steps back to the entrance, and he followed her, occasionally steering her in the correct direction when she turned the wrong way.

They reached the lobby and Lincoln went to go gather their food while Jane paid for her new-old book, then they stepped outside, where they found Victor waiting.

"Home, Mr. Lincoln?"

"Yes, thank you, Victor."

The smiling driver opened the door, and Jane slid inside, clutching her latest purchase to her chest and her shopping bag in her other hand. Lincoln deftly maneuvered into the seat next to her. With little afternoon traffic, the trip back to Lincoln's was surprisingly short.

"Victor, I know you're off tonight. Can you make sure Alexei knows to pick us up at seven sharp tonight?"

"Yes, Mr. Lincoln. You all have a nice afternoon," he said as Lincoln climbed out, offering his hand to Jane to help her onto the sidewalk.

The pair walked through the beautiful lobby and waited for the elevator. With a ping, the doors whooshed open, and they stepped inside.

Lincoln performed the ritual to allow them up to the penthouse, and away they flew. She looked up at him, certain he was about to say something, but then he looked away. A small voice in her head kept muttering to her, but she stared down at her shoes instead until the doors opened again and they had arrived.

The apartment was grayed by the skyline outside, but it was still as beautiful as she remembered as they walked into the kitchen, where an overhead light warmed the room with its golden glow.

Lincoln watched Jane unpack her ingredients. Reading with her had been one of those moments he'd never expected to have, but suddenly found himself wanting more of. The warmth of her next to him felt right, felt more like home than anything had in years. With a shake of his head, he realized she was watching him.

"What?" she asked, cocking her head to the side.

"Nothing," he assured quickly. "Just thinking." He grabbed his own shopping bags. "Should we have some music while we work?" Tapping his fingers against a small panel on the wall, a burst of vintage Christmas music filled the room.

"Whoa," Jane asked, looking around.

"Built-in sound system," he explained proudly. "Definitely one of the things I like most about this place. Is this okay with you? I told it to start with some old-school songs since they're my favorite."

"Mine, too. There's some great new stuff but it's hard to beat the classics!"

He tapped her nose with the tip of his finger. "You have good taste. Now, we should probably get to cooking. I think your stomach was a bit vocal about its needs."

She laughed, but threw a nearby towel at him, which he barely dodged as it flew across the room. "I'm sure glad you cook better than you throw," he teased, pulling pans out of the cabinets. "So, all your pots and pans are here." He turned to a tall cabinet and pulled, revealing a double-sided pantry shelf stocked with every spice, herb, and other cooking accoutrement she could have asked for. "And here's all the spices and oil and stuff you might need. And I've got the double oven if you need to bake anything." He spun the dial of the upper oven to preheat it.

Jane was already at work, chopping mushrooms and

onions atop a heavy wooden cutting board. In no time, the kitchen was filled with warm aromas and their voices as they sang along to the sound system.

Jane watched Lincoln eagerly as he sang. He was swishing around the kitchen, tossing out his best moves as he did.

"You sure you shouldn't be a dancer?" She grinned as he did a tap-dancing circle around the counters.

"Oh now, don't mock," he replied, doing a ballerina twirl. "How's lunch coming?"

"Almost done," she replied, stirring a steaming pot at the back of the stovetop. "And dessert?"

He checked the timer on the oven. "Nearly there, too. Are you going to tell me what it is?"

"I guess," she teased, as she began to serve. "My grand-mother's beef stroganoff, thyme, and mint English peas, and onion roasted potatoes."

"Wow!" Lincoln admired her handiwork as she passed a plate across the counter to him. "This looks delicious, Jane." He took a forkful of the stroganoff, twirling the long noodles. "Mmm! This is heavenly."

"Just old family recipes. My favorites."

"I can see why. The sweet onions and salty mushrooms, the tender steak and creamy sauce. It all just works together."

"I feel like that's significant praise coming from a chef like you."

"I mean it! I'd order this at a restaurant!"

"You're being kind."

"No one has ever told you how good this is?"

She blushed brightly. "I've never made it for anyone else before."

"Well, now, I'm extra flattered," he admitted.

"What did you whip up?"

Drawing a casserole dish from the oven, the fragrance of

cinnamon, nutmeg, and cloves swirled around them. "My YaYa's spiced apple crumble. I thought you'd like it."

"We both managed to make family food," she considered, heart full.

"I think being with yours for Thanksgiving inspired me."

With a tap on the control panel, he cut off the music wafting around them and turned on the massive television as they settled in front of the screen.

"Christmas movie?" he asked, flipping through the hundreds of channels. "Oh!" he exclaimed, stopping as a tall elf marched through New York City.

"Perfect!" Jane approved, "Great accompaniment for such a feast." They tucked into their meal, pausing to quote the movie every so often.

Lincoln glanced at his watch and realized how late it had gotten. "Yikes. We're supposed to leave for the show in about an hour and a half." He looked around. "Did you bring something to change into?"

"I did." She gestured to her bag. "I tried to come prepared."

"I'll clean up here and you can get ready in the guest room."

"That's not fair, for you to have to do all the cleaning."

"Nah. It'll only take me a bit to get ready. I don't mind. Go, go!"

"Alright," she acquiesced, grabbing her bag.

In the quiet of the guest room, she withdrew the one nice outfit she'd thought to pack for the trip; a lovely green velvet cocktail dress. She'd found it at a vintage shop and fell in love with the fitted sweetheart neckline and swirling circle skirt. Paired with her silver flats, she felt elegant and classy, certainly enough for a classy concert. Her dark red curls were twisted into a chignon at the nape of her neck, with a few left loose around her face.

"Jane? Are you ready? The car will be here any minute."

"I'm ready," she called, opening the door and stepping gracefully back into the main hall. She could hear him draw in a sharp breath as she turned to him.

"Does it look okay? It's new, well, new to me, and I'm never sure how things will fit me."

He took her in, standing bashfully in his front hall, looking for all her awkwardness, like she had just stepped off the red carpet. "You look incredible, Jane."

She smiled, noticing that he had changed into a dashing, charcoal gray suit with a black collared shirt. "You don't look so bad yourself, Bainbridge."

He quietly held out her coat as they stepped into the hall. He summoned the elevator, sneaking glances at her. The sleek black town car was waiting, a muscular blond man standing by the back door; she presumed this was Alexei. The man nodded to Lincoln as he opened the door for Jane, who gracefully bowed into the car. Lincoln moved to the other side, sliding onto the seat next to her, and taking her hand.

"It's been a while since I've seen one of Winslow's shows," Lincoln said, his thumb brushing across Jane's knuckles. "They're pretty fantastic, though."

"I've wanted to see him for ages, but tickets sell out so fast when he's in Atlanta."

"We're here, Mr. Bainbridge," Alexei called over the seat. They slowed to a halt, and Jane could see twinkling lights through the tinted windows.

"I will help the lady out, Alexei." The driver nodded and Lincoln climbed out of the car.

Jane's door opened, and she stepped out into the bright lights of the marquee. The lobby was packed as they hurried past the crowd. Lincoln waved two tickets at an usher, who immediately led them into a box of their own.

"Wow. You will never cease to amaze me," she said, hugging him tightly. "Thank you for this, for everything."

The band began the cacophony of warming up and Jane dropped into her seat, eagerly watching the stage. Down went the house lights, and the concert began, the first song one Jane knew well.

As the lights flashed for intermission, she noticed people watching Lincoln as he led her to the lobby.

"Can I get you a drink?"

"Cosmopolitan, please?" she asked, as he moved off to the nearby bar. She watched people passing by, couples and families alike, before she noticed the cluster of women about her age across the room. The four of them seemed to be whispering to each other, but they kept glancing in her direction.

When Lincoln returned, drinks in his hand, she took his arm and they moved past the gossiping girls, but not before Jane overheard one whisper, "Ugh. She's not even pretty. Lincoln Bainbridge can't be dating *her*!"

Like arrows through her sternum, the harsh truth of reality sank in. For all the delight of the time she was spending with him, she knew it wasn't going to last. He was a celebrity, internationally famous, and she was just Jane. "No point in fighting reality," she muttered. "And we're not dating, anyway". No point in being upset about something that wasn't true.

Finale

Jane was the first to arrive on the last day of the competition. The studio was dark, and only a few crew members bustled about, pulling cables and moving cameras. Tying on her apron, she double-checked their supplies. She noticed they'd moved Findlay to the other end of the studio, leaving the two empty kitchens between them. Across the room, she spotted Eliza, the director, and waved.

"Hey, Jane," Eliza greeted, approaching the kitchen. "You're here early."

"Couldn't sleep."

"Nervous?"

"Terrified. Excited. Anxious. Thrilled."

"Sounds about right," Eliza laughed. "I'd think you didn't know what you had gotten into if you weren't a little scared, but I'm glad you're also excited. You've done so well, though. Everyone's impressed."

"Not everyone," Jane countered. "I'm not sure Mr. Perandin is a fan."

Eliza shrugged. "I wouldn't worry too much about him.

It's the judges who make that decision, and even Rahul admires your work."

"I guess we'll see. Any hints on the theme today?"

Chuckling, Eliza shook her head. "No secrets from me. I'll let you get back to prep. Good luck!"

"Thanks!" Jane replied, reaching for her sketchbook to doodle.

"Mornin', lass!" Findlay's voice boomed through the studio. "Are ye ready for today?"

"I hope so. Gonna have to be on our a-game to beat you and Sarah."

"Aye, we've been thinking the same thing. Your pretty castle was fair play!"

"Thanks, Findlay! Y'all's garden was gorgeous, too."

Sarah and Findlay nodded to her as they huddled over their sketchbooks and supplies, as Nia entered, clad in a neon pink 'I <3 NY' t-shirt.

Seeing the look on Jane's face, Nia groaned and explained, "Eddie bought it for me. I know it's hideous, but it was so sweet and I promised him I'd wear it for the competition."

"I love it. It's adorable," Jane laughed, hugging Nia. "Are you ready?"

"Ready as I'll get."

The pair set about completing their prep, straightening and organizing tools into a system that would allow them to work quickly once the show started. Crew and other staff were gathering, setting up their own tools as Antony marched in. Jane avoided his eyes as he surveyed the room.

"Where is he?" he hissed under his breath, standing in front of her station. "Don't play games with me, little girl. I know you've been with him. Where is he?"

"I don't know, Mr. Perandin," Jane answered quietly.

"Don't give me that! I know he took you to a concert last night and—"

"Antony!" Lincoln's voice echoed through the room.

Jane exhaled. Antony retreated, and she watched the pair muttering animatedly, both clearly upset.

"Jane, we'll be starting in about ten minutes," Eliza called as she passed their kitchen, clipboard in hand. "Do you have everything you need?"

"We're all set. I'm sure there's stuff in the pantry if we need things for the theme."

Eliza nodded and headed off, chattering into her headset as she went. There was a flurry of movement over the next few minutes as the judges arrived. They were seated behind their long table as Eliza ordered everyone to get to their places.

"All right folks, we're ready in three, two..." She motioned with her hand as Lincoln stepped to his mark. He delivered his usual introduction, with the pauses for prior footage.

"Today, we've got a heck of a finale and guest judge for you. As always, we're joined by our illustrious judges: Rahul Ingram, Dan Greenberg, and Belinda Wilson."

Belinda stood and addressed the two finalists. "Competitors, you've both worked incredibly hard so far. Congratulations. Today, our guest judge is a renowned scientist and explorer, having firsthand experience with the theme you'll be recreating. Please help me welcome National Galactic Agency public relations director and retired astronaut, Olin Yamoto."

The group applauded as a middle-aged, well-dressed Japanese gentleman stepped into the bright studio lights, smiling and waving. "Good morning, competitors. Your challenge today is to take to the stars and transform them into a cake masterpiece. We want to see your interpretation of outer space."

"Your requirements are the same as always. Your cake must be at least six feet tall and feature at least one extreme element. You will be judged on your creativity, execution, and how well your cake captures the theme. And remember, this is the finals, so we're expecting big things from you all. As before, we're giving you ten minutes to plan and sketch. Go!" Lincoln announced. Both teams scribbled furiously, muttering to themselves as they worked. The ten minutes passed quickly before a buzzer sounded.

"All right teams, your prep time is up and it's time to get to work. We'll be looking forward to what you both create. Eight hours are on the clock. On your marks, get set, *go!*"

There was a flurry of motion as everyone set to work. "I'll get all the layers covered in their base colors," Jane called to Nia, holding up her sketches. "Will you get the sugar rings put together?"

"Sure thing, boss. The asteroid belt, too?"

"Yeah. I'll get the moon done next."

Nia hesitated, glancing at the complicated design Jane had crafted. "Are you sure Jane? This is a risky plan."

"I know," Jane admitted quietly. "But I want to go all in. Leave everything out on the floor, you know?"

"You're right," Nia agreed. "If we're gonna do it, let's do it big!"

By hour three, the cakes were all covered with fondant and buttercream, rising high above the stainless countertop in a towering structure. Across the room, Findlay's creation was tall, but all the layers were on their own platforms and resting at off kilter angles. Jane could see intricate details on what appeared to be a spaceship off to one side and an adorable four-armed creature on top of their large base cake.

As she tightened the dowel through the middle of the asteroid belt, one of the small sugar rings snapped in half, dropping the tiny asteroids to shatter on the floor. "Crap! I'm gonna have to redo the ring to fix this."

"Do we have time?"

"If you can get the details on the outer planets done."

"Sure thing. Fix the ring and we'll go from there.

"Thanks, Nia. Did you see theirs?"

"It's looking good, but I wonder if it's stable like that."

"Guess we'll see. Not like ours is going to be the most stable."

Jane quickly melted isomalt on the stove, watching Nia paint red and copper stripes on a large layer designed to look like Jupiter. A new set of tiny asteroids emerged from the molten sugar, and Jane gently positioned the piece around the cake dowel. She added another set of sugar rings to the layer painted like Saturn, ensuring they were secure as well, before taking a moment to pore over her checklist, marking off the tasks they'd finished, and checked the time.

"Three hours to go, competitors!" Lincoln announced, making her jump. She heard Sarah cry out from their kitchen and knew something had gone wrong. Not a lot of time to fix things now.

"Nia, I'm going to rig up the rocket. Is it ready?"

Her partner looked up from her painting. "Yeah, it's on the drying rack. The little Pluto layer is too."

"Sounds great."

Jane gathered a tangle of wires and a metal platform; they'd found a lifting platform in the supply pantry and planned to rig it to hoist the miniature sugar-paste spaceship. Nia had done a brilliant job covering the smallest cake tier in a mottled grey fondant, so Jane began sliding the copper wires through the sugar paste. Applying silver dust to the covered platform, Jane tucked the wires away and attached the rocket. Once she was confident it was secure, she pressed the button on the remote.

The ship lifted slowly, and Jane did a little happy dance.

Nia high-fived Jane. "We did it!"

"We're not done yet. We've still got to get the layers together and stacked. And did we finish the moon? That's still got to be hooked to the wire to rotate."

"On the drying rack for when we get everything stacked, boss." Nia glanced at the clock. "We've got forty-five minutes. Let's start stacking."

Slowly, they positioned the large Jupiter layer on the wooden dowel and carefully set the next set of dowel rods in a square around the middle.

"Nia! Did you tighten the dowel platform under the asteroids?" Jane started to panic, even as she placed the second largest layer, making sure not to bump the sugar rings around the planet.

"It's as solid as it can be, Jane. I promise."

Jane took a deep breath. This was just like a big wedding cake. There was no time to freak out. She stole a glance toward the far corner where Lincoln was standing. He smiled slyly at her, flashing her a covert thumbs up. Her nerves ebbed for a moment, replaced by warmth.

"Jane, I can't place this one alone. Come on."

Together, they lifted the next two tiers, one with a third set of sugar rings, and positioned them atop a second set of dowel rods. Careful not to smudge Nia's beautiful swirling paint job, Jane tucked the fondant edges in under each cake.

"Thirty minutes to go!"

Brushing a stray curl from her forehead, Jane situated the wires for the platform out of sight, and sculpted sugar rocks camouflaging them along the back of the cake.

"Ten minutes, competitors!" Lincoln's voice boomed.

Jane stepped back, taking in the completed cake. She knew it was ambitious, the massive layer of the sun as a base with each planet represented in a layer. From the ten-inch Mercury to the four-inch Pluto, the cakes centered on a solid central dowel rod with a sugar ring asteroid belt at the center.

"Now we just have to move the thing," Nia said behind her.

"Yeah. No stress there," Jane agreed. They both circled the

towering sculpture. Nia straightened an asteroid, and Jane smoothed a splotchy patch of buttercream near the edge of Venus.

"Times up, decorators! Step away from your cakes!" Lincoln called.

Jane spotted a powder-covered Findlay brushing something from the side of their massive confection, but Lincoln caught her eye. Grinning, he touched his cheek and nodded at her. She mimicked his action to find a blob of frosting, which she tried to wipe away.

As the judges settled into their places, the competitors took a moment to perch on the metal stools, waiting for the tedious moment they had to move their work.

Dan stood from their table and addressed the pairs. "Decorators, time to move your cakes. Jane, you're up first." The partners looked at each other, took a deep breath, and gently lifted the wooden base. Even compared with their previous two cakes, this was weighty. Shuffling from their stainless counter toward the judges' table, Jane and Nia gripped the board between them, willing it to stay level.

She heard Nia breathe in sharply, and hissed at her to stop. The cake swayed between them for a moment, then stilled. With a thud, they slid the base across the butcher block counter until it was centered and they heard the judges applaud. Both women grinned at each other, embracing.

"We did it, Jane!" whispered Nia excitedly. "We really did it!"

"Now, Findlay, if you'll move your cake, please."

The cake, seven layers of wild colors and textures, wobbled as Findlay and Sarah lifted it from the counter. Jane held her breath, watching the wire-suspended stars on the topmost tier as her competition slowly moved across the room. She heard Nia gasp and Findlay swear as something fell off the side, cracking as it hit the tiles. The cake slid across their judging table at last, and Findlay wrapped his arm around Sarah's shoulders, admiring their work.

"Competitors, you can go take a break while the judges examine your work close up and we'll call you back in for judging. You've both done a great job here."

The foursome trooped back to the green room, sinking wearily into the armchairs.

"Well, that was just a walk in the park, wasn't it?" Findlay chuckled, rubbing his hands. "I don't know the last time I piped that much in one day."

"You're not kidding," Jane agreed. "Sugar paste work usually takes me several days. Phew."

"It looks gorgeous, though," Sarah praised. "I'm sure the judges are going to love it."

"What fell off yours?"

"Oh, a little gum paste star. Fortunately, it wasn't anything big. I feared the whole spaceship was coming off for a second. The wire into the motor isn't very sturdy. I hope it doesn't fall when I turn it on!"

"The whole product looks amazing, Findlay. I think you have this one wrapped up."

"Nay, lass. Yours is too good to write off."

One of the production assistants poked her head into the room. "Findlay, time for judging."

And off they went, leaving Jane and Nia sitting anxiously. Jane knew their work was good, but she was always surer of her flavors in baking than her decorations.

"Jane?" the assistant called after a moment. "You're up."

She shook off her nerves as they walked back into the studio, their cake sitting before the judges. Belinda addressed them first.

"Ladies, first, I just want to say how overall beautiful this cake is. You have done some incredible work." Dan and Rahul nodded in agreement. "We would like to see your extreme element, please."

Nia handed Jane the small remote, but when she pressed the button that should make the rocket lift, nothing happened. She tried several times before checking the back of the cake, where one of the wires was frayed and hanging loose.

Turning to face the judges she apologized, "I'm sorry. Something must have happened when we covered the wires."

Rahul spoke up. "I did see the ship rise and fall when you installed it. It is a shame that it longer works."

"In spite of that," Dan interjected, "the way you represented outer space here, with the representations of the planets and the daring the stack them the way you did, it's really fantastic. I have to say, Jane, you've really impressed me in this competition."

"Thank you so much," she gushed. "It's been an honor to have the three of you judge my—our," she added, motioning to Nia, "work. It really means the world to us."

"Cut!" yelled Eliza. "That was great, everyone. Let's set up for the winner reveal. I want the cakes beside the competitors and slightly back." She motioned to the assistants as Findlay and Jane took their places on duct tape floor markings.

"Okay, everyone," Eliza called again. "Quiet. Judges ready?" They nodded. "Lincoln?" He stepped into his position, brushing a stray hair off his face.

"Action!"

"Ladies and gentlemen, we've seen three amazing cakes from each of our competitors, from wild 80s neon to elegant weddings in castles to the galaxy itself, but only one can have the sweetest tooth and take home the prize." He turned to face Jane and Findlay. "Findlay. Jane. The judges have discussed your work and have decided that..." He held this pause for so long, Jane wanted to throw her apron at him.

"Our winner, with the sweetest tooth, is... Findlay!"

Jane swallowed and then grinned at Findlay. "Told you!" She hugged him, then stepped back so he could take his crystal trophy from Lincoln and accept a hug from Sarah, too. She found Nia standing beside their cake.

"You okay?" she whispered.

"Yeah," Jane replied, as Findlay celebrated a bit for the camera, and Lincoln did his sign-off.

"Cut. That's a wrap-thanks everyone for your hard work."

Jane and Nia turned to leave, dropping their aprons atop the countertop, when Nia hesitated. "You gonna be okay? Eddie and I are going to a movie tonight if you want to join us."

"I'm fine, Nia. Go have fun with your sweet man."

As Nia disappeared into the hallway, Antony appeared in front of her station, arms folded. "Well, tough loss, Miss Mullins," he said, smiling, "but you did better than anyone thought you would."

"Thank you," she replied, refusing to back down from his glare. "I'm proud of how we did. I wish the rocket would have worked, but I'm glad Findlay won. His cake was the best today."

"Shame about that platform. You just never know with technology, do you? Sometimes it works fine and sometimes it just *cuts* out." She eyed his sarcastic smile.

"It does indeed." Jane noticed Lincoln crossing the studio toward her.

"Well, it was a pleasure meeting you, Miss Mullins. Have a safe trip home."

"Thank you, Mr. Perandin, for everything." His shoes clicked on the tiles as he exited the studio.

"Was he messing with you?" Lincoln asked as he reached her.

"No," Jane chuckled. "Just being his charming self."

"I'm sorry," Lincoln murmured so no one could hear. "I thought your cake was better."

She shook her head. "Our extreme element didn't work. That's part of the brief and we didn't fulfill it. Findlay deserved it. And I never thought we'd win," she admitted. "I didn't really think we'd make it past the first round, but I never thought that I, with my skill level, would beat out pros."

"You never give yourself enough credit, Jane." Lincoln argued, shaking his head. They stepped into the hallway lights. "When do you fly home?"

"Tomorrow," she answered quietly.

"What's going through your head?"

"Nothing. Everything. I'm proud of our work, but sad we lost. Worried about the money for the bakery because we really could use that prize money. Angry that the platform didn't work at judging, especially because I think it was messed up deliberately." She turned to face him as they emerged onto the street. "Dreading having to leave y—New York."

He hugged her. "One last night in the city. Do you have plans?" he asked.

"Only if you do,"

He took her hand in his. "I've got an idea. Come on."

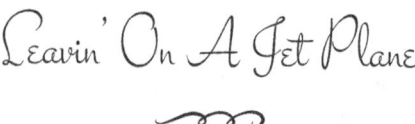

Leavin' On A Jet Plane

"Wow. It's a lot bigger than I thought it was," Jane breathed.

"Yeah, pictures and even video don't really do it justice, do they?" Lincoln asked, watching her face light up in the glow.

She took his hand as they stood beneath New York's famous Christmas tree. "Thanks for bringing me here. I've always wanted to see the tree in person and today was a great day for it." Scatters of snow still littered the ground around them and, despite the disappointment of the day, Jane felt content.

"I feel bad. It's not nearly as flashy as our other outings."

"It's still perfect, Lincoln," she assured, tapping her head sideways against his shoulder. "Can we make it even more touristy and find one of those famous New York water hot dogs?"

He smirked, taking her hand, "As you wish!"

They swept off down the streets, hunting for a hot dog cart and scoping out the beautiful holiday window displays on the way. It took a few blocks, but the pair finally found their quarry and settled onto a bench to eat.

"Okay, I guess these are good," Jane said skeptically, "But they really just taste like boiled hot dogs."

Lincoln clasped a hand to his heart in indignation. "Heresy! New York hot dogs are sacred!"

Jane rolled her eyes. "I wouldn't tell a New Yorker that, but I figured it was safe information with a friend."

"A friend, huh?" He raised his eyebrows as she wiped away the last of a dab of mustard at her lip.

"That's what we are right?" she asked tentatively. "Friends go to hockey games and concerts and eat hot dogs together?"

"They do, but maybe I was trying to impress you." Jane snorted. "What? I can't impress a lovely woman?"

"You can, but we both know that's not me."

Lincoln sobered quickly, staring at Jane's face, hoping to find levity there, but she was serious. "Why not Jane?"

"Because you're you," she said, matter-of-factly, staring straight ahead at an illuminated billboard. "And I'm me. And guys like you don't worry about impressing girls like me. Don't get me wrong, I have loved every minute of being with you, but I don't have expectations of anything after this."

Gently, Lincoln took Jane's chin in his hand, turning to meet his own. "Guys like me?"

"Oh, don't pretend you don't know you're a heartthrob," she shrugged. "If I didn't know you were a chef, I'd think you were an athlete."

"My buddy Diego would laugh at that, but thank you. I still don't understand why that means I can't have been flirting with you."

"Because," Jane said, adamantly, shaking her head free of his grip, "No one would look at the two of us and think we belong together."

"Jane."

"And they'd be right!"

"No, they wouldn't," he argued, even though he knew

what she meant. He remembered the waitress in Atlanta, and he'd overheard all the comments directed at her in the city. "Look at me. Please, Jane."

Hesitantly, she faced him. "It's okay Lincoln, really. I'm okay."

"Jane. I know what people have said to you. I know what that asshole ex-boyfriend of yours said, too. But none of it is true." He lifted his hand and cradled the side of her face. "I think you are stunning, brilliant, and kind. When I saw you in that dress the night of the concert, I was floored by how gorgeous you looked. And I have, in fact, been trying to impress you while you've been here."

"What?" she whispered, leaning into his palm.

"Jane Mullins, I wanted to impress you and I don't know, maybe be more than your friend. I don't have a lot to offer, and I don't know how we'd make it work with me here and you in Atlanta, but I really like you, okay?"

She shivered, and he wasn't sure if it was the cold, or his admission. "This doesn't feel real," she admitted. "But God, I want it to be."

"It's real," he grinned at her, warmth in his eyes. "And I'll work on proving it to you. Let's grab some ice cream and head back to the apartment. Stay with me tonight." Jane nodded happily and took his hand as he stood. Hand in hand, they headed off to catch a cab.

* * *

Jane and Lincoln sat cozily on his long sofa, a Christmas movie playing merrily on the television, spoons digging into the ice cream they'd picked up on their way back to the apartment.

"Man, I'd forgotten how delicious cookie dough ice cream is," Lincoln said, grinning, a bit of cookie dough stuck in his smile. Jane laughed. "What? Do I—" he ran his tongue over his teeth, wiping away the offending candy.

"Nope, you're perfect," she said, still giggling and blushing when she realized what she'd said. "I mean, you got it out of your teeth... I mean..." she stammered for a minute before scooping a huge spoonful of toppings into her mouth and turning back to the movie. And she snuggled closer to him.

"You don't have to be so nervous around me, Jane. I hope you know that by now."

"I do, I do." Swallowing and regaining her composure, Jane took a breath. "So, what's the weirdest story you have from working with Culinary Channel?" she asked, turning to face him.

"Wow. There are so many," he chuckled. "Most of them are from the early days, when I was still really young and uncertain. On one trip, they actually convinced me it was a good idea to wear a fanny pack to carry my things. And not just a fanny pack, a lime green fanny pack."

Jane snorted, taking another bite of her ice cream. "And you fell for it?"

"Again, I have to stress that I was really young and stupid," he laughed at himself. "I probably would have worn clown shoes if they told me I needed to. Oh!" he exclaimed; his eyes bright. "My first trip overseas, we were in this huge bazaar in Morocco, vendors shouting, animals roaming around here and there. I was scoping out this spice stall when this chicken began to peck at my feet, clucking pitifully, but as I reached to pick it up, a woman reached it, yelling at the poor thing and with one swoop, grabbed the beast by the neck and snapped it. She turned back into the crowd and disappeared into the throng. I was so dumbfounded; I stepped backward, away from the angry chicken woman, but stumbled over myself and landed on a stack of brilliantly woven rugs next to the spice man."

Jane patted his shoulder. "Poor you. That must have been traumatizing."

"A little," he admitted, "I *had* seen chickens killed before, when we did a special on free-range birds when I first started with the network. It was just a shock to see this woman just walk up and snap the poor bird in front of me. What about you, Miss Mullins? Funny stories?"

"I mean, there are always baking mishaps. Wrong ingredients. Someone puts salt instead of sugar, you know. But the best," she giggled at the memory, "was about a year after I opened the bakery and we were filming a promo spot for Good Morning Georgia. They had toured the bakery and interviewed me and my staff, but they wanted to do a witty 'back to the studio' moment so the reporter—I think his name was Ben—decided he would hit a cupcake back to the camera with a hockey stick."

"He didn't," Lincoln said, incredulously.

"Oh, he did. I tried to tell him that it wouldn't work, that the cupcake would be too soft, but he insisted. So, we got one of our jumbo cupcakes because he thought that it would show up better for the camera, and he set up the shot. The time comes for him to make the shot and he rears back, swings, and the cupcake splatters everywhere."

Lincoln roared with laughter. "It didn't fly at all, did it?"

"It must have flown a little bit because the circle of frosting was pretty wide, but no, it couldn't have gone more than a few inches from where it started."

Their ice cream was gone, empty cups on the table, the movie forgotten in storytelling.

"I wish you didn't have to go back to Atlanta tomorrow," he said quietly, so quietly he wasn't sure she heard him.

"Jane, I've been happier with you here than I've been in... Well, a long time." He leaned toward her, the room melting away as he looked at her. He brushed a wayward curl from her face. "Can I kiss you, Jane?"

She nodded and his lips were on hers, soft and lush, moving expertly with her own. One of his hands wove into her hair, the other around her waist, pulling her to him. The softest groan met her ears as she leaned into him, her heart racing as she found herself in his lap.

It took a moment to register the noisy tune emanating from her cell phone. Jane drew the interrupting object from her pocket and answered the ring. "Hello?" The disappointment was obvious in her tone. "Oh, hello, Mr. Perandin." Lincoln's eyes widened, his hand brushing hers as she continued. "Oh," her smile faded. "Yes, of course. Yes, sir, we can be ready. I'll call her and—yes, sir. Thank you."

Lincoln watched her hesitantly as she began to gather up her things. "What's wrong? What did Antony want?"

He heard the cracks in her voice as she answered. "He said that Nia and I need to be at the airport in 45 minutes. They bumped up our flight to tonight. We have to go." She quickly typed a text to Nia. "She'll be heartbroken. It's been hard on her since Eddie started his program here."

"And you?" She finally looked at him, and the tears in her eyes hit him like a gut punch. "Oh Jane," he wrapped his arms around her. "I don't want you to go."

"I know it's only a day early," she cried, "But..."

"It's too soon," he agreed, stroking her hair. "Come on. I'll go with you."

A short train ride and a rush of packing things later, Jane and Lincoln waited anxiously at the airport for Nia, who arrived breathlessly, sans boyfriend.

"I knew I wouldn't get on the plane if he came," she said simply. "I know he'll be home in a month, but I didn't want to leave." Jane nodded, watching Nia step away to check in.

"I guess this is goodbye," she murmured, offering her hand

to Lincoln, who eyed it. He brushed her hand away and wrapped his arms around her tightly.

"I'll see you soon, Jane. I promise," he kissed her cheek, and then her hand, which he held until he couldn't reach her as she walked away.

146

Families and Funerals

～～

She was dozing on the sofa, reruns playing low on the television when her phone rang, jolting her awake. Without checking the caller ID, she tapped at the green button.

"Hello?" she answered groggily.

"Jane?" a somber voice asked.

"Lincoln?"

"Yeah. I hope you don't mind. I didn't want to bother you, but..."

She sat up, rubbing her eyes. "It's not a bother. What's up? Is something wrong? You sound upset."

He was quiet for a moment. "My grandfather passed away yesterday."

"Oh, Lincoln, I'm so sorry. Was he ill?"

"No. It was really unexpected, and I wasn't even there. My whole family is a mess." He was sniffling as he spoke.

"Oh, honey," Jane murmured. "Is there anything I can do?"

"I..." Lincoln paused between sniffles. "I know it's a lot to ask, and you can totally say no, but I don't think I can do this alone."

147

It was a minute before what he was asking registered with her. "You want me to come to Nashville?"

"Yes. Well, to meet me there. I'm at JFK now, waiting on a flight down. And only if you're okay with it. I know you hardly know me, but...you were the first person I needed to talk to." He sounded like a lost child as he rambled; she couldn't help but feel sorry for him.

"I can be there in four hours. Will that be okay?"

He breathed a deep sigh of relief. "You are amazing. I should be there in about two. I'll text you the address so you can put it in maps. Let me know if you have trouble."

"You got it. Call if you think of anything you need," she said gently.

"I will. Thanks. And Jane?"

"Yes?"

"Have I mentioned you're incredible?"

She smiled. "Not lately, but I'll take it. See you soon."

"Bye Jane."

She hung up the phone and hesitated. They hadn't talked about their kiss in New York, had barely talked at all in the week since she'd gotten home. Was she reckless to take off across state lines for this guy, long time crush or not? Deciding she'd do this for any friend who needed it, Jane scrolled through her messages, finding her group chat with Nia, Trevor, and Rayna. The bakery was closed on Sundays, but she always worried about orders coming in. She asked them to check the bakery voicemail for the next few days because she'd be out of town for an emergency and, as she sent the message, her phone pinged with a text from Lincoln with the address as he boarded his flight. She smiled at his next message.

Lincoln: You have no idea how grateful I am for you.

"I guess we're doing this," Jane said to her empty room, ignoring the flutter in her belly at his words.

In her room, she grabbed her favorite black dress and a

pair of black heels, tossed in a few sweaters, a pair of jeans, her Converse, and a pair of pajamas into a small overnight bag. She checked her current outfit, gray corduroy pants, and a deep green sweater, and declared it car trip worthy. Suddenly, she found herself in a rush to see him, to make him feel better. He had been so lost, so desperate on the phone. Her heart ached for him.

Her bag dropped into the backseat as she lowered it behind her and cranked up the car. And she was off, zipping up the highway, through the city and into the sparse but autumnally beautiful northern Georgia mountains. As she had predicted, about four hours on the road, and she was nearly within the city limits of Nashville. As she turned off into the area where a sign announced 'Belle Meade', the houses grew further apart and far larger. Winding through sidewalk lined streets with towering oak trees, she found herself in front of a beautiful villa, complete with a stone fountain in the center of the circular driveway. Loose stones crunched under her tires as she pulled her car into the drive alongside several expensive vehicles.

Jane panicked for a moment, noticing multiple doors nearby, none obviously the front door, until she saw the familiar head of dark curls hurrying toward her. She was barely out of the car when he wrapped his arms around her, holding tight.

"I'm so sorry, Lincoln," she murmured, her hands trailing up and down his back, running along the grooves in his knitted sweater. She wasn't sure he'd heard her until she realized he was crying silently into her shoulder. A bitter breeze made her shiver, and he pulled back, eyes red, and she noticed how young he looked.

"God, I'm sorry," he muttered, wiping his eyes. "I'm a damn mess and I dragged you all the way here and I'm keeping you out in the cold and—"

Jane cut him off with a soft kiss on his cheek. "There's nowhere I'd rather be right now."

His face softened, tears threatening again as a woman called for him.

"Lincoln? Honey, it's cold out here. Come back inside." A pretty woman, graying blond hair swept out of her face, wearing dark trousers and an elegant blouse eyed Jane suspiciously. Given the little Jane knew of his last relationship, she was neither surprised nor insulted that his family would be wary of another woman.

"Coming, Mama," Lincoln called back, chuckling. "Figures she'd catch me getting a kiss from a pretty girl. Can I get your bags?"

"I just have the one," she said, suddenly embarrassed by the threadbare duffel.

"Here." He quickly grabbed the bag from her. "I should warn you. Most of the family is here. And this is my dad's family, so there's a lot of us. But that," he nodded to the woman waiting on the porch, "is my mother, Claire." They walked a few more feet before he spoke again. "Mom, this is my friend Jane Mullins from Atlanta."

The woman smiled, the faintly visible lines at her eyes crinkling. "Welcome to Nashville, Miss Mullins. I'm afraid we're full to the gunnel, but I'm sure Lincoln won't mind sharing with you."

"Oh," Jane paused, her face flushing a little, "I'm not... I mean..." she sputtered.

"We'll sort it out," Lincoln said, eyeing his mother. 'Don't worry,' he mouthed as his mother turned to reenter the house.

The pair, hands clasped, stepped across the threshold behind the matriarch and into an open room filled with people who all turned to look as they came in.

From a straight-backed armchair across the room, an older woman asked, "Well Lincoln, who is your lovely lady friend?"

Jane opened her mouth to reply, but Lincoln replied, "This is my friend Jane Mullins from Atlanta. She happened to be visiting a friend here and dropped by." His smile was strained, and he didn't glance at her as he lied.

She felt the dozen or so eyes boring holes into her, and she silently pored over the entirety of her wardrobe, wishing she'd thought to wear something nicer. Without another word, Lincoln grabbed her hand and drew her into a sunny, beige kitchen and up a set of narrow, pokey stairs that opened onto a landing and another flight of stairs. He turned to start up them, but in his haste, Jane tripped on the lowest stair and crashed to the floor.

"Oh, god, Jane, I'm so sorry." He kneeled to help her up.

"I'm okay." She pulled herself into a sitting position on the step, dusting off her knees and palms. "But would you mind telling me why you lied to your family and then rushed me out of the room like they were going to shish kebab and serve me for dinner?"

He looked away, embarrassed. "I'm sorry. I just thought the less I told them, the fewer questions they would ask. And, that the less time they had to interrogate you, the better it would be." Taking her hands, he drew her to her feet.

"And just where are you leading me, Mr. Bainbridge?" she questioned as they moved up the second flight of steps. "Do you intend to imprison me in the tall tower?"

He snorted. "Hardly. I just thought my room was the safest place in the house at the moment." She gulped and hesitated. He noticed the look on her face and stopped as well. "What? Is something wrong?"

"Your room," she mumbled. "I just never thought I'd be in your room. Won't your family think we're up to something?"

"Maybe, but we won't be and we know that. What does it matter what they think?"

"I don't want them to think I'm some kind of... I don't know... Gold digger."

Lincoln laughed out loud. "I'll never get that song out of my head now, thank you"

She swatted his arm. "I'm serious. I don't want people to think I'm that kind of girl."

"What kind of girl, Jane? You're no gold digger. You just came to help someone you—to help a friend. What does it matter what my family thinks about my girlfriends? Do you think I care that much?"

"Because I care!" she cried, exasperated. "I don't want them to think I'm after your money or for what I can get from you, or them." She paused, realizing he'd alluded to her as one of his girlfriends. Before she could ask about that, he continued.

"Jane, if you're going to put yourself in a position where people don't know you, like the competition, like what I do, you have to accept that people are going to form their own opinions of you. And you probably won't like some of them, but you know the truth, and your friends and family will know the truth and sometimes that's the best you get. Honestly, you'd be the first girl they liked who *wasn't* using me." He spun around and marched up the steps.

Jane stood there, watching him go, knowing he was right. She worried way too much about what other people thought, instead of just living her life knowing the truth. She called for him as she hurried up the stairs.

"Lincoln, I'm sorry, I—"

At the top the of stairs, she froze, caught in a storm of light; the fiery red-gold of the setting sun blazing through a bank of windows along one wall. Two opposite walls were a dark charcoal gray; the last was the faintest shade of green. A big bed was tucked into the corner opposite the windows, and three rows of shelves hung above the headboard, lined with books and action figures. Lincoln was sitting on a low, hunter green sofa hidden from the sun by a folding partition, facing a television's black screen.

"Wow. Now this is a bedroom," she murmured. He turned to face her. They both spoke at the same time, smiling awkwardly before he nodded and gestured for her to continue.

"I'm sorry. I sometimes get so set on something that I refuse to bend to it at all. And I should know that as I go down this road, different people, people who I have never met and who don't know me beyond a picture or an article, will be conjecturing about me. They may not come up with the truth, but I have to be prepared to face what comes."

"And I shouldn't have been so testy with you." He motioned for her to sit next to him, which she did. "I get so used to the people who live in my world, who put so much stock in appearances and status, who say one thing and do another, that I get so exasperated with it all. I'm still not used to how—"

"Weird?" she interjected.

"*Different* you are," he finished. "You aren't like most of the people I deal with on a daily basis. Being with you," he took her hands in his, "Is like being home, here where people just know me, where they mean well, even when they are nosy and sarcastic and obnoxious. The people I worked with here are honest and trustworthy and loyal instead of only concerned with their own success or career." He sighed. "I never realized how much I miss this life, this calm, until I spent time with you."

Jane leaned her head on his shoulder and closed her eyes, their hands still paired. Lincoln looked over at her. The sun caught in her coppery hair as it fell lazily over her pale skin, past her shimmering rose-hued lips, and onto the collar of her deep green sweater. Without thinking, he reached his hand up to stroke her hair. "You look really pretty, by the way," he murmured.

She blushed, her heart rate speeding. "Thanks. I just grabbed something warm when you called."

"You're always warm." He tugged her closer, tucking her head under his chin. "I love that about you."

Jane looked up at him, his blue eyes locked on her green ones. She stretched up toward him, closing the remaining distance, when a knock sounded at the door. Lincoln leapt away from her, straightening his shirt.

"Lincoln, honey, dinner is ready," Lincoln's mother announced as she opened the door. She eyed both of them.

"We'll be right down, Mom," Lincoln replied. "We were just putting Jane's things away."

"I'm sure. Don't dally. You know your grandmother doesn't like to wait."

Heartbreak and History

Jane watched Lincoln as he moved around the church hall, talking to different people, shaking hands and offering embraces. His eulogy had been moving, even for her, who had never met the Bainbridge family patriarch, but surely had been difficult, given their strained relationship.

"Jane?" Lincoln's mother stood behind her, a glass of tea in each hand. "Will you take a walk with me?"

Smiling, Jane replied, "Sure." Claire passed her one of the tea glasses as the pair exited the sanctuary and stepped out into a high-walled courtyard lined with tall maple trees. The sky above was a cloudy blue-gray, but all around them was a blaze of gold and red from the trees and even a few late-blooming roses.

"This is beautiful," Jane remarked, as Claire took a seat on a wood and wrought-iron bench.

"It's a memorial garden," the older woman explained quietly, her eyes falling on an aged bronze plaque set in the wall across from her seat. Jane stepped closer to read the inscription.

"In loving memory of Nora Pauline Hardaway. Loving

mother and grandmother, faithful servant, and loyal friend. 'It will be alright in the end. If it's not alright, it's not the end.'" Jane read.

"My mother," Mrs. Bainbridge said, gesturing for Jane to sit with her. "She's the one who really taught Lincoln to cook. Once I left home, and especially once I got married, I preferred to go out or have someone else cook. It was just something I never really had a passion for. But my mother would have Lincoln in the kitchen every weekend learning something new. His father was furious—Phillip never felt that men belonged in the kitchen. The only time he ever worked with food was if he was grilling. And then Lincoln decided to leave the business and go to culinary school and... Well, I suppose he's told you all of this."

"He's told me a little, but not much. I know his father and grandfather more or less cut him off when he left for culinary school. And I know that's why he doesn't come home much."

"That's a kind portrayal of what really occurred," Mrs. Bainbridge commented, half smiling. "He's a good boy to be so nice to them after everything they put him through."

"It must have been unpleasant for all of you."

Shaking her head, Lincoln's mother continued. "They were so proud of him in high school, if you don't count the fights over cooking. And the time he chose to take home economics over auto shop. But he was—is—brilliant. Excellent grades, honor society, class president all four years of school. They had the plan all set for him. He would graduate with honors, attend Vanderbilt like they both had, study business and economics, graduate from there with corresponding honors, then come back to the business and be groomed as the second in line to the whole affair. And for at least a while, Lincoln was alright with that plan. He was dating a lovely girl who was from a prestigious and powerful family here, and the men, especially my father-in-law, sought to do everything in their power to ensure the eventual union." Jane nodded, taking in this insight into the back story of her new companion while his mother continued her tale.

"They probably would have succeeded, if not for two events during his freshman year at college. Lincoln was studying hard, but he wasn't enjoying anything, while Isabella was carefree, partying and apparently, she wasn't very understanding of his study habits and efforts. Then one night, Lincoln had finished his work, so he decided to surprise her and take her to a nice dinner, but when he arrived at her apartment, he found her...*indisposed* with a senior boy from one of her classes."

Grimacing, Jane took in the fact that there was far more hurt in Lincoln's past than he had shared. "I can only imagine how hard that must have been for him," she responded.

"I think they'd been growing apart for some time, and that he would have been able to deal with it just fine if his grandfather hadn't stepped in. Phillip demanded that Lincoln get back together with Isabella, that he overlook her *indiscretion*. They fought more than once over that, but it got worse quickly when Lincoln realized that he didn't want to go into business." Claire shifted on the bench, uncomfortable at the memories.

"I wasn't entirely surprised when he stood up at Thanksgiving his senior year and announced that once he graduated, he wasn't going into the MBA program. He'd be attending culinary school."

"I'm guessing his dad and grandad didn't take that very well," Jane mused.

His mother chuckled darkly. "You'd be right. His father simply left the table in silence, but his grandfather flew into a rage and began yelling that Lincoln was a terrible disappointment, that if he wanted to pursue that career then he could do it on someone else's dime and surely Phillip and I wouldn't tolerate this blatant insubordination and mutiny against all this family stands for. To his credit, Lincoln folded his napkin and laid it across the table and calmly told his grandfather that he understood the ramifications of his decision, that it wasn't treason against the family, and nothing should preclude him from seeking his own happiness, his own life. But Grandfather Bainbridge was far too riled to handle Lincoln's confidence. He bellowed that Lincoln was no grandson of his and ordered him out of the house. About that time, Phillip finally came back into the room and I thought he would restore some order and calm his father down, but instead he stood there, his eyes blazing, and demanded that if Lincoln intended to follow through with his plans, Lincoln should pack up his things and be out of the house in a week. He stipulated that there would be a clear list of what Lincoln could take and what must be left here, and the whole time he's listing things, I can see the tears in my son's eyes and I didn't even try to stop the whole thing. I've never had any authority when my husband laid down the law. Finally, Lincoln just stood up and left. I heard the front door close before Phillip walked out of the room again and our maid came in and started clearing the table." Jane shuddered at the thought of someone being kicked out of their own family just for following their heart.

A breeze rustled above them as Claire grew quieter. "I should have followed him. Chased him down. Called my husband the bully he was and demanded that they allow my son to follow his dream. But the truth is, I believed, on some level, that they were right. I thought he was being ridiculous, going through some phase after breaking up with Isabella. And I think I believed that he would walk around the block and change his mind; see his own folly. After several hours, Mom finally stood up and said, 'This is ridiculous. I'm going to find my grandson.'" Jane saw her hands twisting, bending a funeral program, and laid her own on top.

"It had gotten cold a few weeks before, and there was patchy ice on the streets, particularly after dark. My mother had taken the old Buick she drove and headed for the public library downtown where Lincoln loved to spend his time, but she hit a patch of ice hidden in the dark shadows of an overpass and crashed into one of the concrete pillars supporting the bridge. " Claire was silent again. Jane draped her arm around the other woman and embraced her encouragingly.

"I know what it's like to lose your parent like that," Jane offered quietly.

Claire nodded. "Lincoln mentioned you lost your father when you were very young. I initially thought that was why he'd asked you to be here." Jane opened her mouth to repeat his earlier lie, but Claire raised a hand. "I know you weren't just 'in the area.' He's a terrible liar, that one. But I saw the way he looks at you," she faced Jane, taking in the younger woman's face. "I've never seen him look at anyone that way. Like he feels safe with you. He's certainly never looked like that around here."

Jane pressed the palm of her free hand against her chest as her heart raced. "Thank you for trusting me. I know it has to be difficult to tell this story."

"I should have been with her. Really, I should have never let her leave the house when I knew what the roads could be like," Claire muttered.

"You can't blame yourself for that."

"It's taken me almost ten years and three therapists to accept that," the weary woman sighed. "But my boy. He still blames himself. After the funeral, he took everything his father would allow and moved in with his friend Watson near the culinary institute. He was determined to make it because she said he could; she told him that he would be the biggest star the culinary world had ever seen. I know she used to tell him she just knew he would have his own show one day. And, as usual, she was right."

Jane smiled wistfully at the thought of Lincoln's determination and his love for his grandma. "She'd be proud of him. He's one of the most popular hosts on the network."

"Oh, she would be. Even prouder than I am. But I think," Claire patted Jane's arm, "and this is why I'm telling you this, that he is unhappy. He would never want to sound ungrateful for the opportunity, but he has so much creativity and they don't seem to be letting him embrace it." Her grey eyes met Jane's green ones. "I think Lincoln stays at the network because part of him believes that this is what his grandmother wanted for him, so he should stay. And another part of him still believes what his father told him the day he moved out, that his good looks and charm would only get him so far before he failed."

Jane shook her head, tears forming. "Poor Lincoln. I can't... He never lets on."

"He won't, Jane. In that, he is his father's son. And I believe that you can help him, that you can show him how pursuing his real passion is what he needs to be doing."

Jane stared at her hands. "He barely knows me. I mean, we only met a few weeks ago."

"Sometimes that's all it takes for the heart," Claire said, patting Jane's knee.

Both jumped as the door from the building creaked open and Lincoln stepped out. "Mom? Mr. and Mrs. Bannister would love to see you. They're in the corner near the drinks."

Claire squeezed Jane's shoulder. "Duty calls. Thank you for listening, Jane."

"Anytime Mrs.—Claire."

Lincoln sat down next to Jane as his mother disappeared back into the swarm of family, friends, and colleagues. "What were you two talking about?"

"Oh, nothing much," she replied. "I think she just wanted to know more about me. How are you?"

Lincoln sighed, resting his head on her shoulder. "I should feel terrible that we hadn't spoken in so long, but I just feel separated from him. Maybe because we weren't ever close, I never had to feel as if I'd lost something."

"Your eulogy was beautiful," she said, absently stroking his hair. "I know it must have been difficult for you to stand up and speak so kindly of him after everything."

"Well, honestly. It's easy to praise his business acumen and his philanthropic efforts. He was a great man. He was just so stubborn and set in his old ways."

He closed his eyes for a moment. "Thanks for being here, Jane. I couldn't have faced any of this by myself."

She wove her fingers through his. "My pleasure."

Hallowed Halls

~⚬~

"Lincoln," Claire called, stepping away from an impeccably dressed couple. "Your grandmother is staying with us for a while, until she decides what to do with the house. She doesn't feel comfortable staying there, even with Mrs. Cullman and the Fosters. Would you go to the house and get some things for her? It'd be an opportunity to show Jane your grandparents' home."

"I'm not sure that's a positive thing," Lincoln muttered out of the corner of his mouth.

"What, dear?" Claire inquired absently, eyeing the crowd of congregants expectantly.

"Nothing, mother. What does Grandmother need from the house?"

"She made a list as your grandmother would." Claire rolled her eyes mildly, drawing a folded sheet of paper from her clutch. "As always, she is very specific. Mrs. Cullman should be able to help you if you have trouble. When you get back, she'll be staying in the green suite. We will not have a formal dinner, but I'm certain there will be plenty of food left for the two of you to eat. Jane, will you be staying with us again tonight?"

"She will," Lincoln replied quickly. "We'll be back soon." He swept Jane from the room without another word

"Do you not want me to go with you?" Jane asked quietly as they approached the car.

Lincoln glanced at her, noting the disappointed look on her face. "No, no," he corrected swiftly. "I want to spend every minute you're here with you." He took her hand, squeezing it gently. "My grandparents' home is one of the largest in Belle Meade. It's borderline ostentatious, especially in this day and age. It is impeccably maintained, mostly by Mrs. Cullman, the housekeeper, and Mr. and Mrs. Foster, the groundskeeper and cook. They live in rooms on the property, like servants. And to be honest, my grandfather always looked at them as such. It was a subject he and I butted heads on many times."

Jane grimaced, opening the door. "I see." She slid into the passenger seat and Lincoln took his place behind the wheel. "Let's go get things for your grandmother, then we can go back to your parents and watch a movie or something. You've had quite a day."

Lincoln nodded and started the car. He held her hand, Christmas music playing softly on the radio as they drove to the Belle Meade neighborhood. As they grew closer, Jane found herself awed by the houses they passed. Huge mansions, some crafted into traditional plantations, others like Mediterranean villas. Lincoln turned left into a short drive and stopped at an ornate, wrought-iron gate. Rolling down his window, he reached for a small keypad, where he quickly typed in a well-memorized sequence of numbers. The gate slowly swung open, allowing the car to pass quietly through before closing behind, as the pair wound through an orchard lined drive.

"Whoa," she gasped, as the house came into view, the rows

of trees giving way to the tableau of an enormous home, cream and tawny colored stone with a grey-blue roof; a home that would not have been out of place in Louis XIV's France. Windows as tall as a man covered the front facade of the main house, with a garage to one side, and a cottage-like building to the other. Lincoln smirked as he pulled the car through a stone arch and into a cobblestone courtyard.

"I did try to warn you. My great-grandfather started building this house for his wife, who was obsessed with everything French. It is actually modeled after an aristocratic villa, down to the carvings in the front hall. Grandfather inherited the house when his father died, and took to renovating the interiors, adding some modern conveniences and planting the garden on the far side of the swimming pool for Grandmother. For the most part though, the house is as it was when my great-grandparents moved into it in the 1920s."

"It's one of the most beautiful places I've ever seen. This is where your father grew up?"

"Yes, and my aunts and uncles." He climbed out of the car. "Come on. If you think the outside is something, wait until you see the inside."

He led her through a small but ornately carved wooden door back to the main driveway. They approached the double doors, which stretched higher than Lincoln was tall; he leaned to his right and pressed a gilded button. Resounding chimes echoed behind the doors, which promptly opened, revealing a short woman, tight grey-blonde curls framing her narrow face as she smiled widely when she saw Lincoln.

"Lincoln! Sweet boy, it's been too long!" She pulled him into a smothering hug. "I'm sorry about your grandfather. He was a good man."

"Thank you, Mrs. Cullman." He pulled Jane closer to him. "This is my friend Jane Mullins."

The older woman's smile grew even wider. "Pleasure to

meet you, Miss Mullins. It's always nice to meet a friend of the children. Now, why are you here, dear? I thought you'd all be at the church until later."

"Grandmother is staying at my parents' for a while and she needs some things while she's with us."

"Mrs. Grace is staying with y'all? She didn't mention that to us."

"Honestly, I think my father may have had something to do with her decision. I heard he and Uncle Miller discussing the estate and they're planning on having some company meetings here, which is always easier when she is not."

"I see," she replied, frowning. "Well, I'm sure Mrs. Grace gave you a list of the things she wants." Lincoln nodded, holding up the paper with his grandmother's elegant, swirling script on it. "I'll take that and pack her things. Why don't you give Miss Jane here the tour? It'll take a bit."

"That would be lovely, Mrs. Cullman. Thank you." All three stepped inside the house, the sunlight dimming in the dark paneled hall. The housekeeper bustled off, up the stairs, leaving Lincoln and Jane alone.

"She's adorable." Jane smiled, wary of Lincoln's frown and narrowed eyes.

"She is. She was always great to us kids, even when we were little terrors."

"What's wrong?"

"I don't know. Didn't think I'd ever be back in this house. Not after that Thanksgiving. Honestly, if Grandfather were still alive, I probably wouldn't be. He was staunch about his disowning me. Not great memories in these halls." He looked at Jane, curious that she didn't seem surprised by his words.

Sensing his question, she explained, "Your mom pulled me aside at the church. She told me the story, about your grandfather and your dad, about losing your grandmother."

Lincoln turned, glaring now at a carved coat of arms above

a dark wood table. The heraldic marker bore deep blue and green hues, a shield with three golden axes at its center.

"*Fides et officium familiae super omnia,*" Lincoln recited bitterly. "Loyalty and duty to family above all else. The noble motto of the house of Bainbridge. Of *this* family Bainbridge anyway. Any time we wanted to do something that wasn't our grandfather's idea, this is what we were told, and what was held over our heads."

She touched his arm. "I'm sorry. We can just sit and wait for Mrs. Cullman to get your grandmother's belongings. I don't want you to have to relive the hurt you felt here."

He shook his head. "No, it's alright. It's been ten years. I moved on. I made a career, made a life for myself, made myself successful. Most parents would be proud of that."

"Your mother is proud of you. I could tell it in the way she spoke to me today."

"Maybe." He turned his back to the carving. "This is as good a place as any." He gestured to the large room that opened to the left of the front hall. "This is the formal receiving room."

The dark paneling continued, with deep red carpeting topped by an intricate rug. All the furniture was delicate, dark wood with golden metal work; converted gas lamps accented the tables with their milky glass housings.

"Grandmother and Grandfather entertained here with social gatherings that would be attended by the crème de la crème of Nashville society. She would hire a pianist to come and play here." Lincoln turned and pointed across the hall to a smaller room, with a hardwood floor, also covered in a beautifully patterned rug, that housed a glistening black grand piano. "Bainbridge Christmas parties were rather legendary. The mayor of Nashville used to attend. For several years, the governor of Tennessee attended as well."

"That must have been quite an experience for a child."

"Oh, we weren't allowed to attend until we were twelve, and then we were stuffed into flawless, tailored clothes, and were told not to speak until spoken to."

"So not fun times then." She laughed, trying to lighten the mood. Taking some initiative, she walked down the front hall, which opened into a high-ceilinged ballroom, with floor to ceiling windows overlooking the swimming pool and gardens.

"This is where the Christmas tree would be," Lincoln described, joining her. "Family Christmases were better with all of us together. Even my grandma, who would sit at the piano and play carols for us to sing, which drove Grandfather crazy, but somehow we managed it every year."

"The gardens look lovely, even in autumn. Mr. Foster must be quite the caretaker."

"They were really designed that way. There are certain elements in the garden designated for each season, so it never looks empty or dead. Grandmother wouldn't have liked it to look empty, especially since the ballroom overlooks it so grandly."

In the golden rays of the late autumn afternoon, Lincoln studied her as she moved almost reverently around the room, admiring the paintings and family portraits. The slant of a sunbeam caught the red of her hair, silhouetting her face in the glow, and suddenly he saw her, clad in an elegant ball gown, laughing, swirling around the famous Bainbridge Christmas ball, mingling with the rich and famous who frequented the party. Crossing to her, he swept her into his arms, spinning her about the floor to a silent waltz.

"Lincoln, what on earth?" Jane gasped, laughing as she followed his steps. She spun neatly under his arm as he moved her around the floor. "Who knew the culinary Casanova could waltz?"

"I can do a passable foxtrot, too." He smirked. "But you do not want to see that."

"I mean, I might."

"Not if you don't want your toes squished."

She smiled as they came to a stop, facing each other. "Why thank you, sir." She curtsied prettily. "You are too kind."

"I guess we should go and see the rest of the house," he suggested.

"I suppose so," Jane replied wistfully. Lincoln led her off to the side of the ballroom, describing the kitchen as they approached a dark wooden door and stepped into a bright, open area.

Cream cabinets wrapped around three walls, with heavy marble countertops lining their tops. A massive stainless-steel stovetop stretched wide beneath an elegant range hood, while two large ovens, stacked one on top of the other, framed the space. Jane assumed the tall cabinet to the right of the stove was a custom fronted refrigerator, larger than any she'd seen outside a commercial kitchen. The marble topped island workstation housed a deep stainless sink, with room for four stools on the far side. Far simpler than the formal dining table they'd passed upstairs, a table for six was nestled alongside the windows.

"The Fosters and Mrs. Cullman eat here, and we did when we were little and too immature to eat with the adults."

"Did you ever cook with Mrs. Foster? Is that where you learned?"

"God no," Lincoln replied adamantly. "My grandfather would never have allowed it in his house. My father certainly didn't in ours. I learned mostly at my grandma's apartment, and then in my own kitchen in college. I pretty much watched the entire Culinary Channel lineup at the time."

"It's a beautiful kitchen. So much room to work."

"Mrs. Foster certainly made the most of it. They hire in help for big events, but she did everyday meals on her own and they were always fantastic. We can head upstairs from here," he said, gesturing to a stairway in the far corner.

The pair climbed the two sets of stairs until they opened on the second-floor hall. "There's a dozen bedrooms up here, all decorated in the same style but with different colors. He opened the nearest door, revealing a sumptuous arrangement: dark wood floors laid with thick carpets in shades of blue and green, a large bed, a tall tester of cherry wood rising as spires at each corner, matching tables at each side.

"Whoa," Jane breathed. "It's like something out of Versailles." She stepped into the room, treading gently. On the bed was a small army of pillows and cushions, which matched the small pillows tucked in the window seat that overlooked the gardens. "It's so lovely. All the rooms are like this?"

"Most of them. My grandfather's room is less flowery, more masculine. His office is on this floor, too. He wanted people to make the trip up the stairs. He said it was more intimidating that way."

"Your grandparents had separate bedrooms?"

"Yes, from the time they were first married. My great-grandparents did the same, and grandfather doesn't like to mess with the way things are." He stopped. "Didn't. He didn't like to change things." He guided Jane from the blue room, shutting the door behind them, and down the hall to a different room. "My grandmother's rooms. She has an attached bathroom here; only a few of the other bedrooms have their own."

This room was larger than the other, with more windows, but they also overlooked the backyard and gardens. A lavender damask wallpaper covered the walls to match the darker lavender carpets. Here the bed was a wider canopy style, with a light, floating cream cloth wrapped about it. A marble fireplace dominated one wall, an ethereal impressionist painting hung above it. Another window seat, this one cushioned in a pale toile fabric, spanned the length of the windowed wall. She peered around an open door, admiring a polished white bathroom, with glistening countertops and a clawfoot bathtub in the center of the windows, which were hung with translucent drapes.

"It's so classic." Jane gazed around in awe. "A page from a romance novel, where the heroine is carried away by the handsome and charming rogue." Turning slowly to take in the decor, she caught Lincoln's expression. His dark brown eyes were locked on her, a soft, warm smile had replaced the painful look from earlier.

"What?" she asked, blushing as he stepped toward her.

He embraced her, arms tight around her waist. "I was just thinking how different you are from the people who are normally in this house. Not a lot of dreamers around here when your life is planned out for you in your infancy."

"I can't imagine that," she admitted. "Even if I'd had a 'family business' to go into, I can't believe I wouldn't have dreamed of something else at some point in my life."

"Well, of course, you can't imagine it if you didn't experience that feeling," he snapped, pulling away harshly and storming out of the room, his footsteps echoing down the hall.

Dumbfounded, Jane stood, staring out into the hallway, listening for Lincoln to return, but all she heard was an echoing slam. She stepped back out of the bedroom, closing the door behind her, looking at the empty hall. Her eyes began to well with tears; she hadn't meant to be rude or insensitive, but she wondered if her big mouth had gone too far.

Faintly, she heard a thud down the corridor. She moved quickly toward the opposite rooms, pausing at each door. Near the balcony at the top of the front hall staircase, a set of double doors caught her eye. Reaching for the curved handle, she stopped when she heard gulping sobs from the inside.

Jane raised a hand to knock, but stopped. He was already angry with her. Interrupting whatever he was doing would likely only make matters worse. A hand on her shoulder startled her.

"He needs you," Mrs. Cullman whispered. "I'm sure by now you've heard the stories, but this is harder for him than he'll admit. I heard him earlier, but dear, he's not upset with you. He's mad at his grandfather, at his own father. And he has every right to be. He needs someone from outside this circle, outside the people who hurt him."

Jane sniffed, but nodded. "How do you know I'm the right person?"

The older woman offered a half smile, "He's never brought another woman here. He has to trust you to have done that." She disappeared around the corner without another word.

Breathing deep, Jane knocked tentatively. "Lincoln? Can I come in?" No response from the other side. She tried the handle; it opened noiselessly into what had to be Grandfather Bainbridge's office.

The room was a sight. Dark wood paneled walls set with floor to ceiling bookshelves, the floor a thick, dark gold carpet. Tall windows faced the front courtyard but were mostly obscured by long, heavy curtains. An imposing desk, a solid mahogany behemoth, consumed most of the floor on the far side of the room. Other than the furniture, the room appeared empty. She took a step into the office, closing the door behind her.

"Lincoln?" she asked again, her voice muffled in the room.

Sniffs and quiet sobs came from behind the desk. She rounded the desk and saw him sitting with his back against the desk drawer, head in his hands.

Tucking her feet beneath her, and arranging her dress across her knees, she pulled him close as he continued to cry.

Tears fell fast on the shoulder of her black sweater, soaking it to her skin.

"It's okay, Lincoln," she murmured. "It'll be okay."

"I hated him," Lincoln choked, still sobbing. "I hate the old man. He... He was..."

"I know. You have every right to hate him."

"I hate him, but I don't," he explained, lifting his head from her shoulder, and wiping his eyes on the cuffs of his jacket. "He was my grandfather who taught me the value of running a strong business and who encouraged me to go to college and study business and marketing, who had every intention of training me to run at least part of the company, alongside my brother and my cousins. I grew up here, in this house, under his eyes almost as much as my own parents."

Jane studied him as he looked out the window. The man in her arms was far away, lost in his memories and pain. She took his hand, trying to pull him back.

"But he stifled us, all of us." Lincoln's ire continued. "He even went so far as to try to force me into marrying a woman who not only didn't love me, but who was unfaithful to me. He pressured my sister to stay at home and have children instead of taking my place in the business. And the day he disowned me, he sent my grandma out of this house for supporting me and she died out there." His voice was harsher now; Jane shrank away. "It was his fault. It was his FAULT!" he bellowed, slamming his fist on the floor.

"I'm sure he didn't mean to hurt you the way he did," she whispered. "That he was just doing what he thought was best for you and your family."

"By forcing us into his ideals? By turning his back on me when I dare to want something outside his parameters?"

"Maybe he saw it as what he felt was best for you. Imagine someone of his generation, someone who saw more value in their business than in cooking, especially cooking within the confines of a medium that was still very new. Perhaps he thought not that you would fail, but that this concept of food on TV would fail and you would be left behind in a career."

"And the rest?"

"He wasn't perfect, Linc. He certainly said horrible things to you, but he was your grandfather. And he raised your father, who raised you. There must have been something good done in that sequence."

Lincoln looked at her, his eyes red, calm trickling through him at the thought of Jane's use of his nickname. "I'm not a good grandson. I'm not even sure I'm a good person."

"Of course you are," she insisted, her hand on his. "You're here, aren't you? After what was said and done, most people would not have come back."

"I should have been here sooner," he muttered. "Before it was too late." He reached for a large book next to him on the floor, handing it to her. For the first time since she entered the room, she noticed the thick leather tome.

"What is this?"

"Open it."

Gently, she lifted the cover, revealing faded pictures of a curly haired little boy, at a birthday party, a Christmas dinner, a family portrait. She flipped pages, and the boy grew older; the pictures reflecting graduations and achievements. Jane paused at a picture that could only be from Lincoln's graduation at Vanderbilt. His dark curls pressed beneath the black mortarboard, grinning broadly standing between an older couple, dressed flawlessly who had to be Grandmother and Grandfather Bainbridge.

"They look so proud of you." She smiled.

"They were. That was a week before I announced that I was going to start culinary school instead of the Master's program at Vandy. I graduated early after everything with Isabella. I'd taken extra classes. Before..." he stopped.

Jane shifted the book to close it, but a photo slid from between the back pages. It was a faded magazine article cut out of Lincoln from his very first competition win. When she turned the page of Lincoln's graduation, she found even more; photographs and articles about his meteoric rise in the culinary world, a detailed memoir of his career to date and a fairly recent feature piece from the local paper about the home-grown star's success.

"He knew. He kept track of everything." Lincoln uttered, eyes filling with tears again.

"Looks like it." Jane kept turning pages, revealing more and more of this homemade archive of Lincoln's life. "He even printed some of these international articles." She gestured to one from a French magazine.

"I want to hate him for what happened before I left, but this? I think I hate myself for not coming home when Mom first said he was sick. For not coming home years ago."

"Don't hate yourself. You didn't know. He never reached out, right?"

"No, never."

"For all you knew, coming home would have been more like that Thanksgiving. But at least you know he loved you. That he was proud of you."

"I didn't know," Lincoln repeated, fingers running along the edge of a photo.

"I didn't know him, but it seems like he raised a family as stubborn as he was." Jane half-smiled. "I don't think he'd want you to hate yourself. He wanted you to be happy, and it seems like he was happy that you'd found a passion and a calling."

Lincoln leaned his head down, resting it on Jane's damp shoulder. "Thank you."

"For what?"

"For being here. For not running away when I bit your head off or when you walked into my hysterical sobbing. For just being Jane Mullins, the kind-hearted woman who cares about people and who believes the best in them. And I'm sorry for yelling at you. You deserve so much more than I'm giving you." His gaze met hers, and he leaned in pressing a soft kiss to her lips, when there was a knock at the office door. His shoulders sagged at the interruption

"Lincoln, love, I've got your grandmother's things and your mother just called. Mrs. Grace is anxious to settle in so she wants you to get back."

"Thank you, Mrs. Cullman," Lincoln replied, sighing. "I guess that ends the tour of the Bainbridge mansion."

"It is a beautiful house. Thank you for showing it to me," she gushed as he helped her to her feet. He laid the scrapbook on the polished desktop.

"It is, memories and all. Let's go get my grandmother her things before she has to sleep on 300 thread count sheets," he joked.

"Oh, heaven's no!" Jane replied, laughing as they headed out the doors. She hesitated a step behind him, pressing her fingers to her lips. Their kiss in New York had been hot, passionate, but this one felt like a promise and she needed to find out who was promising what.

Wake Up Call

Finishing a quiet, reserved dinner back at Lincoln's parents' house, the family sat around the ornate dining table, the subtle notes of silver touching china the only sound.

"Thank you for the dinner, Mrs. Bainbridge. It was absolutely delicious," Jane offered, laying her fork across her plate.

"I'll be sure to tell Mrs. Frambert," Lincoln's mother replied, smiling. "She always does well, but this is exceptional."

"Well, she *is* a cook," Emily retorted derisively. "If she wasn't good at what she did, she'd likely be searching for a new job."

"Emily—" her grandmother began, a tone of warning in her voice.

"Just being honest, grandmother. The food is good."

"May we both be excused, Mom?" Lincoln interjected, laying his napkin beside his plate and pushing his chair back.

"Of course, darling."

He took Jane's hand, and they both hurried up the stairs to his room, closing the door behind them.

"Your sister really doesn't like me, does she?" Jane

muttered as she sat on the edge of the bed, staring out the windows at the sparkling skyline.

"Emily? To be fair, she's a terrible snob and doesn't really like anyone. Even when she was a girl, she'd turn her nose up at dolls she felt were inferior."

Jane giggled. "I guess I'm in good company, then?"

"The best! Some of them were lovely dolls." He yawned as he dropped onto his bed. "God, what a day. I've done competitions that didn't leave me so exhausted." He patted the space next to him and Jane stretched out beside him, holding his hand between them.

"I haven't stopped thinking about New York," Lincoln murmured, squeezing her hand.

"Me either," she whispered.

"I think it was the best kiss I've ever had."

"You think?" Every nerve in her body stood on end waiting for his answer.

"Well, more in-depth study would have to be done to be conclusive," he teased, raising up on his elbows to look at her.

Drawing in a breath, she leaned up to meet him. "By all means then."

It was as if no time had passed. He wrapped around her, lips roaming her mouth, her throat, a small spot behind her ear that made her offer the most delicious moan.

"I thought you were tired," she said between kisses, running her fingers through his curls.

"I am. Tired of being alone, tired of not being with you." He tucked his head against her shoulder. "I mean it, Jane. I don't think I even knew how lonely I was before I met you." He yawned again and snuggled against her. "Please don't take that as an assessment of your skills," he insisted. "It's just been a hell of a day."

"I understand. We should watch a movie or something,

just chill after everything." She paused. "Don't sleep on the sofa tonight."

Lincoln raised his head to look at her. "I don't want you to be uncomfortable."

"I won't be, and neither will you."

He nodded. "I'm going to go take a quick shower if you wanna get changed."

"I am dying to get out of these heels," she replied. "Go bathe, you smell!"

He threw his shirt at her as he disappeared into the bathroom. Tugging Lincoln's shirt off her head, she took a deep breath of the subtle smell, his smooth but spicy cologne, clean laundry detergent, and the softest hint of cloves. For the first time since arriving, she felt comfortable at home with him.

"Well, don't you two look cozy?" Jane jumped at the sound of Emily Bainbridge's voice behind her.

"Hello, Emily. Lincoln is just taking a shower before we watch a movie. Do you need something?"

"Not from my dear brother, but you? I need you to stay away from him. I thought you might be up to something with my dear brother, but I didn't think you'd be so bold as to do it in our parents' house."

"We're not 'up to' anything, Emily."

"That's not what it sounded like a few minutes ago."

Jane blanched. "Nothing happened."

"Right. I think, Ms. Mullins, that you're after money or fame or both through my brother, and you should know that it absolutely will not work. He might find you sweet enough now, but he'll get bored. He could have his choice of women, and I doubt his options would include you."

Jane felt hot tears forming, not at any insult intended but at the truth in Emily's words. She swallowed before replying.

"Emily, I have no pretensions on your brother's affections.

We are friends and whether you believe me or not is your decision. I assure you I am well aware of his options, and that I am no supermodel or heiress. I am here because he asked me to be. Now, if you'll excuse me, I need to get ready for bed. It's been a long day and I have a drive ahead of me tomorrow."

Emily snorted derisively, but disappeared down the hall as Jane sat on the edge of the bed. Her tears dripped onto the hem of her skirt, darkening the fabric. Emily was right. What could happen between them? This was only going to break her heart in the end. She heard the shower cut off and hurried to pull on her baggy t-shirt and leggings, wiping her eyes.

Lincoln, drying his hair on a towel, poked his head into the room. "How do you feel about *Hard Time to Die*?"

"To be honest," she mustered a smile, "I've never seen it."

Lincoln clutched his chest. "Never seen *Hard Time to Die*? How is that possible?"

"I guess we need to remedy that."

He pulled her onto the bed with him before he noticed the redness of her eyes. Jane tried to turn away, but he took her chin in his hand gently.

"What's wrong?" She shook her head. "Janie, what's wrong? We were laughing when I left the room."

"I'm fine," she whispered. "Really, I am."

"Was it my sister?" He knew the answer when she hesitated. "Damn it, Emily. She just can't let me be happy!" He started for the door.

She grabbed his arm. "No, Lincoln, I'm fine. Please don't let this be a fight between you, not now when you're coming back to your family. It's alright. I just took something she said too much to heart. I'm okay."

Lincoln pulled Jane close, his arms firm around her waist. "It must have been something to hurt you. I don't want anyone to hurt you."

"I'm fine, probably just overtired. Let's just get in bed and watch the movie."

"If you're sure."

"I am. You've got to introduce me to *Hard Time to Die*, remember?"

They tucked into bed, snuggled together in the darkening room, Jane's head on Lincoln's shoulder as the watched the action movie.

"You called me Janie," she commented softly, breaking the silence between them.

"You used my nickname. Seemed only fair to use yours. Unless you don't want me to."

Sleepily, she rushed, "No, no. It's fine, I was just surprised. Only the people who love me have ever called me that."

"I think I'll use it more," he replied, sliding his arm around her waist. It only took about half an hour before he noticed her soft, slow breaths beside him.

Kissing her forehead as he turned off the television, he spooned against her.

"Goodnight, sweet Jane," he murmured into her hair.

* * *

When her alarm blared from her phone the next morning, Jane found herself alone in the bed. Had she dreamed last night? Had he almost said he loved her? Golden sunlight filtered through the trees, casting a soft pool of light on the empty spot beside her. Jane dressed quickly, tossing on her jeans and a chunky knit sweater for the drive home, and hurried downstairs, where Lincoln sat at the kitchen counter.

"Good morning!" she said brightly.

He nodded, sipping his coffee, eyes locked on something outside the window.

"Did you sleep okay?"

180

Another nod. Even this early, Lincoln was usually more talkative than this. She reached to touch his arm, but he pulled it away.

"You're going home today?"

"Uh, yeah." Jane replied, surprised by his demeanor. "Soon if I wanna beat traffic."

"Good. Thanks for coming up."

Tears stung the corner of her eyes. What the hell had happened? Where was the man who'd held her when she fell asleep? Who'd been worried about someone hurting her? The one who'd cried on her shoulder the first night?

"I guess I'm... I'm gonna go." She looked at him; he didn't even turn.

"Drive safe. Goodbye."

She couldn't get to her car fast enough. Flinging herself into the driver's seat, she slammed the door and cranked the car. Once she was out of sight of the mansion, she pulled off into an empty parking lot, letting the tears flow.

* * *

She was crossing the Tennessee-Georgia line, the last few leaves twisting ruby and copper in the December breeze, thoughts ricocheting. She knew being with Lincoln had been a beautiful dream, but at least they'd been friends, right? But then he'd shrugged her off this morning. Worse than shrugged her off, he'd acted like she was a complete stranger, not the woman he'd kissed, the woman he'd slept beside the night before. Maybe Emily had gotten to him. Maybe he believed she'd come just to get something from him.

As she considered this, the sound of her ringing phone echoed in the car. Lincoln's name flashed across the screen, superimposed over the photo she'd taken of him at the hockey game. What on earth could he want from her? Taking a deep breath, she pressed the 'answer' button on her steering wheel.

"Hello?"

"Jane," his familiar voice sounded relieved, its resonance sending a warm tingle down her spine. "I'm glad you answered. How... How are you?" Now he sounded nervous.

"I'm fine, Lincoln. Just came down from the mountains at the border, actually. How are you?"

"I'm a jerk," he admitted. "Totally and completely. I have no excuse or even a real reason. I panicked when I woke up next to you this morning. Believe it or not, that's really unfamiliar territory for me and I had some sort of flashback and just..."

"Freaked out?" she supplied.

"Freaked out. And you deserved so much better than that. You came all the way here four days before Christmas. You dealt with my family drama, dealt with me. And I just brushed you off as if nothing happened. I am so unbelievably sorry."

Her heart pounded. Did she believe him?

"Jane?"

"I'm here, sorry. It's alright." Her doubts lingered, but he seemed sincere.

His exhale filled the car. "No, it's not. You deserved better. I'm so sorry. I can't say it enough. I want to make it up to you."

"You don't have—"

"Yes, I do, and I want to. I'm going to stay here a few more days to help get things settled, but I was thinking I'd come to Atlanta and spend Christmas with you, if that's okay. Might not get there until Christmas Day, but I want to be with you."

"I... You ...Sure," she sputtered. "We do Christmas Day with the family."

"I was honestly hoping that was the case," he replied, and she could tell he was smiling. "I am going to help my mother take care of some things, but I will talk to you later. Text me when you get home so I know you're safe, okay?"

"I will," she assured him.

"Bye, Janie."

"Bye, Lincoln."

The city was grey as she turned onto 16th Street and then Holly, a chilly mist swirling by. Christmas lights twinkled in the darkening afternoon, and Jane realized she hadn't put up the first decoration.

"Guess that's tonight's project," she said to herself. She'd check in at the bakery tomorrow; they'd be closing up now anyway. The Santana's, the family two doors down, had outdone themselves this year, with a small army of inflatable reindeer on their roof and a massive illuminated Nutcracker by their driveway. Jane parked her car in the narrow spot by the house and, grabbing her bag, walked out to check her mail. Several bright envelopes announced Christmas cards, but it was a long white envelope with her landlord's return address she was concerned about. Without waiting, she slid her finger beneath the envelope closure and tore it open.

"Dear Ms. Mullins," the letter began, "Due to circumstances beyond our control, we will no longer be renting out the property at 1247 Holly Street, effective February 28. We apologize for the inconvenience and late notice, but will be reimbursing moderate moving costs incurred by this change. Thank you for your excellent tenancy, and we wish you the best in the future." The familiar signature of Mr. Huber, the sweet old man who owned her house, swirled neatly across the bottom of the paper.

"Great, first the bakery, now this?" she muttered, unlocking the door and letting herself inside. She dropped her bag in the hall and sank into the armchair. "What am I going to do?"

It hadn't been easy to find a place near the bakery to rent

to begin with. Even the apartments, small, cramped studio spaces, were thousands of dollars per month, and with the bakery's rent going up? Her phone chimed before she could tumble further into the gloom.

Trevor: Closing up for the day, boss. Everything is set for tomorrow's orders. Oh, and Mrs. McElveany called and asked specifically to speak to you. I told her you'd be in tomorrow, but if you're not, you should call her. – T

Margaret McElveany was one of the leaders of the Atlanta Junior League. Jane had designed a cake for their annual winter gala for the past five years, before the bakery had even opened. It was late in the season for them to be planning the event, but they were important clients, so rather than wait, Jane decided to call.

The phone rang three times before the polished voice answered, "McElveany residence, Margaret speaking."

"Good evening, Mrs. McElveany. This is Jane Mullins from The Puck Stops Here Bakery. I'm sorry to bother you at home, but I had a message from my assistant that you had called for me."

"Ah, Jane. Yes, dear, I know it's dreadfully late to call about the gala; it seems to have crept up on us this year. But due to new member dietary restrictions, I'm afraid we're not going to have a cake at the event this year."

Jane's heart sank. "Oh, well, we'd certainly be happy to accommodate any—"

"It's alright, dear. We're working with a company that specializes in these things. And I'm sure your holiday schedule is filled to the brim already. Have a lovely night!" Then a click and silence.

The Junior League event was the order that pushed the bakery through the January slump every year. Losing the gala wasn't just losing the order, though; serving at the gala always produced more orders for the rest of winter and into the spring. The bakery had even done the cakes for several high society weddings thanks to meetings at the gala.

Her heart sank lower than the couch cushions as she dropped onto them. She gripped a throw pillow, hugging it to her chest as she began to cry. The weight of the past twenty-four hours fully crashed into her as she drifted off to sleep.

Crumble

~~~

Bleary-eyed after a third fitful night's sleep, Jane sat in her office, searching for a new place to live while the order she was working on— a huge variety of muffins for the Statesman Distillery Holiday breakfast— was baking. She checked her phone for the umpteenth time, remembering Lincoln's promise to join her for Christmas, but as had been the case since their phone call, nothing. Still, she thought about what she could get him as a gift.

Outside her office, she heard the first sounds of holiday dissent in the kitchen. Inevitably, as Thanksgiving passed and the Christmas rush began, tempers began to flare a bit in the shop. Opening the door, the voices she had heard battling suddenly dropped to a hush. Nia and Trevor were standing close together, Trevor's hands tightly behind his back.

"What is it?" Jane asked nervously. Every day since New York, there had been articles and blog pieces popping up about her performance in the competition, the surprise come-back she had made, or her least favorite—articles about Lincoln that mentioned her.

"Nothing, boss. We just couldn't agree on what shade of

blue for the edging on the Mordacha Hanukkah cake," Nia said quickly, as Trevor twitched, trying to conceal something.

"You're a terrible liar, Nia. What's wrong?"

"I... There's..." Nia stammered before her shoulders dropped in resignation. "Show her, Trevor."

From behind his back, Trevor produced his cell phone, the screen bearing a webpage splashed with a lip-locked couple, their faces far too familiar to Jane. "Simple Starts chef reunites with supermodel love," she read quietly from the screen. She hastily scrolled through the article, naturally accompanied by more photographs.

"Culinary Channel darling and all-star chef Lincoln Bainbridge was spotted this week at La Provence in Nashville with ex-fiancée and supermodel actress Railey Richards-Grant. The pair, who haven't been seen together since the mysterious end of their engagement two years ago, was first spied by an amateur photographer who caught the couple in a firm embrace outside the Bainbridge family home late Friday afternoon before climbing into Bainbridge's car and heading toward the downtown area," Jane read aloud. "The duo was captured at La Provence having a quiet dinner that night, and Ms. Foster-Grant was seen leaving Lincoln's home early the next morning. Inquiries to both parties have been met with no comment, but it certainly appears that the glamorous power couple has worked out their differences and is back on the radar." Jane laid the phone back on the counter.

"Well. I guess that explains the radio silence." For a moment, the only sound was the buzz of the overhead lights and the hum of the working oven. "Trevor, did we get that shipment of fondant that we needed?"

"Uh, yeah, boss. It's in the stockroom," he answered as the door buzzer sounded. "I'll get that." He disappeared through the swinging door, grabbing his phone on the way.

Nia watched Jane, who was staring at the counter, unmoving and unblinking. "Jane, you're not okay."

Jane jerked her head up. "I'm fine. I always knew this is how it would go, Nia. He's Lincoln Bainbridge for heaven's sake! What did we expect? A happily-ever-after where I ended up with the celebrity I've been in love with for years? Right. Nia, even my imagination can't fathom that." Jane turned to return to her office.

"Jane, I think this is all a setup or something. It doesn't feel right. I saw the two of you in New York. He likes you, Jane. I think he might love you."

Without turning, Jane spoke calmly but forcefully. "Stop it, Nia. I don't ever want to hear that again. Go help Trevor with the customers." She heard Nia start to rebut, but kept walking into her office, shutting the door behind her. At her computer, she hastily typed in the address for the celebrity gossip website she knew the girls favored. Sure enough, there were the same photographs of Lincoln and Railey splashed across the main page, with matching headlines flashing. One even mentioned her, though not by name: "We wonder how Lincoln's mystery hockey date is taking the news."

Jane could feel her heart thumping slowly, even as she was trying to take deep breaths. Friday night. She'd spoken to him just that morning, when he'd apologized to her and asked to spend Christmas with her. He'd gone out with his ex that night. That explained why she hadn't heard from him since then.

Mercifully, it was almost six, and once Trevor helped the customers, she would send them home. The shop was clean; all she would have to do was count down the register and pack up the muffins for pick up the next day. The door buzzer sounded, and after a moment, she heard Trevor and Nia return to the kitchen.

"She'll be okay, Trevor. She's a tough cookie."

"I know, but this isn't just some guy, Nia. This is the guy she's pined after for years. And you know he had something with her. You saw them together. And we know she loves him."

"I know she does. But right now, she won't think about it. She'll throw herself into the holiday rush, and that's okay. We have to let her deal."

Jane heard the rustle of jackets being gathered, and bags being picked up.

"Boss?" Nia called through the office door. "Everything's ready to go except the register. Oh, and Trevor didn't lock the front door because he forgot his key. You alright to handle it?"

Summoning up a smile, Jane opened the door. "Sure. Y'all head on home before it gets any colder. Trevor, you're coming tomorrow morning to finish the Randall cake, right?"

Befuddled, Trevor replied, "Yes, boss. Have a good night."

The pair disappeared through the back door, and Jane, dropping the gargoyle smile, headed for the front to finish up her work. Her fingers moved quickly across the keys of the register, running through the day's receipts and totals. She was nearly finished when the buzzer on the door sounded.

Without raising her head, she called, "I'm sorry, we're closed."

"I'm sorry, Miss Mullins. I know you are closing up, but I had to wait until your assistants went home," a smooth voice intoned from the doorway.

Gulping, Jane looked up from the bright computer screen to see the smirk splashed across Antony's face. "Good evening, Mr. Perandin. What can I do for you? I feel like this is a bit unusual for you to be visiting someone who didn't win their competition," Jane greeted the man coldly.

"Ah, Miss Mullins, I see you're still upset with me from your time in New York. And that's just fine, because honestly," he stepped aggressively toward the counter, his smile changing into a glare which made her want to cower in the corner, "I'm not your biggest fan, either. Obviously, you figured out that you weren't supposed to make it past the first round and that your little castle cake ruined some major plans of mine. I could have dealt with that—I can make my own contingency plans—but then you had to go and be all cozy with my star and start turning his head. And Miss Mullins, I just can't have that."

"What?"

"Don't play coy with me, little girl. Your fat ass made puppy eyes at Lincoln and then started spewing nonsense about passion and dreams and desires into his ears. And vitriol about me. You're an ungrateful, unattractive little bitch, and I should have found some way for them to disqualify you for it, but that would have really only caused me more trouble." His eyes narrowed, and he grabbed her hands. "However, if you come anywhere near Lincoln again, I will make sure that you not only never work on my network again, but that your reputation everywhere is decimated. I will wipe you off the map, Jane Mullins. Do you understand me?"

For a moment, she looked ready to burst into terrified tears, but then the memories of the judges in New York revived her confidence and she pulled herself up straight, yanking her hands away from the steel-eyed executive.

"I know you sabotaged my final cake, but I won't pretend that I have enough influence for that to hurt you. But I will not allow you to stand in my store and insult me. I am good at what I do, and I don't need your approval to succeed. And as for Lincoln," her heart hurt to say his name, "You don't have to worry about me. It doesn't matter that we got close. It doesn't matter that I love him. Given that he and his ex-fiancée were spotted together outside his house three days ago, you don't have to worry about me. He's back where he belongs and I won't be your problem anymore. Now, get out."

"I see we understand each other better than I thought, Miss Mullins." Antony dipped his head and walked back out the door without another word.

Jane quickly locked the door and turned out the lights in the front of the store. It wasn't until she slipped back through the swinging door back into the kitchen that the ramifications of the situation finally assaulted her. She slid down the wall onto the tiled floor, sobs choking her as she tucked her head into her knees and wept.

* * *

Christmas Eve morning found Jane curled tightly under the blankets in her old bedroom at her grandparents'. The bakery closed at noon for the holidays, so she decided to stay at the house an extra night, not wanting to be alone after Antony's visit. She stared at the ceiling. From the bedside table, her phone began to vibrate and her heart fluttered.

Seeing the unknown number on her phone, she took a deep breath and pressed the green answer button. "Good morning, this is Jane."

"Miss Mullins? Jane?" a familiar voice replied.

"Yes? Who is this?"

"This is Dan. Greenberg. From the competition?"

The world around her stopped. "Of course, Mr. Greenberg. How can I help you?"

"Please, call me Dan. I'm sorry to call while you're in the middle of the holidays, but time is essential, so here we are. I am co-hosting an international cake consortium in London, starting on the twenty-eighth. There will be speakers, demos, and tons of swag, but we are short one cupcake demonstrator for a beginner's session. You would have one course, the very first day, then you can check out the rest of the conference yourself, and spend some time seeing the sights of London. Unless you've been here and seen all that."

"I've never been to London," she breathed, hanging on every detail.

"All your expenses would be covered, flight, hotel, food. And you can bring someone along with you as well. What do you say?"

"Yes," she replied without hesitation. This was the biggest opportunity she had ever encountered, and she wasn't about to pass it up, not that she could even begin to think of a reason to do so.

"Excellent! I will have a courier get the tickets and information to you first thing tomorrow. See you in London!"

"Definitely. Thank you so much!"

She'd barely hung up the phone when she leapt from the bed and raced into the living room, squealing and rocking excitedly on the balls of her feet as she reiterated the entire conversation to her confused grandparents who, once the situation was explained, were jabbering excitedly as well.

"Gramma," she said, turning to the older woman relaxing in a deep red recliner, "I can take someone and I want you to go with me."

Her grandmother stared at her for a second, dumbfounded. "Are you sure, honey? You could take Nia, or even that nice young man of yours..."

Jane shook her head. "You and I have talked about going to London since I was a little girl. Grampy has been, and Daddy had been, but you and I, we just got to listen to their stories and dream of the city. We get a week in the city and I only have to be at the convention the one day then we can explore. We can go see Westminster and the Tower of London and the palaces. We can even hire a car and go out into the country to see whatever we want."

"Are you sure?"

"Of course! I know it's Christmas Eve, but why don't we go and buy anything we need for the trip, so we don't have to worry about it later?" She embraced her grandmother, grinning. "You're alright with this, aren't you, Grampy? I wish I could take you both—"

"No, sweetheart. You're right. I've been to London, spent time there. I'm glad your grandmother will finally get to go. Maybe you could take this opportunity to visit your mother."

Jane froze. She hadn't even thought about the fact that she'd have the time to see her estranged parent. Her grandparents were watching her, both of their expressions soft.

"Maybe you're right. It's been a long time," she agreed, hesitantly. "Thanks for suggesting it, Grampy." He nodded and kissed Gramma's hand. "Y'all go shop 'til you drop. Just don't forget the kids will be here about seven."

* * *

Jane sighed, the winter wind biting at her toes. They had successfully gotten everything they should need for their trip, and the evening with everyone had just been lovely. Christmas Eve was always one of her favorite times of the year; all the kids and grandkids spent the night at the house and then Christmas morning breakfast woke everyone up again. But tonight? Tonight, her heart ached, and she didn't want to bring anyone down with her, so she was wrapped up, slowly swaying on the swing in the garden.

There was a creak across the space, and she jerked her head up to see a shadowed figure making its way across the moonlight.

"Jane?" her heart leapt at the voice that called through the darkness. Traitorous warmth seeped through her as she heard the garden gate open.

"Lincoln?" Her throat constricted and her fists tightened. "What in God's name are you doing here?"

He didn't miss the stringency in her tone. "I told you I was coming for Christmas; I just got here a little early. What's wrong, Jane?" he asked tenderly as he swept aside the long strands of willow branch. "Gramma said you were out here and that you were upset about something."

She reached for the ledge where she tucked away books and grabbed the glossy-fronted gossip rag and tossed it at his feet.

Lincoln quickly scanned the magazine's pages, grimacing at every word. "Jane. You can't really believe this garbage."

"How did they get the picture then, Lincoln? What really happened?" She didn't sound angry, just defeated and sad.

"Railey showed up, unannounced, at the house and cornered me. She insisted that we had to talk, that she couldn't leave without talking to me, so we went to dinner. I know the executive chef at La Provence, so it seemed a logical option, plus I didn't even imagine that there would be paparazzi skulking around somewhere I wasn't supposed to be. I've never had issues with them in Nashville before."

"So, you went, just believing you wouldn't be caught. Okay."

"No!" He exclaimed, frustrated that she didn't believe him. "We ate dinner, were ambushed by cameras, then went back to my house to finish our conversation before she left and went back to her hotel."

"The next morning? I get it. She came back, apologized for everything, and you're taking her back. You didn't have to come all the way down here just to tell me that. It's fine. I hope you're happy with her."

"My God, you are stubborn, woman. That's not what happened at all."

"Then why even see her? When I first met you, you

couldn't even mention the woman's name without getting upset, but somehow you managed to not only have dinner with her, but take her home with you. Why?"

"I," he hesitated, his face screwed up in thought, "I can't tell you that. She didn't want me to tell anyone."

"So, your ex-fiancée told you some great secret and then swore you to secrecy? And then spent the night at your house? You know you can just tell me the truth."

Lincoln groaned, obviously irritated. "I wish I could tell you, but I can't. She didn't spend the night. I don't where that part of the story came from. She needed a friend because she's dealing with something big, I just can't tell you what it is. Can't you accept that?"

"I can't do this. I know it makes sense. The two of you make more sense." Silence hung heavy over them, punctuated by the crack of branches in the wind. "Gramma and I are going to London the day after tomorrow for the International Cake Baker and Decorator Conference in London and we'll be gone until after New Year's. You can go back to Nashville and be with your family, or back to her in New York. But you don't have to be here to placate me." She turned her back to him, gaze lingering on the fairy tale book on the shelf.

"So, Dan called. He said he would," Lincoln smiled weakly.

"He called and I'm going. And I..." She was trying desperately to hold in the tears. "I need you to go, Lincoln. I can't play second fiddle to her. I can't... Just go, please"

"You don't play second fiddle to anyone, Jane. Nothing happened." His voice was hushed. "I thought you believed in me." He stepped closer to her, reaching his hand out to brush her hair away. I thought we were more than a passing thing. I lo—"

"Don't. Please don't say it." She stood, moving out of his reach,

"Jane, please," he begged. "Don't push me away."

"Please, just go." She heard the soft thud of something hitting the ground behind her, but didn't turn to look.

When she finally heard his footsteps falling away along the flagstone path, she turned, tears in her eyes, and picked up the small blue box he had dropped. She debated even opening it, but she pushed open the lid and gasped when she saw its contents.

Inside, on a bed of jeweler's fluff, lay a necklace; a beautiful silver chain from which dangled two small pendants in the form of gingerbread people, one set with a sapphire, the other with an amethyst. Her stare moved to the opened fairy tale tome on the shelf.

"*It is enough for me that I have been able to live on the same counter with him...*" Jane whispered a line from *Under the Willow Tree* into the night air.

Her fingers brushed across the shimmering stones; the sapphire, her birthstone and the amethyst, his. The small sapphire figure, who wore a tiny bow atop her head, seemed to glare at Jane, who sank into the hammock behind her, head in her hands, and for the second time in as many days, sobbed for what she had lost.

Taking Off

The airport bustled with post-holiday travelers, their bags rustling as they scurried from check-in to the trains to their gates. The domestic terminal had seemed far busier, but the high-ceilinged atrium of the international terminal was still plenty full of harried travelers.

"What time does our flight leave, Janie?" Gramma asked, wheeling her new navy-blue suitcase toward the British Airlines check-in kiosk.

"Nine," Jane replied, her dark green bag careening along behind her, clutched in her left hand. Their tickets, which had been couriered to them the afternoon before, were held tightly in her right. "We're supposed to land in London about eleven at night, local time."

"May I help you?" A woman with salt and pepper curls asked warmly, in a British accent.

Jane handed her their tickets and IDs. "Yes, ma'am. We're checking in for the nine o'clock to London."

The woman, whose name tag read Iris, glanced at their passes and her fingers flew across the keyboard. "Yes, Miss and

Mrs. Mullins. Everything is in order here. You have bags to check?"

Jane hoisted hers and Gramma's bags onto the checking platform and Iris looped tags around the handles of each.

"Very well," Iris acknowledged, as the bags vanished into the back. "You will be in the first loading group, but in the meantime, your passes will gain you entry into the Queens Club Lounge, which you will find to the left of the gate."

Jane stopped. "What?"

Iris smiled. "All first-class passengers are granted access to the lounge whilst they await their departure. Beverages and hors d'oeuvres are also available and free wireless internet as well."

Gramma was grinning eagerly; Jane was simply dumbfounded. She hadn't noticed the tickets were first class and she couldn't believe that Dan had set up such an extravagance.

"I... Thank you, ma'am," Jane managed, accepting the passes Iris handed back across the counter.

"My pleasure, dear. Have a lovely flight and thank you for choosing British Airlines!"

As they walked toward the security checkpoint, Gramma said excitedly, "First flight, first class! I am a lucky woman."

Jane grinned. To see her grandmother so happy, so eager to visit a place she had dreamed of for years obscured all the unpleasantness of the last week. Grampy had bought his beloved wife a new camera to capture all the places Jane had planned for them on her detailed itinerary, and Jane knew her grandmother was giddy about trying it out.

They reached gate 5A and noticed only a handful of other passengers had arrived. A family of five was clustered around the windows, two little boys excitedly watching planes in the rising sunlight, while a pink wrapped infant slept in the mother's arms. Two black suit clad businessmen dozed in the chairs along the wall, small briefcases at their feet. To their left was a dark wood door with a small placard set in the center; the words "Queen's Club Lounge" engraved upon it. Checking her watch, Jane saw they still had almost an hour before their flight left.

"Gramma, shall we go check out the lounge? We've got plenty of time before our flight leaves."

The older woman nodded, and they both entered the room. As the door closed softly behind them, they both let out an involuntary exclamation of surprise and awe. The room wasn't large, but it was so unlike the airport outside, Jane fought the urge to step back out of the door to confirm that they hadn't inadvertently stepped into another world. Dark wood, the same as the door, paneled all four walls, with one large window set into the outside wall overlooking the tarmac. A large leather couch stretched along one wall, with a handful of matching armchairs grouped around it, an impeccably dressed set of women, in their late thirties, as best Jane could tell. Two bulky wooden desks lined another wall, a tall bookshelf filled with leather-bound tomes in between them, while the last wall, to their right, was occupied by a bar and a man in a tailored white coat serving a martini to another black suited businessman. A glass case filled with pastries, sandwiches, and bottled drinks sat at one end of the bar, and a small oven sat on a counter behind the serving man. Jane's stomach rumbled. Breakfast hadn't been a priority when they had to be at the airport at seven that morning.

Gramma seemed to think along the same lines. "Do you think we could get a muffin or something, Janie? I'm completely starved!" She giggled, and Jane followed her.

"Good morning, ladies," the bartender said. "My name is Ben. How can I serve you today?"

"Morning, Ben," Jane said brightly. "Could we get two cinnamon muffins, a coffee, two creams, and an earl grey tea?"

She reached for her wallet, which was tucked into the top of her carry-on bag, but Ben stopped her.

"I can get all of that for you," he said, smiling, "but you don't pay. It's included, ma'am."

"How lovely!" Gramma remarked, taking the steaming cup of pale coffee from the counter. "Thank you, Ben." She settled herself into an armchair and sipped her coffee.

Ben popped the muffins into the small oven, then turned back to Jane. "Would you like your tea straight, or could I interest you in a London Fog latte?"

Jane grinned. "I'd love one. It's rare to find someone who actually knows what one is."

"I love them! They are so creamy but tangy. Perfect for a cold winter morning." He began mixing up her latte. "So, you're off to London? Business or pleasure?"

"Both actually," Jane replied. "I've been invited to an international convention for bakers and sugar artists, but we also have a fairly full itinerary of places to visit." She smiled. "I've always been a bit of an Anglophile; I get it from my grandmother." Jane inclined her head to where Gramma now sat, lost in one of the books she'd had Jane add to her new e-reader.

"What are you most excited about seeing?" Ben asked, passing her a steaming, frothy beverage.

"Oh, there's so much!" Jane responded dreamily. "The palace, of course, and Westminster and St. Paul's. The Tower of London. The museums, definitely the British Museum and the Victoria and Albert. Oh, we're supposed to have tea at Fortnum and Mason one of the days at the end of the trip. And that's on top of the actual convention." She stopped. "Sorry, I'm babbling."

Ben was grinning. "No worries, love." He dropped his voice conspiratorially. "Most of my clientele are stuffy work travelers. It's refreshing to hear someone so pleased and obviously thrilled about her trip."

"We are. This is the first intercontinental flight for both my grandmother and me, her first flight ever." Ben passed the two drinks and muffins across the counter and Jane retreated to the chair beside Gramma, sipping her latte.

"Attention passengers on British Airlines, flight J923, nonstop to London. Boarding will begin now for first class and Queen's club members. Please make your way to the counter at this time please.," a cool, clipped female voice announced over the intercom.

Jane eagerly returned their cups and plates to the bar. Ben smiled at her, pulling her empty cup back across the counter.

"Have a lovely trip, Miss," he said. She reached into her bag and pulled out five dollars, which she dropped into a glass tip jar at the end of the bar.

"Thank you, Ben!"

They stepped back into the terminal, the clutch of business people behind them. Approaching the counter, a pretty young woman with long, dark hair greeted them.

"Good morning ladies, Welcome to British Airlines, may I see your boarding passes please?" Jane passed over the two sheaves of information. "Miss Jane Mullins, and Mrs. Annette Mullins, seats 3A and 3B. The flight attendants will direct you to the appropriate section. Enjoy your flight!"

They moved down the narrow tunnel to the plane, emerging into the chilly interior of a luxurious plane. Jane had flown before, but always in the tiny and cramped economy seats. The section before her was open, sunny in the bright morning light. Instead of sections of multiple seats together, there were ten ample chairs, more like armchairs, or even small loveseats, one on each side of the plane.

A navy-clad attendant approached them, checked their passes, and gestured to the seats on either side of the middle row. "Please take your seats and let me know what I can get you to keep you comfortable."

The women nodded and settled into either chair. Jane tucked her messenger bag into a niche at her feet and looked out her window. The sun was up over the tarmac, and she could see planes moving along the runways.

"Janie, I think once we get in the air, I'm going to catch some sleep. I didn't get much last night; I was packing."

"That's fine, Gramma. I might do the same."

"I know you haven't been sleeping well since you two had that fight."

"How did you—"

"Oh, honey, I raised a family of kids. I know. I wouldn't worry, though. That boy is so head over heels in love with you that I can't imagine him not apologizing soon."

Jane smiled halfheartedly. "I don't know, Gramma. I think he's made his decision. And I can't blame him."

They both fell silent as more passengers filed onto the plane. Most of the businessmen and women they had seen took seats around them in first class, but a steady stream of others filed past them, looking at their accommodations enviously. It was about twenty minutes before everyone was loaded and situated, Dennis and the flight attendants settling things and ensuring the plane was ready to take off.

"Ladies and gentlemen, thank you for choosing British Airlines. We will be departing shortly for London Heathrow, where we are scheduled to arrive at approximately ten thirty in the evening, local time."

* * *

The sky was dark, but the city twinkled merrily beneath them as they descended into Heathrow.

"Ladies and gentlemen, we are arriving at London

Heathrow airport," the warmly accented voice of the captain pronounced over the PA system. "The local time is currently 10:04 p.m., and the weather is a brisk 5 degrees Celsius. We do hope you've enjoyed your flight with us. Thank you for flying British Airlines and have a pleasant evening."

Gramma looked at Jane across the aisle and grinned broadly. "We're here!" she exclaimed quietly.

Jane smiled back, every bit as wide. "I know! I can't believe it!" There was a small jolt as the plane landed, and a gentle lurch as they slowed to a stop at the terminal gate. At the flight attendant's permission, they removed their seatbelts and gathered their bags.

"Let's go," Jane cried exuberantly, her messenger bag snug over her shoulder. They followed their flight companions down the narrow tunnel, through a cold steel door, and emerged into the terminal at Heathrow.

For a moment, Jane stopped, completely lost in the bright room and the buzz of unfamiliar accents, but the polite "ahem, pardon me" from the suit-clad man behind her broke her reverie and she followed Gramma on to the baggage claim and customs area. Finding their things and going through all the proper checks took far less time than she had thought it would, and within the hour, they were standing in front of a large diagram of the London tube system.

"The hotel we're staying at is The Wolf and Rose Hotel at Canary Wharf," Jane noted, reading the information that Dan had sent her. "Oh, goodness, Canary Wharf. It's on the absolute other side of the city from here," she chuckled, "but I think it will give us plenty of time to enjoy the famous tube. It looks like we'll travel from here to the South Kensington station. From there we will change to this green line—"

"The District line, this says," commented Gramma.

"Right. We'll take the District line to the Tower Hill station. At Tower Hill, we'll change to the DLR—not sure what that is—and take that to the Canary Wharf station. That's not so bad," she smiled. Gramma was smiling too.

"I don't care if we have to change trains a dozen times," her grandmother remarked. "We're in London. The actual, real London."

Jane grinned so excitedly her nose wrinkled. "I know! Come on, let's catch our first train."

They hurried to the platform, their ample suitcases rolling in their wake. The first train was rather full, with all the travelers leaving the airport for their respective destinations. The further they traveled, however, the crowd thinned. A half-dozen people poured off at their first stop, but a handful more joined them. Jane stood next to Gramma, clutching a tall post, reading the advertisements around her and dreaming about all the stops they were passing.

They finally arrived at the Canary Wharf station and took a moment to sort out which direction their hotel was in. The air was frosty. Not that either of them minded one bit. As they approached the beautiful building, Jane sighed contentedly.

"Gramma, did you ever think?"

"Good evening, ladies," the doorman, a tall man with short, dark hair, greeted them as he held the gilded glass door open.

"Thank you," both women said before stopping dead in the middle of the lobby. Jane had seen some beautifully apportioned places in New York, and this put them all to shame. Before them rose a magnificent suspended staircase; stone, glass, polished, and a mulberry-colored carpet creating a functional piece of art. The lobby was tiled in a cream stone, with columns of medium wood and pale paneling. The wood repeated in the fine receptionist's desk, and Jane could see more of it leading into what appeared to be a bar and restaurant.

"Wow," she whispered, trying to compose herself. 'Get it

together, Jane,' her mind prodded her. 'You're a professional adult, for heaven's sake.' She smiled and stepped up to the reception desk.

"Hello, ladies," the concierge greeted them. Dressed in an impeccably tailored navy suit, the woman, whose name tag read 'Millicent,' smiled at the new arrivals. "Welcome to The Wolf and Rose Hotel. May I have your name, please?"

"Jane Mullins, though the reservation would have been placed by someone else," Jane explained.

"Yes, Miss Mullins, I have you right here. You and an Anne Mullins?"

"Yes, ma'am. That's my grandmother."

Millicent nodded, typing information into the sleek silver computer. "Miss Mullins and Mrs. Mullins, we have your rooms all ready for you. Thomas will take your bags up." She gestured to a uniformed young man who sprang forward with a silvery baggage cart. "You will be in rooms 813 and 815. I think you will find the view lovely in the morning. Please let us know if there is anything we can do to make your stay more comfortable."

"Thank you," Jane replied, taking two keycards from Millicent and shifting her bag over her shoulder.

"This way, ladies," Thomas said, waving a hand toward the elevators. He led them to an elegant elevator that opened silently, revealing the matching wood paneling inside, and slid closed behind them. Thomas pressed the round button for the eighth floor and they slowly rose. The doors opened again onto a plush carpeted hall with wood doors, each set with a brushed silver number and handle. The bellhop led them down the hall to the far end, where 813 and 815 sat side by side.

"Your rooms, ladies," he said. Gramma opened hers first, revealing a spacious room, a large bed with a desk, and a smaller door leading, presumably, to the bathroom. Thomas set Gramma's suitcase at the foot of the bed, asking, "Anything I can get you, ma'am?" Gramma shook her head.

"Thank you, Thomas," she said, smiling.

"Thank you, ma'am. Miss, if I can show you to your room?" he said to Jane.

"Yes, Thomas, thank you. Gramma, why don't you settle in here? We both need to try to get some sleep tonight."

"I was just thinking the same thing, dear. I'm more tired than I thought I'd be. Think I'll send a message to your grandfather, then settle in and watch some television. Goodnight, dear." They closed the door and stepped to the room beside it.

Jane opened the door of her room, which was laid out opposite of her grandmother's; the key difference was a large cellophane wrapped basket on the desk, a bright blue folder lying next to it, and a magnificent bouquet of lavender roses. As he had done before, Thomas rested her rolling bag at the foot of her bed, and she dropped her messenger bag atop the coverlet.

"Oh!" Thomas exclaimed, moving toward the windows. "I forgot to show your gran, but here," he swept the long curtains back, revealing a beautiful view of the Thames, glittering with the lamplights.

Jane's heart fluttered. "What a view," she whispered as she moved toward the glass, pressing her fingers to the icy surface. "Thank you, Thomas," she said quietly. "You're a peach," she told him as he let himself out, chuckling.

Jane turned and began to unpack her bag, hanging outfits in the small closet, and arranging her makeup on the counter in the bathroom. She changed into her nightgown, grabbed her laptop, and settled herself in the narrow window seat overlooking the window.

London stretched out before her, aglow in the post-Christmas cold. Buses trundled across the bridges, cars zipping around them and up and down the narrow streets. A few boats drifted along the river, their lights reflected in twinkles on the water's waves. She had dreamed of this view since she was a little girl, reading about the Pevensies and the Royal family. But it was overlaid; the lights sparkled like the lights in New York had, the traffic rushed the same way.

Her heart ached. Whether she'd meant to or not, she'd fallen in love with him, with the real Lincoln Bainbridge, far more than the image and the distant person she'd had a crush on. And she missed him, how she missed him.

"But he went back to her," she confided to the empty room. "As he should. He went back to the woman he'd loved before."

Reaching into her carry-on bag, she drew out the small blue velvet box and opened it, the silver cookie man and woman resting neatly on the black velvet background. In spite of everything, she hadn't been able to get rid of it.

Her fingers brushed across the cool metal. "I can't regret it," she promised herself. "I won't regret it." Unhooking the clasp, she draped the necklace's chain around her neck, pressing the pieces to her chest where they lay at her sternum. "It can remind me that maybe there is someone out there."

Glancing at the clock, she realized it had grown late while she was lost in her reverie and, as she planned to be up early in the morning, it was time to retire. Jane opened her suitcase, laid out her outfit for the following day, and climbed into the sumptuous bed, her cold toes snuggly warm beneath the thick blankets.

"Tomorrow is a big day," she whispered.

Bittersweet

~~~

The sun was rising, a glittering copper orb above the river, as Jane checked her messages. There were several from work, mostly confirmations of events taking place after her return home. One was from Nia, letting Jane know that they had scheduled a wedding tasting for the second week of January, and one was from Grampy, asking how they were doing and how the food was. Jane chuckled at that. Checking the clock on the bedside table, she decided it was time to go; she was supposed to be at the convention center at nine a.m.

The jet lag seemed to be at bay, for now, though she knew her grandmother would likely sleep most of the morning before visiting an old friend while Jane was at the convention. Gramma had mentioned visiting the Science Museum the following day, too, before the pair had time to explore together.

She knew she shouldn't, but her mind wandered to Lincoln. Was he still in New York? Or home in Nashville? She grimaced as she wondered if he was in Los Angeles with Railey.

A flock of birds fluttered by, startling her.

"Time to get ready," she said to herself, rising from the window seat.

She dressed in her favorite grey tweed skirt and a deep green turtleneck, fleece-lined black tights, and her black knee-high boots. The folder of information slid into her messenger bag as she grabbed her coat and headed out the door. It was a short ride from Canary Wharf station to the convention center, where she found a mass of people filing through the glass-paned doors.

Languages swirled around her, some she easily recognized, others not so much. A large banner announcing registration in a dozen languages caught her eye, and she moved through the throng toward it. The line was long but moved quickly and soon she had reached the table, now clutching her portfolio of information.

"Name, *s'il vous plaît*," a grey-haired woman asked, so quickly her words seemed to roll into each other.

"Jane Mullins."

"*Oui, Mademoiselle* Mullins. Your badge, and your itinerary. Also, I was asked to pass this along to you," she added, and handed Jane a bright red envelope with a laminated name card on a pink lanyard, and a sheaf of papers.

"*Merci, Madame*," Jane said, moving quickly to allow the next registrant to the table. The woman smiled as Jane walked away.

Down the hall a few hundred yards, Jane found a corner and looked over her materials. The pink cord of her lanyard identified her as a cake artist and, from the looks of her itinerary, she'd gotten into all the breakout sessions she'd wanted, including a highly coveted spot in cake legend Seymour Panucci's class on fillings and frostings. The session in which she'd been asked to present was one of the first of the day, but she was thrilled to see her name alongside other decorating legends. She slid a finger under the sealed lip of the crimson envelope and opened it to find a folded white card.

'Welcome to London, Jane,' she read in Dan's handwriting, his scrawl making her smile. 'I hope everything has been great for you so far and your accommodations are to your taste. Lunch today will be a slightly bigger group than just the pair of us; I hope that's okay with you. We'll be in the Waldorf room, on the third floor at one o'clock, after your second session. If you get lost, just find one of the volunteers with the bright blue ribbon in their lapels and they'll get you to us. Have fun today! Dan.'

Checking her watch, Jane saw she had only ten minutes to get to the other side of the building for the open session she was demonstrating in. She was briefly intimidated as she stepped into the hall, but Greg Givantré, the decorator leading the demonstrations, greeted her so warmly, she felt at home. "You are as talented as Dan promised." The man passed Jane a business card. "If you are ever in need of a new position, please contact me."

Her heart fluttered. The competition had bolstered her confidence, but having a world-renowned expert not only compliment her work, but offer her a position? That was more than she'd dreamed.

Once she'd completed her task of presenting, Jane was able to attend her first session, a lecture on the changing world of local bakeries with Alexandra Messlethwaite, the owner of a chain of bakeries in Ottawa. The meeting room was full. Jane estimated at least a hundred people were seated in the dark upholstered chairs. She settled herself in the first one she found, in the middle of the back row, and took out her notebook and a mechanical pencil.

The chatter ebbed as the lights dimmed. Images appeared

on the projection screen and their speaker stepped up to the podium. Jane felt a little foolish with her notebook at first, but as Alexandra spoke, she could hear the familiar click of keyboard keys, so she knew she wasn't the only one taking notes. For the entire hour, her pencil flew across the page, and she was surprised when the lights came up and the session was over. She followed the crowd back into the hall and made her way to her workshop with Mark Connelly, a cartoonist who got into cake work when his company went bankrupt.

Jane was hoping his workshop 'Night of the Living Cake' would help her improve upon sketches for clients and the handwork on her cakes.

Much like her first session, Connelly's room was almost completely full. Unlike the first, however, this room was more like a classroom, with individual drafting tables, an array of art supplies next to each. She found an open workspace in almost the dead center of the room and took her seat.

"*Buongiorno, bella.*" Jane turned to see a handsome man, probably a few years her senior, grinning at her. His hair was that perfect blend of coiffed and 'just rolled out of bed' and shone like dark gold in the warm overhead lights. Her heart skipped when she met his eyes, the deep green irises fierce.

"Hello!" she replied cheerily, hoping her neighbor spoke English, too.

"Ah, American!" he countered, still grinning. "You make the cakes?"

She nodded. "I own a little bakery in Atlanta."

"Oh, Atlanta. I visited a friend at university there once. It was big, but very hot."

Jane laughed at the accurate assessment of her hometown. "It gets very hot in the summer. Makes the cakes difficult."

"How so?"

"The frosting doesn't want to stay on the cake!" She

laughed again. "I had a cake one day that I thought was completely finished with its base coat of frosting, but when I came back after about an hour, most of it had slid off the sides onto the cake board!"

The charming man laughed loudly. "*Poverino*! That is terrible. I am Ludo Giovanni." He extended a hand. "Head of cake design at Libero in Roma."

"Jane Mullins, owner and head baker of The Puck Stops Here bakery, Atlanta."

"Ladies and gentlemen, let's begin," a voice boomed from the front of the room. A tall, thin man with wire-framed glasses had stepped from behind the front table. "I guess you all know I'm Mark Connelly, cartoonist turned baker. I'm guessing most of you are here to learn techniques for your customer sketches, or maybe for the minute handwork our jobs sometimes call for. I don't expect you to walk out of here ready to be the Picasso of cake, but I hope you can pick something up. Now, I'm going to put up a few descriptions of cakes and I want each of you to choose one and sketch it for me. After a few minutes, I'll put up the pictures of what the client wanted and see how your work compares."

Jane set to work on the cake described as 'wintry pastels, the bride is a writer, no lilies.' Each time she glanced up for a moment, she noticed Ludo watching her, his charming smile lingering on her profile as she worked. When Mark called for time, he changed the slide. A few groans were heard, and Mark chuckled.

"Now, now, don't worry. Interpreting a customer's needs is rarely achieved the first time-sometimes they aren't even sure what they want. I did see one iteration of the spring birthday cake that was spot on." He pointed to an older man in the front row. "Well done..." he paused.

"Ellis," the man replied, nodding his head.

"And one young woman did an even better job of interpreting the winter writer than my staff did." He gestured to Jane, who blushed. "The tiny poinsettia blossoms and the topper with the quill and ink bottle are absolutely lovely, Miss..."

"Mullins," she stated, blushing even deeper pink. "Jane Mullins."

"Fine work. Let's move on to your next challenge." He progressed the slides and everyone went back to sketching, except her neighbor, who was staring again.

"*Bellissima*, beautiful Jane," he whispered.

"Thank you, Ludo," she replied politely, cocking her head to sort out the direction of 'abstract summer.'

"Have dinner with me tonight?" he whispered, softer this time, leaning close to her table.

"No, thank you," Jane answered. "I have to meet my companion back at our hotel."

She returned to sketching, adding a set of gracefully curved arches to her design.

"Oh, *carissima*, you don't have to lie to me." He placed his hand on her arm. "Come with me; I'll make it a night you will always remember."

"No," she said adamantly this time, shrugging his heavy hand from her elbow. "I have to meet someone."

She continued sketching, color blooming across the page, but she knew he was still watching her.

When Connelly dismissed the class, she gathered her notes, the sketches she'd made, and her bag and headed to lunch with Dan. Following the map in her guidebook, she made one turn, and then another before someone grabbed her left arm, tugging her around.

"Sweet Jane, I *must* see you tonight," Ludo said seductively as he drew her close. "Come with me, *por favore*."

"Stop it, Ludo!" She tried to pull free of him, but he was

stronger than he appeared. He leaned in to kiss her as she writhed in his grip. "Stop it! *Stop!*"

With a fierce tug, she freed her right arm, and with a swing that betrayed years of carrying heavy baking pans and tray, slammed a punch into the offender's face.

Ludo yelped in pain and surprise as blood flowed from his nose and his eyes watered.

"You stupid woman!" he bellowed, approaching her again, but she stood her ground, her fingers tight around one of the pens in her tote, ready to use it as a weapon if she needed to.

"Hey! What the hell do you think you're doing?" someone shouted down the hall. Ludo's confident expression returned as he stepped back from her, his charming grin unfaltering as footsteps pounded toward her. Jane was still standing, feet planted, her hand wrapped around the metal barreled pen.

"It was nothing, gentlemen, just a little misunderstanding between my dear heart and myself."

"Jane, are you okay?" Dan's voice was soft. She looked at him, finally dropping the pen, her eyes meeting his, and nodded.

"I'm fine. Just keep him away from me."

"Wait a minute," one of Dan's companions said suspiciously. "Where is your name badge?"

"Ah, I must have left it in the classroom," he said, turning to return for it.

"You look familiar," a woman in the gathered crowd commented, eying Ludo skeptically. "Let me see your license."

"I'm sorry, *signorina*, but I will not." He refused, looking somewhat frightened by her request.

A security guard appeared, observing the growing crowd, and repeated the request. Dropping his head, Ludo withdrew a worn leather wallet and handed it to the guard.

"Feeney McDonagan," the guard read from an ID card he tugged from the wallet. "From Torridon. If I had to take a guess, I'd say you're the Casanova that's been seducing young businesswomen and then stealing their credit cards and using them all over London."

Jane's eyes grew wide. "You're a conman?"

"Aye, lass," he confessed, his Italian accent dropped and replaced with a thick Scottish burr. "Ye didn't think I was really after yer," he paused, appraising her with a rough glance, "good looks?" Jane blanched at his rudeness, ducking her head again.

"Get him out of here," Dan ordered, glaring ferociously at the man. "Come on, Jane. Lunch is served." He smiled, trying to bring a matching expression to her face. She followed him down the hall, not turning her head, even when she heard the guffaw of the man as he spat, "Like I'd ever have a go at her."

Turning into the room from which Dan and the others had emerged, she gasped. The room was lavish, like many of the rooms in the conference center had been, but the crowd at the tables was astonishing. Kristoff Gunnarsson and Rahul Ingram sat at one end of the table, conversing with two women Jane didn't recognize. The empty spot next to Dan was the only one at the table.

"Here, Jane," he said, patting the chair's back.

She sat primly, feeling like a child invited to sit at the "adult table" for the first time. The salad in front of her looked divine, but her stomach was suddenly in mangled knots.

"Sorry for the disturbance, folks," Dan said, chortling. "Jane here was just helping to apprehend a serial identity thief out in the hall here." She blushed scarlet to the roots of her hair.

The crowd clapped and laughed, especially once they saw her reaction. Jane decided the best reaction would be to dive into the salad; at least she wouldn't be expected to answer questions with a mouthful of endive and arugula. The conversation resumed around her and she made out that the unrecognized table partners were acclaimed bakers and decorators in their own countries, from as far away as Kyoto and as nearby as Edinburgh.

"Jane, are you okay?" Dan whispered, not wanting to draw any more attention to her than necessary. "Did he hurt you?"

She shook her head slightly, appreciating the discretion. "Just my pride."

Dan frowned. "Don't take any of it to heart. And maybe don't mention it to your boy back home. He's not the angry type, but I don't think he'd take kindly to someone treating his lady that way."

"My boy?"

"Lincoln," Dan chuckled. "Part of me wondered if he'd be with you, but I guess he's working on the new season of the show?"

Jane gulped. "Mr... Dan... Lincoln and I aren't together."

"Oh. I, uh.... I thought, when I saw him with you in New York..."

"It's alright. I don't think you were the only one who got that impression. But yeah, he's not mine."

Dan offered a look that said he didn't believe her, but returned to his meal. Jane nibbled at her lunch, thoughts racing.

She chimed in a few times to the conversation, offering a small bakery point of view as she seemed to be the only one of them at the table. It was a remarkable experience, and she found herself slightly overwhelmed by the experience. It was something she'd never have dreamed of.

"Miss Mullins, I was thoroughly impressed with your work in the competition," Rahul Ingram's elegant accent reached her from down the table. "Particularly your final cake."

"Thank you," Jane replied, fidgeting in her chair, but

pleased. "We gave our all on those cakes. Findlay's was spectacular, though."

Cocking her head to the side, an elegant woman to Jane's left remarked, "Most competitors would be quick to praise their own work over a rival."

"His work was fantastic. I even asked his assistant how they assembled it because we get requests for wobble cakes, but I always have trouble getting the dowels right," Jane insisted. "Even if our rocket had worked, I think they might have beaten us." The woman nodded politely, then returned to her conversation.

"Ladies and gents, the next sessions are due to begin in ten minutes, so I believe we will have to end our lovely luncheon. Thank you for joining us, and I hope the rest of your conference is amazing." Dan's cheer was infectious, and Jane noticed smiles and laughter as the room emptied.

"Thank you so much for the invitation, Dan. This was a once-in-a-lifetime moment for me."

"It doesn't have to be," he replied, grinning at Jane as she gathered her things. "You're a brilliant baker, Jane. Still a little new to the process, but wicked talented all the same. I doubt this is the last time you'll be in a room like this."

"I hope you're right." She shook his hand proudly. "I better get going."

"What does your afternoon look like?"

"The main session speaker on changes in baking and the workshop on sugar work."

"Sounds great. Have fun! And Jane?" She turned at the door. "I get that you're not together, but I've never seen Lincoln look at someone like he looks at you. And I saw him with the model."

She drew in a sharp breath. "Really?"

He nodded eagerly. "Really. Do with that information what you will."

Closing her eyes, she saw the glossy gossip site, Lincoln and Railey's faces on the top. "Thanks, Dan!" she called, hurrying out the door.

She turned his words over and over in her mind for the rest of the afternoon, in between thoughts of sugar paste flowers and new metal cookware.

Reunion

The tube was full of passengers, most looking as if they were heading off to work on the bright December morning. She studied her written directions carefully, knowing she had to make sure she got on the right train at Tower Hill since the District line ran in several directions on the west side of the city. The first train that arrived was heading southwest, to Richmond, but a few minutes later, a train bound for Edgeware Road and Notting Hill Gate arrived and, nervously, Jane boarded it.

Gramma was exploring the Natural History Museum for the afternoon, having said flatly that she would not accompany Jane on this visit.

"You have to do this on your own, Janie. I can't do this for you," the older woman had insisted.

So, she sat, swaying with the train's movement, the written address clutched tight in her hands.

Fourteen years. It had been over a decade since she last saw her mother shouting at her on the cafeteria patio. Her mother had three children now. Marco was fifteen, Margaret was thirteen, and Elizabeth was eight. After Grampy's suggestion,

Gramma had unearthed the address she'd tucked away; apparently, the Dunmire's had been living in the same house since Jane was a teenager.

Her mother and her new husband—referring to a man she'd never met as her stepfather felt odd—lived in a townhouse near Kensington Palace with their three children; somehow Jane doubted their townhouse was anything like the one she resided in. Carter Dunmire was one of the foremost import and export dealers in the city, an occupation Jane always suspected drew her travel-hungry mother to him.

A glossy magazine cover in the hands of the grey-haired woman sitting opposite her caught her eye. The bright smile of Railey Richards-Grant taunted her next to a headline in shocking red: "Soap Star Pregnant with Director's Baby!"

The woman holding the magazine was staring at Jane. "Oh, I'm sorry," Jane apologized eagerly. "The headline just caught my eye. I thought she was seeing that chef." She tried to sound nonchalant, but her heart was racing.

Softening her gaze, the woman replied, "Oh, that's alright. Apparently, she's been with this director bloke for a few months, but the stupid paparazzi kept linking her with her ex, that Bainbridge boy."

"Does the article say why she waited to make the announcement?"

"Says she was afraid she'd lose her role in her soap opera if she was pregnant, but I guess they must have sorted it, because she seems really cheery." The woman shrugged.

"Good for her," Jane said thoughtfully. Her mind raced, but her heart ached. He'd been telling the truth, and she'd refused to believe him. Lincoln had been a good friend to the woman who broke his heart, and Jane had just dismissed him for it.

"You alright, dear?" the woman asked kindly, watching Jane's now crestfallen expression.

"Oh, yes. Just thinking about a friend of mine," she added, summoning a smile. "Thank you for sharing your magazine with me." As the train slowed to a stop at the Victoria station, the woman gathered her bag.

"You're welcome. Have a lovely day," she said as she stepped from the train onto the platform.

Jane hugged her bag to her chest; she'd been an absolute idiot. She had to talk to him, see him. She had to apologize. Instinctively, she grabbed her cell phone and scrolled through the phone book to find his number. Without hesitation, she called and listened to the ring. After a dozen rings, she heard his voice and her heart skipped.

"Hi, you've reached the phone of Lincoln Bainbridge. I'm probably elbow deep in my kitchen right now, so if you'll leave me a message, I'll get back to you as soon as possible."

Jane hung up before the beep could sound.

'I'll call him tonight,' she told herself. 'Tell him everything.' Wringing her hands, she noticed that they were approaching High Street Kensington station, her stop.

She emerged from the station into the grey winter morning, and made her way toward Kensington Court, just a few blocks over. Jane was awed by how large the townhouses were as she wound her way through the streets. Most were at least five floors, all façade in aged red brick with white trim. As she stopped in front of number forty-three, she had to smile. Though it was the icy dark days of winter, she knew the flower boxes at the window ledges would be full of something bright and cheery come springtime. Time may have changed things, but her mother would always love flowers. In the bay window, which extended halfway to the street, sat what appeared to be a large Christmas tree, multicolored lights sparkling in the overcast day.

Jane took a deep breath, stepped up to the door, and knocked. Over the rumble of cars in the street behind her, she heard a clatter of footsteps slow to a stop on the other side of the door.

"Who is it?" a small voice called.

"Jane Mullins," she answered. A round face framed by light brown waves peeked around the dark blue curtains at the window by the door.

"Mummy!" the little girl yelled back into the house. "There's a girl here to see you!" Jane chuckled, assuming that the doorkeeper was her youngest half-sister, Elizabeth. There was a louder rumble of clamoring footsteps to the inside of the door, followed by a much slower march of feet.

"Behave yourselves," a woman directed in a hushed tone, before there were a series of clicks and the door opened.

Framed in the doorway was a slender woman with shoulder-length blonde hair. Flanking her were two teenagers: a tall, dark-haired boy with dark brown eyes and a girl, long blonde hair and hazel eyes with unreadable expressions on both their faces. The little lookout stood closest to her mother, her eyes wide.

The woman smiled nervously. "Jane. You made it. Won't you come in?" After so many years, her mother's accent took her by surprise with its elegance.

Jane nodded and stepped into the front hall. The house was immaculate; nothing seemed out of place in the white foyer with a tall honeyed wood staircase rising before them.

"We can sit in here," her mother said, gesturing to the sitting room where the Christmas tree stood. The oldest kids sat on one short sofa against the wall, while Jane settled herself in an elegant antique chair, and her mother and Elizabeth took the longer sofa facing the tree and the front bay window.

There was an awkward silence before little Elizabeth asked, "Is this your friend, Mummy?"

Her accent was adorable, making Jane smile. She could see

her mother in each of her half-siblings, assuming the dark hair was a trait they inherited from their father.

"No, dear," her mother began slowly, looking from face to face of her children, the oldest both wearing looks of great curiosity. "Maggie, do you remember a few months ago when you asked me what the M stood for in my signature?"

The teen nodded. "You said it was your maiden name, but I don't think that was right."

"You're quite right, sweetheart. I should have told the three of you ages ago, but somehow, it never felt right, and your father and I don't talk about it much. I was married once before I met and married your father."

All three children gaped at her.

"What?" Marco yelped, his face sour at this revelation. "So, you're divorced?"

Jane got the feeling from his tone that divorce was not a normal occurrence in their circle.

"No," his mother answered calmly. "When I was just a few years older than you, I was the daughter of a small family in Birmingham, Aurelia Walsh. You know that much. What you don't know is that I met a lovely American man named Joshua Mullins who was in London for business and we fell in love and were married. I moved to the States to live with him in Atlanta, and we had a little girl named Jane." The children's eyes swiveled to Jane, who was listening to her mother's retelling of the story with great interest. "When Jane was five, her father was killed in a car crash." Again, three sets of eyes stared at Jane for confirmation; she nodded. "I was still young, younger than Jane is now, and I was very lost and confused. My husband was gone, and I was alone in a country I was still adjusting to with a five-year-old. To get my head together, I left Jane with her grandparents in Atlanta, and came back to Birmingham to see friends and decide what I wanted, which is when I met your father." Jane wiped a stray tear at the memory of their shared loss.

"When we decided to get married, we were faced with how to handle Janie. Your father was traveling constantly in those days, and honestly, I wanted to travel with him to China and India and all the beautiful places he visited and I knew we couldn't do that with a small child in tow. It wouldn't have been fair to Jane either, to take her away from her friends and everything she knew. It would have been like uprooting the three of you to Spain when you were little."

The tense silence settled again.

"It was the right decision," Jane agreed, meeting her mother's gaze. "For both of us."

Her siblings looked at her. Marco cocked his head, then stood and walked across the parlor, hand outstretched.

"It's a pleasure to meet you," he said politely, shaking Jane's hand. "I'm Marco."

Jane grinned. "It's lovely to meet you, Marco. You are... Fifteen?" she asked. He nodded, resuming his seat next to Maggie. "And you must be Maggie," Jane continued, noting her middle sister.

Maggie smiled and nodded. "And I'm thirteen. And the doorkeeper is Ellie."

"I'm eight!" burst Ellie.

"She's eight and likes to keep watch for Papa to get home," Aurelia added. "We are very glad you're here." Her voice caught at the end. "Will you three give us a minute to talk? It's been a very long time since we've seen each other. Ellie, you can see much better for Papa out the front window in the study." The three filed out and up the stairs quietly, and Jane heard doors open as they reached their destination.

"You look beautiful, Janie," Aurelia began, after a pause. "Your grandmother sends me pictures and things, but you are so much like your father. Anne told me about your competition."

Jane smiled proudly. "I like to think he'd be proud of everything I've been able to do."

"You should have won," her mother said.

"No, it was right for Findlay to win. That last cake he made was masterful. And even coming in second has been great. I mean, getting to be here, meeting bakers and decorators from all over the world. It's so much more than I ever dreamed."

Aurelia gazed wistfully at her oldest child, "Your father was always the dreamer... You remind me of him so. I'm sorry Janie. For everything."

"I'm sorry, too. I was awful to you the last time I saw you and—"

"No, you were honest," Aurelia insisted. "It was beyond ludicrous of me to expect a thirteen-year-old who hadn't seen me in eight years to pack up and move to a completely different country."

"Well, yes," Jane acquiesced, "But I should have treated you better, more respectfully at least. You were trying."

"You do know I love you. I always have. And Carter didn't not want you." Jane opened her mouth to reply, but Aurelia barreled on, "I know you've believed that for a long time, and I never did anything to disabuse you of that fact. The truth was, Carter would have made it work, if there hadn't been Charles and Anne to take you, if I had insisted on it. He pressed me to bring you here more than you know. But, Janie..." She was quiet.

"I reminded you of Dad," Jane finished.

"Every day. Every smile. And while I love Carter, your father was my first love, and I was haunted by him constantly with you. I will not say it was right, but it was a choice I made. Janie, you need to know that I did love your father and our life. I know you heard our fights and my immaturity. Your father was doing his very best for both of us, and I loved him for it."

Jane nodded. "I know. It was hard to understand at five, but now... I can understand the hardship y'all faced."

"I have something I want to show you," Aurelia said softly, reaching behind her chair and drawing out a box, the leather shell worn at the corners. "I had to dig it out of the attic when you wrote that you were coming." Jane moved to sit beside her mother, who slowly opened the lid, revealing a trove of memories; photographs, dried flowers, and what looked like letters filled the chest to the brim. "These are things from your father that I saved. The flowers from our wedding." She tenderly held out age-dried lilies, faded to mauve from the years.

Jane's eyes filled with tears. "I can't believe you saved these," she whispered. "I don't think I've ever even seen a picture from your wedding. I know it was small."

Aurelia dug into the box and pulled out a glossy snapshot of a young man in a crisp suit and a young woman in a lacy blue dress, clutching a bouquet of lilies.

"Our wedding day," she said, watching Jane's expression. "And here is when we first moved to Atlanta." Another photograph of the young pair, lugging cardboard boxes into the old apartment. "And this is the day we brought you home from the hospital."

She handed Jane the last photo, Aurelia and Joshua sitting on a floral-patterned couch, tiredly but lovingly gazing at the red-headed bundle in their arms. "You were so young," Jane murmured. "I always forget how young you both were."

"We were, but I never regretted it. Neither did he."

Jane nodded, unable to speak. She brushed a fingertip over her father's face.

"Oh!" Aurelia exclaimed. "I'd forgotten this one. I think you're three years old here." She held out another photograph to Jane. The same couch featured in the photo, with Jane curled into her father's lap while he read to her from a familiar book.

"Daddy," Jane said tearfully, one hand reaching to the silver chain at her throat.

"You loved that book."

"I still do," she said. "I found an almost identical copy when I was in New York."

"And your necklace is the gingerbread people, too. Did he give that to you?"

Jane wiped her eyes. "Dad? No—"

"The man from the show," Aurelia asked, passing a handkerchief to Jane. "Anne mentioned that you and he were seeing each other."

"I don't know what we were, but we're not anymore."

"Why?"

"I made a mistake and yelled at him and pushed him away."

"Did you apologize?"

"I... I tried to call him on my way here, but he didn't answer."

Aurelia studied her daughter, her strong, vibrant girl. "Do you love him?"

Jane took a deep breath, recalling the way he looked at her in New York, in Nashville, then the shattered look on his face when she pushed him away on Christmas Eve. "I do. But I hurt him. A lot."

"Try him again."

Jane grabbed her phone, dialing Lincoln's number again. It rang and rang before clicking to his voicemail. She hit the end call button before the beep. "I can't tell him I love him in a voicemail."

"One more call?" Aurelia suggested.

More rings, still no answer. Jane gulped, tears threatening.

"He probably hates me. I'm sure he doesn't want to talk to me."

"It'll be alright, Janie. Give it time. Maybe when you get home."

"Maybe."

"How long are you and Anne staying?"

"We're here through the day after New Year's. We're actually supposed to have tea at Fortnum and Mason on New Year's Day."

"That will be *lovely*! It's been ages since I've done that."

"I know it's mostly a touristy thing, but since we are tourists, and there's no telling when I will be able to get back here, it seemed like a great plan."

"And is Anne enjoying the trip? I seem to remember her being quite the fan of all things British."

"Definitely a trait she passed on to me," Jane admitted. "It's been a wonderful trip, honestly. Hard to believe we go home the day after tomorrow."

"I hope it won't be won't be the last time you're here to visit," Aurelia commented softly. "I hate to think of it being another decade before I see you again."

Jane leaned forward, taking her mother's hands in her own. "It won't be, Mom. I don't know when I'll be able to come back, but I'll come as soon as I can."

Eyes full of tears, Aurelia gently touched her eldest daughter's cheek. "You called me Mom."

"Because you are, and always will be," Jane promised, her heart full of affection, even as her mind was racing with thoughts.

The Sacking of Antony Perandin

Lincoln sat in Antony's opulent office, waiting for the man to make his appearance. Natalie Ramos, Antony's bookkeeper, had called him and said that the network executives wanted to meet with them before everyone left for the New Year's holiday. Though he figured on a solo night of takeout and watching the ball drop on TV, Lincoln assumed it was an important subject if the studio people wanted a meeting during the holiday rush.

Silence stretched taut in Antony's corner of the offices, which was opposite of its norm. Natalie and Fred Greenbaum, Antony's stylist, tried to look busy, typing nervously while watching the door. Julia was conspicuously absent, but it was the holidays, so there could be a perfectly good explanation for that.

Even so, Lincoln grew more and more uneasy the longer they waited. His cell phone buzzed insistently, but he shoved it in his pocket, ignoring what was probably a zealous telemarketer. Staring out the window, he watched fat snowflakes fall, trying vainly not to think of an eager smile summoned by the snow, of Jane's cheerful spinning in the flakes.

229

After ten or so minutes, the elevator dinged and Antony stepped out, crisp as always, in a dark suit, white shirt, and dark silvery tie, his Italian leather loafers tapping hurriedly across the cold tile floor.

"Bainbridge! Good to see you, son. Any idea why Geoff and the big boys called this meeting? Seems odd this time of year."

"I thought so, too. They're usually too busy with the holiday lineup and the New Year, New You specials. Must be something important to call us in."

The elevator dinged again, this time a group of men and women emerged, all in various states of dress. For all their prestige, most of the Culinary Channel network executives were far more casual. The glint of one businesswoman's red hair caught Lincoln's eye, making his stomach flip and his fingers tingle at the memory of red curls twisted between them.

Natalie and Fred tucked their heads into their computers while Antony stood up, grinning his slick smile. "Gentlemen, ladies, come on in. Bainbridge and I were just discussing the holiday lineup."

Not one of the men or women returned his smile; Lincoln's stomach turned.

"We didn't call you both here to talk about the lineups," Geoff Edwards said solemnly. "It's come to our attention that someone has been appropriating and misusing company funds."

Lincoln gasped, staring at each boss in turn. When he looked at Antony, he was startled to see the man still had his cool smile on his face. "And you came to see if I knew who it was?" Antony clarified, no trace of fear in his voice.

"No, Antony," a woman Lincoln recognized as Faith Mountebank, the CFO of Culinary Channel. "We're here because we know without a doubt who it is. You've been embezzling funds from all of your shows for the past three years. We also know that you've been taking far more than your allotted percentage from Lincoln and Jeannie Anne." An iron glare replaced Antony's grin, and Lincoln remembered why people found the man so intimidating.

"You don't have any evidence of these accusations," the stone-faced man said confidently, his hands tight on his leather desk chair.

"We didn't," agreed Leon Andresskar, the head of the legal department. Leon was always a very happy-go-lucky guy, but not a trace of that showed at the moment; his dark eyes were fierce as he addressed Antony. "Until someone brought to our attention a trip you made to Atlanta last month." Lincoln spun back to face Antony. When had he gone to Atlanta?

"That was a scout trip for Sweet Tooth. Lisa Pegg flew to Ireland, too; are you accusing her of embezzlement?"

"It wasn't the scout trip, Antony."

For the first time, a tiny glimmer of fear shone in Antony's eyes. "What trip are you talking about?"

Lincoln wondered the same thing, forcing himself away from thoughts of his own time in the city. "Why would Antony have made a trip to Atlanta?"

"We'd like to know, too. It wasn't even an overnight trip. He flew out on the red eye and flew back in that night. It was a few days after filming in New York wrapped. Lincoln, you were in Nashville at the time."

Lincoln turned to Antony, fire blazing in his eyes. "You went to see Jane."

"Of course I did! That chunky little cupcake queen was a hairbreadth from ruining everything I'd built in you. I thought it would be enough to cut the wires on her little rocket, that it would break her spirit but no. And I could see you questioning the show and the choices we'd made. You were in love with her, and not the kind of sappy little puppy love I'd dealt with Railey, and if you fell in love with someone so intrinsically sweet and loveable, all your female fans would have disappeared. I couldn't take that chance. I knew she was feeling very unworthy of you, so all I had to do was fuel the fire. Then Railey called me, looking for you, and it was too perfect."

Lincoln leaped from his chair, knocking the heavy wooden seat on its back. "You planted the paparazzi outside the restaurant and my house. You wanted it to look like we were getting back together, like she'd spent the night at my house," he bellowed.

"It was too easy. Then I flew to Atlanta and simply kindled the fear that little idiot already had. She never even questioned it. Though I will say she was a bit fiercer than I'd expected when she ordered me out of her crappy little shop."

"You heartless *bastard*," Leah Markowitz muttered from the back of the room.

"Took the words right out of my mouth, Leah," Lincoln said, still glaring at Antony. "Geoff, is he fired?"

Geoff stepped forward. "We can fire him from all capacities at the network, but you and Jeannie Anne are the only ones with the authority to fire him from his management duties. We spoke with Jeannie Anne this morning and she assured us her lawyer would deliver a formal letter of release first thing after the holiday."

"Oh, he's fired," Lincoln spat. "I can't believe I ever trusted you. I don't ever want to see or hear from you again."

"Oh, boohoo. Two chefs and a mediocre network are firing me. I'll go somewhere bigger and better. Where I won't have to constantly fight to keep my clients under control."

"What?" Lincoln replied, confused. "I never fought you. I always trusted that you knew best."

"Oh, you're so simple. You kept pushing about your family and being home. I knew if you asked to move the show back to Nashville, or wherever, you'd be freer and I would lose that authority. So, I kept telling you that we had to keep the show in the city."

Lincoln's eyes blazed. "You kept me from my family. Selfish egotistical ass." He looked at Geoff. "Could I have moved the show?"

Geoff nodded, "We actually had a meeting to discuss moving the show to Nashville since your roots are there, and Antony assured us you only wanted to stay in the city."

"When was this?"

"Twice, actually. Once, about five years ago, when you were working on Slice N Dice and we started discussing your show and then again last year after your relationship ended. We thought you might want to get out of the city."

There was a heavy silence in the office. Lincoln remembered a long stretch of days, alone in his apartment, wishing he could get away from the city and all the memories it was full of, and to know that all that time, his manager, his alleged friend, had possessed the ability to make that happen.

A ding and a chorus of loud footsteps echoed through the stony silence. Lincoln spun around to see a fleet of navy clad men marching through the front office; Fred and Natalie both leapt from their desks as men began to gather folders from atop them.

A short, stocky man stepped into Antony's office first. "Antony Perandin?" he inquired, looking straight across the room and across Antony's massive mahogany desk.

"What do you want?" the ferocious-looking Antony demanded. "What the hell are you doing with my files?"

"Confiscating them," the man said gruffly. "Though we have enough evidence against you already collected to put you away for a very long time. You're under arrest for money laundering, embezzlement, extortion, and tax evasion." He handed the thick pale blue wrapped warrant to Geoff, who showed no trace of surprise.

Antony's face had paled, but he still held his ground. "You've got nothing. And if you take me, you've got to take at least the girl, too," he gestured at Natalie, who was avoiding his glare, but eagerly trying to help the agent at her desk. "The girl's been in on it for years; she knew!"

"Wrong again, Mr. Perandin. Natalie came to us the first time you asked her to illegally transfer money from the show to your own account. We were fairly certain we could take you down on what she'd brought us, but we were lacking anything completely concrete to seal the case. Until that flight to Atlanta. When we confirmed with the network financial office that this was not the trip you were approved for, we knew that we had the link finally."

"If we could ask you gentlemen and ladies to step outside," a tall agent asked quietly, as Antony clenched his fists around his desk chair's tall leather back.

Lincoln followed Geoff and the others into the front office. Natalie reached Geoff first.

"Mr. Edwards, I'm so sorry I didn't come to you, but they told me not to tell anyone because it might jeopardize their investigation, but I promise I made sure that they knew you guys didn't know anything was going on." She was almost in tears by the end of her tumbling speech, and Fred had joined them by then.

"I didn't know! Mr. Edwards, I swear on every Prada shoe I picked out for that man that I didn't know." The executives chuckled at this. Geoff raised his hands to quiet them both.

"I know you both were either unaware of Antony's choices or simply doing what you had been asked to do to ensure his eventual arrest. I promise that neither of you are in any sort of trouble with the network. And I will do everything in my power to relocate you, either within our network here, or with a contact of ours elsewhere. In the meantime, go home. Enjoy the New Year with your families." Both nodded, gathering their coats.

"Thank you, Mr. Edwards, everyone," Natalie said, Fred nodding in agreement. They turned toward the elevator, but Natalie stopped, turning back. "And Mr. Bainbridge?"

Lincoln looked up from his phone that he'd pulled from his pocket, startled to see Jane's name on his missed calls list. Three missed calls.

"Natalie, after this long, you can call me Lincoln."

"You should know that she does love you; that she still loves you. He raged about it when he came back from Atlanta. He seemed confident that she wouldn't act on it, because she was so convinced you'd gone back to Railey and 'where you belonged,' but Antony said she blatantly told him she loved you, but that it wouldn't matter to you."

There was a long pause and Lincoln was sure every eye was on him, even the FBI agents.

"Make it matter, Lincoln," Natalie said, as she stepped into the waiting elevator.

Sparkle

Waiting nervously, her grey-gloved hands wringing in her lap, Jane looked at her grandmother. The older woman, impeccably dressed in a tailored hunter green skirt and blazer, stared out the window, eyes wide, reminiscent of a child taking in the sights of a city she had longed to see since her earliest years.

The door opened from the outside, the chill biting through her thick grey and blue coat as she stepped onto the curbstone of Piccadilly in front of the imposing brick facade of the tea shop, the windows dressed with giant festive teacups in their trademark green and white.

Nigel, their driver, shut the door behind her and quickly moved to the other side of the car to help her grandmother out. Jane fussed with her dress beneath the coat, made sure her stockings were straightened and her heels clean before her grandmother stepped up beside her.

"It's beautiful," Anne breathed, taking in the store. Christmas decorations still filled the entryway of the ground floor, but Jane could see how stunning the place would be on an average day.

"It absolutely is," Jane agreed. "But we should probably

get out of the doorway since we're blocking everyone else." She giggled at her grandmother.

"Miss Mullins?" a middle-aged man dressed flawlessly in a tan wool suit inquired, eying both women through tortoise-shell rimmed glasses.

Jane gulped. Had they been that disruptive already? And how did they know her name? "Yes, that would be me."

"Ah, good. The gentleman gave me little description of you other than your name and said that you would be in the company of your grandmother. If you will follow me, please?" He turned and began to walk away, but neither woman moved.

Gramma looked at Jane, both of them bewildered. "Ladies?" the attendant called, before tip-tapping back to them. His expression was not annoyed, but rather amused at these obvious tourists. "I'm sorry. I thought you knew. I should have explained myself better. My name is John Hale and I'm here to escort you to your private reserved table for tea."

"Reserved? I didn't reserve a table. I was told it was unnecessary, as long as we arrived early."

"You were rightly told, Miss, but we received a phone call this morning from a gentleman wishing to ensure a flawless experience for you and your grandmother and he reserved the table. Everything has been arranged and settled in advance."

Jane looked at her grandmother, dumbfounded. "Would Grampy have called?"

The older woman shook her head. "No. Grampy is on a fishing trip with your Great-uncle Frank this week." They both turned to Mr. Hale.

"I was sworn to secrecy," he said with a smile. "But if you'll follow me ladies, tea time approaches." They followed to the imposing staircase in the center of the room, twisting around and around as they made their way to the Diamond Jubilee Tea Salon on the fourth floor.

The restaurant was teeming, holiday revelers scattered at the tables filling the room. Jane eyed the tables they passed, gorgeous tablecloths set with magnificent settings of china and crystal, until John stopped beside a table set for two, a single lavender rose at one setting. Pulling the first chair back from the table, he gestured for Gramma to sit. Once she had, he pushed the chair gently toward the table. The sound of a piano swirled around them.

Jane timidly raised her hand, gesturing to the closest staff member, a dainty sprite of a girl. "Pardon me, we do not have menus here."

"Ah, Miss, we have special instructions regarding your table, if it pleases you."

"Of course. I suppose we will simply have to wait and see. Thank you." Gramma was looking at her as she turned back to the table and the flowers.

"Did the gentleman who invited you to London do this, Jane? Would he have wanted to treat you?"

"Dan is a very kind man, but I don't think he would go to all this trouble."

Suddenly the young lady reappeared with a tower of treats — perfectly piped tan macarons, delicate petit fours, golden scones, perfectly cut sandwiches, and a beautiful tea service.

"Ladies, your tea," she presented with a flourish. With a jolt, Jane realized everything on the trays had been specifically chosen for them: cinnamon and licorice macarons, scones studded with cranberries, even a pillowy white chocolate cake. Whoever had set this arrangement knew her and Gramma's favorites.

"And this is for you as well, Miss," she murmured, slipping a small, cream colored-envelope into Jane's hand.

Without hesitation, Jane flipped the parcel over to open it, breaking the small wax seal in the process. From the envelope, she drew a folded piece of paper, the same creamy hue as its holder, and, unfolding it, saw that it only bore a handful of words.

Altitude 360, in the Millbank Tower. 6 o'clock.

"What does it say, Jane?"

"Very little." She turned the card around so her grandmother could read it.

Laying the card aside, both women sipped their tea. "Are you going to go?"

Jane took a small bite of a cucumber and mint sandwich. "I don't know."

"You know who it's from then?"

"I think I do." Her heart was fluttering. Only one person she could think of would have gone to these lengths for her. And she hoped he was waiting at the end of the day.

For a few minutes, the only sound from their table was the subtle chewing and sipping of their tea. The macarons melted on Jane's tongue; the salmon sandwiches were silky and soft.

Finally, the young woman arrived back at the table. Jane noticed, as she leaned in to take the empty plates, that her name tag read "Siobhan".

"Have you enjoyed your tea, ladies?"

"Very much, thank you." Gramma nodded her agreement.

Siobhan cleared the table. "Miss Mullins, I have this for you," she said, passing Jane another cream envelope.

Jane didn't hesitate this time, tearing ungracefully into the envelope. The note was longer this time:

Take this across the street to Miroiter at Burlington Arcade. There will be a clerk named Marilyn to help you. See you soon.

From inside the envelope, she drew a small item tag, bearing only her name.

"Curious," her grandmother, commented when Jane showed her the note and tag. "Sounds like some sort of secret admirer," she commented, winking.

Jane didn't argue. Everything had been absolutely delightful, but her mind was racing, filled with a velvety voice, the soft smell of sage, and a smile that warmed her to her toes.

The pair gathered their coats, Jane tucking the rose into her bag, and hurried down the stairs again.

"May I help you?" A middle-aged woman with autumnal-red hair and quirky glasses asked as they entered *Miroiter*.

"Yes, ma'am," Jane replied, stepping closer to the counter, almost bouncing on her toes with excitement. "I am looking for Marilyn. I am supposed to give her this tag."

"Well, you came to the right person, my darling. I'm Marilyn." She inspected the tag. "Ah, I wondered when I would see you, Miss Mullins. Right this way." She gestured to the dressing area. "There are some very comfortable seats here for your grandmother."

Gramma looked at Jane, surely pondering how all these people seemed to know them, but took a seat in one of the squashy hunter green armchairs as Marilyn led Jane to a dressing room at the far end of the row.

"If you need any help, call for me. Your gift is in that bag." She waved at a taupe hued garment bag. She closed the door behind her.

Reaching for the garment, Jane noticed another note taped to it with the instruction: "Not to be opened until after you open the bag."

With some trepidation, Jane drew the zipper carefully down. She gasped as she pulled the hanger from the case, revealing a magnificent dress, the very dress of which she had a picture tacked to her bulletin board at home. Tears filled her eyes; no one, outside of her family, had ever given her something so special.

The frock was knee-length and empire waisted, with a full skirt. It had a V-neck and a wide silver band fitted under the bust, but her personal attraction to the dress was the fact that it was entirely covered in silver and iridescent sequins. Quickly she undressed, hanging her grey sheath inside the garment bag and laying her coat across the damasked chair in the corner.

Gingerly, she stepped into the dress, slipping her arms into the bodice. With her left hand, she tugged the zipper up. It fit her perfectly, hugging every curve; she sighed happily as she looked in the mirror. With each movement, even the slightest ones, the dress sparkled. She was overwhelmed; tears were forming in the corners of her eyes.

"I can't believe he did this," she uttered. Her necklace rested against her sternum, its jewels twinkling in the lights.

Each sparkle and shimmer reminded her of nights in another city, the chill of a snowy day, the sound of festive music. She felt like a princess but still herself, as if her whole story had transformed when she stepped into the dress.

"Jane, dear, are you alright in there?" Gramma Mullins called anxiously.

"I'm fine, Gramma. I'll be right out." Glancing at the garment bag, she remembered the envelope which had fallen to the floor. Tearing it open, she read quickly:

Jane, you look beautiful, but then, I've always thought that. I can't wait to see you.

"Miss Mullins, I also have a pair of shoes for you when you're ready." Marilyn's voice drifted into the dressing room. "I can also have your day things sent back to your hotel."

"Then I guess we should be on our way, Gramma. Apparently, someone is waiting for us."

Emerging from the changing room, she handed the bag

containing her gray dress to Marilyn in return for a pair of silver peep toe heels.

Gramma was staring at her. "Do I look alright?" Jane asked nervously.

Gently patting her cheek, Anne answered, "Alright would be an understatement. Are you ready?"

"I think so," Jane breathed.

A classic black cab waited outside the arcade and the pair slipped in silently, Gramma directing the driver to their location.

It wasn't a long ride to the Millbank Tower, but Jane's nerves were alight with anticipation. When they slowed to a stop at the front entrance, her hands were actually trembling in her lap, causing the sparkles on her dress to shimmer in the darkening dusk light. The driver let Gramma out first and escorted her around the car, before opening Jane's door, offering a hand, and helping her onto the curb.

Even with her nerves, the building mesmerized her. They had spent days touring centuries old locales, and here was an almost brand-new, glass-facade homage to modernity, glistening in the fading sunlight and twinkling, leftover Christmas lights.

"Thank you," she called over her shoulder to the smiling driver who was reentering his vehicle. Gramma was watching her, smiling broadly.

"You look beautiful, Jane. Shall we go in?"

Jane nodded, at a loss for words as she took her grandmother's hand and stepped through the tall glass doors.

She was not disappointed in the lobby, which was a temple of glass and chrome, as they approached the gargantuan desk at its center. A tall, authoritative-looking bald man with a heavy mustache glanced up as they stepped forward.

"May I help you?" he asked, his voice clipped and proper.

"Yes sir. My name is Jane—"

"Mullins? Yes, madam. Nicolas?" he called to a young man, dressed in a flawless black uniform, emerging from a side room, who looked up at his name.

"Yes sir?"

"Please take Miss Mullins and Mrs. Mullins upstairs to Altitude. Ladies." He waved his hand in the direction of the younger man and the elevators. Both women gracefully moved across the room and entered the elevator that Nicolas had called down for them. Once they were all inside, he pressed several buttons on a small keypad and the elevator lurched upwards rapidly.

When the doors opened again, Gramma stepped out first, Jane close on her heels. Both women stopped when they got the first glance of the magnificent view outside the windows of Altitude. Stepping right up to the plate-glass windows, Jane marveled at the sight. It was as if one was floating above the streets of London, above the river. She was completely lost in delight when she heard her grandmother behind her.

"Charles?"

Jane whirled around to see her grandfather, dressed wonderfully in a new, tailored black suit, a bouquet of lilies in his hand, embracing her grandmother. In a second, she was at their side, lost in a six-armed hug.

"Grampy? How on earth?"

"Your old grandfather is full of surprises, kiddo," he said, grinning, his arm around Gramma's waist. "You both look beautiful."

Jane blushed, but her heart sank a little. It wasn't that she wasn't happy to see her beloved grandfather; she just had been expecting something else. Someone else.

"Thanks, Grampy. Are we the only ones here?" She glanced around, seeing only a few servers and bartenders scattered about.

"I guess so," he answered, still smiling. He whispered

something in her grandmother's ear and she began to grin too. "Jane, you really should see the view on the other side of the bar. It's really beautiful."

Smiling, she left her grandparents to their whispers and laughter and moved along the bar to the spot her grandfather had suggested. He was right. The view was amazing, especially as the sun set, and the city came to life in lights, twinkling at her like a million tiny smiles. She stared dreamily across the city, her heart occupied in a very different city, which was, no doubt, also sparkling with millions of lights tonight.

"It's not a bad view, but it's not half as beautiful as you are."

Jane spun around to see Lincoln, roses in one hand, standing against the bar, smiling broadly.

"Lincoln," she breathed, her heart racing. He crossed the space between them in two strides, sweeping her into his arms, dropping the roses on a nearby table.

"I thought you must hate me," she murmured into his chest, as he stroked the red-gold waves spilling over her shoulders. "When you didn't answer the phone."

He drew back and held her at arm's length, eyeing her with concern.

"I'm so sorry about that. I promise there's a reason and I'll tell you all about it soon. But I could never hate you." His eyes lit on the pendant at her throat. "You're wearing it."

"I love it," Jane whispered. "I wish I'd told you that night." She smiled. "I'm so sorry, Lincoln. You tried to tell me that it was all gossip and that you weren't with her, but I didn't stop to think that you were telling the truth. I was so in my own head, convinced that you couldn't ever want me like that..." He slipped two fingers beneath her chin, lifting her face to his.

His deep brown eyes locked onto her green ones. "You are so much more than you think you are, Jane Mullins." He leaned down and captured her lips with his own.

After a few moments, they parted. She snuggled into his embrace and they watched the boats on the river. He reached into his pocket and took out a small box, but Jane didn't notice until he released her and turned her around to face him. She protested for a moment until he dropped to one knee before her.

Her heart and breath both held in her throat as the tears edged their way into her eyes.

"Jane Rosalind Mullins, you said once that you waited for me for twelve years, but I've waited my whole life for you. And I almost lost you once, and I don't want to feel that way again. I don't want to spend a single moment without you in my life. I don't care if we live in New York, Nashville or Atlanta. We'll make a place for ourselves, somewhere only we know."

His hands were warm as he took hers and she thought back to the first time he'd held her hand, and how much they had overcome. She thought she loved him then, but at this moment? She knew, with no doubt, that she loved this man.

"Will you marry me?"

It was the second time in his life he'd asked the question. The first time, he had a massive ring he considered ugly, and the nagging feeling that the woman he was asking was more concerned about which magazines would run the story. But now? This was the love of his life, adoration written in her every expression, and as he opened the jeweler's box, revealing the beautiful vintage emerald ring, he knew he'd never made a better decision in his life.

Jane stood before him, the tears in her eyes sparkling in the lights reflected around them. "Lincoln, I…. It's beautiful."

"It was my YaYa's ring." When she didn't say anything, he blurted, "We can get you something else if you want a ring fancier or bigger or…"

Jane grabbed him, pulling him to his feet and kissing him

fiercely. "Don't you dare, Lincoln Bainbridge. Why would I want anything other than something so important to you?"

"So that's a yes?" He raised his eyebrows.

"Of course, it's a yes, you silly man!" He laughed brightly, spinning her around.

"You should probably pinch me. I just can't believe this is real," Jane murmured.

He laughed, gently pinching her hand where he held it. "Believe me now?"

Smiling widely as he slid the ring on her finger before wrapping her in his arms, she teased, "You may have to remind me from time to time."

As his lips met hers, he whispered, "Every day, for always and ever."

Home

"What do you mean, *closing*?" Trevor demanded.

"Exactly what I said, Trev," Jane calmly replied. "I made the decision while I was in London that I will close the bakery at the end of January. That gives us time to fulfill the standing orders this month and to work through our existing inventory. We'll still do some fresh bakes, but the doors will close then."

"But why, Jane?" Rayna asked, tears at the corners of her eyes. "Is it because I wanted to cut back time? Because I can..."

"No, no," Jane countered, patting the older woman on the shoulder. "It's not because you wanted more time at home with your boys *or* because Trevor is leaving us for a minor league team *or* because Nia is moving to New York." The group looked at each, excitement and sadness both on their faces. "You know we've been struggling this past year, and the rent is going up."

They all nodded.

"If only we had won the competition," Nia bemoaned, offering the obvious solution.

"I know. But honestly, I think I would have come to the

same conclusion then. I have more money in savings, enough to keep going until business picks up. But I don't want to."

The whole group was quiet; Trevor stared at the floor, Rayna dabbing her eyes, and Nia watching Jane, who appeared to be twisting her hands behind her laptop screen.

"The truth is," she began. "Honestly y'all, my dream was always to do more with my family recipes, creating new ones, too. I'm not sure if that will look like a restaurant or what yet. I have loved every minute of this ride with y'all, but I want..." She took a deep breath. "I want to go after that dream now. I didn't think I could do it, and I'm still not sure how to, but after the competition, and everything I learned in London, I think it's time to try. We're all chasing our dreams, right?"

Nia smiled. "You're right, you know."

"It happens occasionally," Jane giggled. "So. Now that we've covered all the doom and gloom..."

"Seriously!" Trevor interjected. "Is there some good news in all of this?" He still looked forlorn.

"Well, I guess a little." Jane lay her left hand on the top of her laptop screen, the new accessory glinting in the overhead light.

Rayna noticed it first, her dark eyes wide.

"Well?" Trevor prompted again. "What's the news?"

Wiggling her fingers again, Jane grinned broadly.

"Oh, my Lord," Nia cried, reaching for Jane's hand. "What? When?"

"What is it?" Trevor asked, staring at the ring.

"He surprised me in London, New Year's night," Jane answered Nia, unable to hold it in. "He had a whole plan with a glamorous dress and dinner at a beautiful restaurant that overlooks the whole city. He even brought my Grampy with him."

"Wait. You're engaged to Lincoln Bainbridge?" The realization finally clicked in Trevor's brain.

She nodded. "I can't believe it either."

Her friends all screamed at once, excitedly bouncing around the room.

"Does that have something to do with the bakery closing, too?" Rayna asked, smiling at Jane's elation.

"Wellll," Jane drew out, "I think it might."

"You think?" Nia questioned.

"Well, it depends on how his meeting with the network executives goes this week."

Trevor's jaw dropped. "Is he leaving the Culinary Channel?"

"No, he'd like to stay with the network, but he wants to do a different show, and he wants to move out of New York." Jane paused. "He's mentioned wanting to open his own restaurant."

She told them everything that had happened with Antony, how the network had promised Lincoln almost anything he wanted to make up for it. Since their return from London, Lincoln had told her all about the dramatic scene in Antony's office and the revelation that he'd not only been stealing from the company, but from Lincoln himself. Surprisingly, he wasn't that angry about the situation; he seemed relieved that he could be free of the tyrant manager that had controlled so much of his life for the last decade.

"If everything goes well in his meetings, and I think it will, he wants to move here. And he doesn't want his show to be all him anymore. He wants to do more creative recipes."

"That sounds wonderful, if it all happens," Nia hugged her boss as she spoke. "But what about your house and everything here? How much planning have the two of you been doing?"

"My house isn't going to be rented anymore, so I needed to find a new place anyway. I know it sounds fast. Believe me, not having extensive plans and research and notes makes me so nervous, but for the first time, I don't know what tomorrow will bring me, and I'm okay with it."

They were all quiet for a few moments, looking at each other, the people that had been their family for the past few years.

Trevor spoke first. "I guess we should open the shop and get to work."

"You're right, and no sad faces!" Jane admonished. "We are all stepping into new challenges and that's no reason to be sad." She clapped her hands and stood. "Let's go!"

The team bustled about, serving customers and finishing up a wedding cake that was being delivered that night. Jane made several signs explaining the bakery's upcoming closure and posted them, stopping to discuss with the regulars, who were disappointed. While most of them expressed how sorry they were to see her close, they all were happy for her and the future ahead.

"Oh! Janie, that is the most wonderful story!" Mrs. Allegheny, a neighborhood resident who stopped in each week for a dozen cream cheese Danishes, gushed. "What a love story! I'm sorry to see you go, of course, but I am so very happy for you!"

By six, the cold sunlight gave way to the twinkle of Atlantic Station after dark; Rayna had gone home, and Trevor and Nia were loading up the Henderson wedding cake to head to the hotel hosting the reception. Jane tossed her bag over her shoulder and climbed into her car, turning the key to start the heat. Her phone began to trill.

"Hello?" she answered.

"Hi, love!"

"Lincoln! How's New York?"

"New York was very, very cold. But things went well. Antony will go to court sometime in the next few weeks, but the network has already put a new producer on the show."

"A new producer already?"

"Yeah, Kelly Radmen. She was an assistant producer on Slice N Dice for a while; I like her a lot, and she's from Macon, so she knows Georgia well. And I talked to Geoff about a new agent, and he recommended the Portman agency."

"I know that name. Aren't they an Atlanta firm?"

"They are," Lincoln replied. "And I have an appointment with them tomorrow. Tonight, I have a surprise for you."

"Wait, you have a meeting in Atlanta in the morning? Does that mean you're here?"

"Yes and no," he chuckled on the other end of the line. "They've okayed the move down here for the show, and a new direction with it, too. But I've got a surprise for you. I'm down near your grandparents—there's a studio kitchen that the network wants to use and I want your opinion."

"You're already here?!" she cried giddily. She turned her car towards the interstate and headed off south. "Why didn't you tell me you were coming?"

"To be honest, I wasn't sure, until the meetings were done. The execs had a lot to talk about with me and with Jeannie Anne, since Antony's actions affected her, too."

"I can imagine. Okay, so where am I going?"

Lincoln gave her an address, vaguely familiar, in the town next door to where her grandparents lived. With little traffic, Jane arrived at a large, empty parking lot in Union City quickly. From the outside, there wasn't much to see, just a large warehouse façade, but she turned off the car and hurried to the familiar silhouette under the building's lights.

"Lincoln!" she cried. Smiling, he swept her up, spinning her effortlessly in his arms.

"Hello, gorgeous!" he murmured as he kissed her cheek. "Did you miss me?"

"Nah, not really," she replied, as he set her back on her feet. He swatted her playfully.

A uniformed man opened the glass door in front of them. "Mr. Bainbridge and Miss Mullins?"

"That's us," Lincoln replied, taking Jane's hand as they entered. The front hall looked like any office Jane had ever been in: nondescript carpet and an empty receptionist's desk, tall ceilings and various art prints on the walls. But they moved down a hallway, past a few closed, dark wood doors, before stopping at a set of metal double doors.

"Mrs. Radmen is already here, sir," the security guard said, as he opened one door, bright light spilling into the hall.

"Thanks..." Lincoln paused.

"Roland," the guard replied.

"Thanks Roland."

"Anytime." Roland left them as they stepped into the room, which was far larger than Jane had expected. A huge, modern kitchen set rested in the middle of the open stage, surrounded by cameras on stands.

"Whoa," Jane breathed.

"Yeah, this is actually bigger than the set I had in New York, but I really like it. What do you think?"

She took in the wide expanse of white countertops, the shimmering stainless appliances, and dark wood cabinets. "It's gorgeous," she said, resting her hands on the counter. "I'd love to work in a kitchen like this on a regular basis."

"So, you like it?"

"I do, but you're the one who has to work in it. It's really different from your old show. I'm really glad they were on board with all the things you want to do." She hugged him as he stepped to her side of the island.

"Well, there was one thing they want to do that wasn't part of my plans."

She looked at him. "What's that?"

"They want me to have a co-host. They think the family atmosphere vibe will work better with a pair."

Nodding, Jane agreed. "That makes sense. Do they have someone in mind already?"

"They do actually. She's from Atlanta, and locally well known, so they're confident she'll work well."

"Really? So, she lives here already?"

"Yeah, she's in the city currently, but I think she's moving down to the southside soon."

"That's cool. What's her name?"

Lincoln looked at her, grinning broadly.

"What?"

"I think you know her name."

Startled, Jane understood. "Me?! They want *me* to co-host a show on the Culinary Channel with you?"

"Yeah. It was Lillian's idea, actually. They were all impressed with how you handled yourself in the competition, especially with Antony meddling with you. And then Dan filled them in on what happened in London."

"Oh. That."

"Yes, that. You know you were the first woman to see through his whole charm routine? Not to mention you broke his nose!"

She shrugged. "I've seen that kind of 'charm' before." She crooked her fingers in air quotes. "I know better than to trust it."

Lincoln kissed her. "I love you, Jane Mullins. So, what do you say? Will you be the newest member of the Culinary Channel team?"

"I'd love to!" She beamed. "I just can't believe they even want me."

"Of course we do," someone interrupted as they stepped into the lights.

A middle-aged woman with short black hair and bright red lipstick reached out to shake her hand.

"I'm Kelley Radmen, the new producer for the show. I am

so excited to meet you, especially after everything Lincoln has told me. I think we're going to have an amazing product here."

"Thank you so much! I'm honored to get to be a part of it."

"We both are," Lincoln added. "And I love the set. It's what I'd wanted in New York for a long time."

"Let me show you the rest of the place," Kelly offered, waving a hand toward another set of doors. The trio moved down a back hall to a vast pantry and food storage area, a set of offices and dressing rooms for them both, and a large area for crew members. "We'll have a receptionist out front obviously, and my office is on that side, and Jermaine Rogers, from Fork Frenzy, and Gio Cortez, from Cuisine, are both assistants with us and they'll have offices, too."

"Excellent," Lincoln commented, looking at Jane. "So?"

"I think it's wonderful. I'm just still in shock, to be honest. But I love the whole place. It'll be a drive from my house, but I don't mind."

"Thanks Kelly. We'll see you soon!" He watched Jane, her expression rapt as she took in the space, her mind no doubt racing at this new opportunity.

"Y'all, too. I'm excited for this, I really am." She headed out the door as Lincoln turned to Jane.

"Think you can stand any more excitement?"

"More than this?" Her eyes widened, and Lincoln pressed a soft kiss to her forehead.

"Come on." They left the building, calling a goodnight to Roland as they did, and climbing into Jane's car. Lincoln tapped his phone a few times, and it began to offer directions to yet another location. Jane followed each turn until they ended up at the edge of a wide driveway up to a brightly lit old farmhouse. A spacious porch wrapped around the front and a swing was tucked under the eaves. Huge trees framed the property, and she swore there was a tire swing dangling from one.

"What is this?"

"Apparently it was on the market long enough that the owners were eager for a solid offer. I've still got to sign the paperwork, but once I do, it's all mine."

"You're going to live here? It's a little bigger than your penthouse"

"Well, I was hoping you might help it feel less empty. It's only fifteen minutes from the studio and only twenty from your grandparents' house and most everything else we need. It's big enough for us both to be comfortable, but not so big we have to walk a mile from one end of the house to the other."

Jane stared at him, awestruck. "You bought us a house?"

"I know. And I know this is a ton to process, and it's wild and probably overwhelming. I just..." He stopped rambling and looked at her. "I just didn't want to wait anymore. I waited to have control of the show. I waited for a place I wanted to live. I waited for someone who loved me for me. Now I have those. And I just want to live. With you."

Jane hugged him tightly across the console. "I know. Life was fine before I finally met you. I had a successful bakery and great friends and family. I had a cozy little house. This," she gestured around outside the car, "is so much more than I ever could have anticipated. Better than anything I've ever planned."

"They left me the number for the lockbox so we can take a look around inside," Lincoln hinted, and they climbed out of the car.

He took her hand as she stepped around the front, adding, "We'll have to get furniture and things, but I just really wanted you to see it tonight."

"I'm glad you did. London felt like a dream, and today feels like it's all really happening. You and me."

He opened the front door, and they stepped inside of the warm, open entryway. She turned to him, snuggling into his arms and laying her head on his chest.

"I love you," he said softly into her hair. "Welcome home, Jane."

The End

Acknowledgments

To my editor for fixing the errors of my ways and helping me make Jane and Lincoln the best they could be.

To the team at Parcel & Page who took a chance on me, there aren't enough thanks to offer.

To Miriam, for being sweet and supportive always.

To Jasmine, without whom this book may never have seen the light of day again, and who is the very first to ever tell me how promising it was.

To Caitlin, for being my cheerleader, my sounding board, and sometimes my calmer. You are a remarkable human and I'm grateful to have met you.

To my granddaddy, for being the best grandaddy.

To my parents, who gave me a lifetime of books and made me want to write my own.

To my sweet daughter E, for sleeping like a champ so Mommy could write at night, and for making this story the second-best thing I've ever created.

And to my amazing husband Michael, who has been my rock and supported this crazy dream. You are my best friend and I love you so much.

Under the Willow Tree:
Andersen, H. C. (Hans Christian), 1805-1875. The Complete Hans Christian Andersen Fairy Tales. New York: Gramercy Books, 2006.

About the Author

Kate Chambers is a wife, mama, and librarian from Atlanta. She's been writing since she was ten years old and always preferred essay tests in school. Besides writing, she loves to read romance, historical fiction, and children's books. She's also addicted to stationery.

When she's not reading, writing, or chasing her little one, Kate can be found experimenting in the kitchen, DIYing all manner of projects, and cheering on her Atlanta Braves.

Somewhere Only We Know is her debut romance novel.